UNENDING JOY

ELIZABETH JOHNS

Copyright © 2025 by Elizabeth Johns
Cover Design by 17 Studio Book Design
Edited by Scott Moreland
Historical Content by Heather King

ISBN: 978-1960794277

All rights reserved.
No part of this book may be reproduced in any form or by any electronic or mechanical means, including information storage and retrieval systems, without written permission from the author, except for the use of brief quotations in a book review.

CHAPTER 1

Joy felt like a fraud as she stood in the glittering ballroom at Grosvenor Square. It was a study in opulence—diamonds glinting under the light of countless chandeliers, silken gowns swishing in rainbows of colours, and the murmur of conversation punctuated by bursts of laughter. None of it held the slightest appeal for her.

Standing near the refreshment table, she tugged absently at the too-tight sleeve of her lilac gown, a rare concession to fashion which left her feeling utterly unlike herself. Her wild locks had been subdued into an elegant coiffure with a thousand pins that dug into her scalp. She felt sure it would not survive the night, and her feet, garbed in delicate slippers, already pinched from the quadrille she had just suffered through.

"Cheer up, Joy," Patience whispered at her side, her voice laced with both amusement and sympathy. "It is the day of your birth. Surely you can find a shred of enjoyment in all this?"

Joy shot her elder sister a glare that lacked any real venom. "I should much rather be mucking out the stables than mincing about, pretending to care for this nonsense."

Patience sighed, though the corners of her mouth twitched. "You might try smiling, at least. It is not so very dreadful."

Joy did not reply. The ballroom was a blur of indistinct shapes and shifting colours, and her head pounded from the effort of trying to distinguish one person from another. The Season would be one endless parade of such events, and her nerves were already wearing thin.

Her thoughts were interrupted by the arrival of Mr. Cunningham, who approached with his usual air of easy confidence.

"Miss Whitford," he said, bowing with exaggerated formality, his grin wide. "Suffering already?"

"Help me to escape, Freddy," she begged. "I do not know how you can stand these confounded events."

"It is all in how you look at them, my dear."

"There is more than one way?" She wrinkled her face, which she knew her governess would have scolded her for.

"You enjoy dancing."

"Yes, but not the stuffy ones where I must hold myself just so, and paste a false smile on." She imitated said posture and flattened her face.

Freddy laughed, as she had known he would. "You could do that, of course, or you could just be yourself."

"People already think I am outrageous."

He did not deny it. "Do you really wish to ensnare someone with whom you will have to pretend to be someone you are not for the rest of your life?"

"No, of course not." A feeling of panic threatened to make her flee the ballroom.

"Joy," he said lightly, though his tone held a note of concern, "are you quite well?"

"I am perfectly well," Joy said quickly. "My next partner approaches."

Joy found herself dreading the dance she had promised Lord Abernathy, a rather foppish young man who fancied himself a wit. As they stepped onto the floor, the patterns blurred and swirled before her eyes, and she stumbled, catching herself just in time.

A murmur rippled through the crowd, and Joy's cheeks burned. Abernathy, oblivious, chuckled and guided her clumsily through the steps, but her humiliation was complete. Now she had almost knocked down two Abernathys: mother at an earlier dance, and now the son. She could not endure an entire Season of this.

Freddy was waiting for her when Abernathy led her from the floor.

She looked down, avoiding his gaze. "The ballroom is crowded, and I was distracted."

"Hmm," was all he said, but his gaze lingered on her longer than she liked.

By the end of the evening, he sought her out, cornering her in a quiet alcove near the terrace. "Joy," he said softly, his usual banter absent. "When will you tell me what is troubling you?"

She opened her mouth to protest but faltered, the weight of her secret pressing down on her. "I don't know what you mean."

"I am your best friend," he said gently, his voice laced with a rare seriousness. "What is it? Your sight?"

She gasped and turned away. "'Tis nothing. Just…an inconvenience."

"It is not nothing," Cunningham said firmly. "Why have you not told anyone?"

Joy glared at him, but the fight drained out of her as quickly as it had risen. "What do you suggest I do? Call off the entire Season? Let everyone know how useless I am?"

"You are the least useless person I know," he said, his tone softening, "but you cannot face this alone. Let me help."

"The doctor said there is nothing to be done. I might be permanently blind soon."

As she looked up at him, his sincerity reflected in his steady gaze, something in Joy's heart shifted. Perhaps confiding in someone wasn't such a terrible idea.

Joy blinked furiously and glanced away while holding her hand to her head where it throbbed. The semi-circular scar left on her temple was a daily reminder of one of her restless escapades. A part of her mind scolded her for making a scene—an entirely new experience for her, for seldom did she care what onlookers thought—but this was different. This was not a trifling matter, such as wearing an unfashionable gown or forgetting a dance step. This was her sight, which seemed to be slipping through her fingers. Freddy reached out, but she drew back an inch, uncertain whether she wanted comfort or the preservation of her pride. Still, the concern radiating from his eyes struck a chord deep within. She did not want to be pitied, and she did not want to air all of this at a Society ball.

Yet Freddy was her dearest friend of the past few years. He had understood her from the first and had never made her feel insignificant or treated her like a silly young girl. He had always been her champion, in jest or in earnest. And here he was again, championing her.

"Joy," he said gently, "why would you suffer through this alone?"

"Please do not pity me," she managed, though her voice trembled. "I cannot abide pity, Freddy."

He shook his head. "Pity is not what I offer. I offer help—or, at the very least, an ear to listen. If you cannot see well, has it occurred to you that spectacles might help?"

Joy gave a bark of disbelieving laughter, quickly muffled by her gloved hand. She had never heard him speak so plainly and so...practically. Spectacles. The very word conjured up the image of a stern governess or an elderly scholar in a dusty library. It was not the sort of thing worn in London's fashionable ballrooms, certainly not by young ladies making their debut. "Do you think I should become an object of ridicule?" she asked, managing a wry smile. "It is hardly the thing for a debutante to sport spectacles."

Freddy's eyebrows arched in gentle amusement. "Perhaps not, but I would argue it is better to see clearly than to fret over Society's silly notions. You have always scorned them, have you not?"

"Yes, but one learns that there are certain...boundaries," she whispered, glancing about to ensure no curious ear lurked nearby. "I do not mind being thought outrageous, but—" She paused, turning to face him fully. "Should I suddenly appear with spectacles, heads would surely turn, tongues would wag. I suppose they already do. I do mind being pitied and coddled. I mind even more losing what little independence I have."

Freddy took a step closer, his voice lowered in confidence. "Let them wag. When have you ever cared about trifling gossip? Were you not the one who climbed a tree in full view of half the *ton*? You braved that with a laugh, I recall."

Joy felt a gentle flush warm her cheeks. She did recall that mortifying moment, though at the time she had laughed it off, unprepared for why strangers of the *ton* would care what a country girl did. Her eldest sister Faith had only smiled in that resigned way she had, while her other sisters had said nothing. And Joy had continued on as she always did.

Yet losing one's sight was not a trifling tree-climbing escapade. It changed everything. "I wish," she said slowly, "it were as simple as a pair of spectacles. But the physician said that it may worsen. Even if a lens aids me for a time, what happens when—when it grows worse?"

Freddy's hand found hers, and she let him gently cradle her fingers, surprised at the comfort it brought. "We shall cross that bridge together when it comes," he said. "But if you do nothing now—if you hide and suffer through these balls and soirées, half-blind and in pain—what will that solve? It will only make you miserable…and very likely more conspicuous than even spectacles themselves."

Her mouth curved into a rueful line. "It is not a thing I wished to share. I suppose I thought that if I did not speak it aloud, it might resolve itself." She sighed. "It has been happening for some months. Some days are better—I can read, or ride astride, or dance without much difficulty. Then, on other days, the world blurs, and every shape merges into an indistinct haze. If I exert myself—ride too hard or dance too long—my sight worsens."

Freddy lifted her hand to his lips in a rare gesture of tenderness. "If—if the worst should happen and your sight fails entirely, I promise I shall remain by your side, whether Society scorns or not. Your friendship has always been precious to me. Nothing shall change that."

She looked away, though she felt a flush heating her cheeks. "That is kind of you," she said softly, unused to tender emotions from her friend.

She glanced down at her slippers, noticing with some irony how much more clearly she saw them than the swirling shapes of people in the ballroom. The floor was an elaborate mosaic in muted greys and gold, though to her eyes it was starting to blur at the edges. "I do not even know where to procure spectacles," she murmured.

With a rueful smile, Freddy nodded. "We can discover that together."

A soft rustle interrupted them. Joy glanced up—or tried to—and discerned, from the drifting perfume and the swirl of pale blue skirts, that her sister Faith had ventured into the alcove. "Am I interrupting something?" Faith asked, her tone somewhere between teasing and concern.

Joy pulled her hand from Freddy's, though she did so gently. "Not in the least," she managed. "You recall, of course, that I wanted to flee this dreadful ball. Freddy only enquires if I have gone mad enough to do so by means of some scandalous route—perhaps scaling the terrace walls."

Faith's lips curved, but her gaze flickered from Joy's face to Freddy's in that shrewd way she had. "Yes," she said dryly, "I can see how that might be a route you would choose. Joy, my dear, I realize this night has not gone as smoothly as one would hope, but truly, there is no need to skulk in corners unless you feel unwell." She stepped closer, then touched Joy's arm gently. "Is your head paining you again?"

Joy swallowed, aware that her sister could tell. Faith was not so easily deceived. "A trifle," she admitted, "though I shall manage. I merely needed some air."

Faith's gaze was all sympathy, though in her measured, elder sister way. "Perhaps a brief walk on the terrace would do. The music and chatter in here grows deafening. Do not be overlong."

Freddy offered an arm to Joy. "Shall we?"

She hesitated, uncertain whether to remain hidden in the shadows or brave the watchful gazes of the assembled guests. But she reminded herself that retreating forever was not an option. So she looped her arm through Freddy's and ventured onto the terrace.

FREDDY WAS MORE than a little bothered by the thought of Joy losing her sight. The notion of sprightly and fearless Joy no longer able to see the world around her—no longer able to engage in all those spirited pursuits that had endeared her to him—was almost unbearable. Joy was lively, forthright, and possessed of an unladylike fondness for galloping across the countryside or tending to horses as though she had been born in the stable yard. She was so full of zest for life that Freddy sometimes wished she had been born a male. Then they might have hunted together or ventured into clubs that were far from proper for a genteel young lady.

But now, everything felt turned upside down. If Joy was indeed afflicted with a malady of the eyes that threatened her vision, why had she not confided in him sooner? Had she believed him too frivolous to be entrusted with such a burden? Had she feared his pity or his judgement? The thought nettled him, though he reminded himself that Joy had always guarded her vulnerabilities as fiercely as she embraced her freedoms. It was not in her nature to lament her own troubles for fear that her family would coddle and shelter her. Surely her sisters did not know, but he could not betray Joy's confidence.

They walked side by side down the garden path in silence. That was another thing about Joy—he never had to talk if he did not care to, and she would not chatter a man's ear off as so many females were wont to do. They stopped before a fountain of three leaping fishes shooting water from their mouths in graceful arcs.

Joy's posture was stiff, as if she were bracing herself for something —or perhaps she was merely weary from the press of the ballroom.

She wore an elegant lilac gown, her generally wild hair tamed into a sophisticated coiffure. To him, she looked terribly uncomfortable.

"Joy," he said softly.

She turned part-way in his direction, though her gaze landed slightly to his left. There it was: the tell-tale sign that she could not quite discern his figure unless she focused very carefully. Freddy felt a twist in his chest at the sight. How had he not noticed before?

"Freddy," she murmured. Her tone was guarded but not cold. "You should go back inside to dance."

He approached, offering a tentative smile. "I will soon. If you must know, I grew weary of listening to Lady Pratt extol the virtues of her niece."

A hint of amusement flickered across Joy's features. "Her niece, is it? Next she shall try to foist her upon you in some manner."

Freddy laughed, relieved at the return of her uninhibited tongue. "Let us hope not. I fear I am too clumsy to evade her machinations should she turn them on me."

A silence settled between them, filled by the night songs of crickets and the distant lilt of the orchestra. Freddy studied Joy's face in the warm glow of a nearby lantern. She looked tired, though she tried to conceal it behind a polite mask. He swallowed, recalling how, earlier in the evening, she had nearly stumbled during a dance—her second near disaster with the Abernathy family. Indeed, her vision must be more precarious than she dared admit.

"Are you feeling better now?" he asked gently.

She fixed him with a look he could not entirely interpret. "Oh, Faith has fussed enough over me. Pray, do not join her in it." She drew a breath, then smiled, but the expression did not quite reach her eyes. "I am exceedingly well, except for the usual vexations of these endless balls."

Freddy's mouth tightened. She was steering him away from the subject, reluctant to speak of her infirmity. Yet how could he leave it unaddressed? Joy had always prided herself on meeting obstacles head-on. Why should her sight be different?

Nevertheless, he sensed that pressing the matter too forcibly might only drive her from his confidence. So he forced a lightness into his tone. "Yes, these events can be tiresome. At least you have your menagerie to return to at the end of the night."

At the mention of her beloved pets, Joy visibly brightened. "Oh, the kittens!" She laughed—a real laugh, this time, carrying that musical lilt he had always found so captivating. "You have no idea how they have grown. They scamper about the house as though they own it. My maid found Camilla perched upon the mantelpiece yesterday! The little daredevil must have leapt from a chair to a bookshelf and then across to the mantel, toppling half the Dowager's porcelain figurines in the process."

Freddy raised his brows in mock horror. "Was there much damage?"

"Shockingly, only one figurine was lost—the small shepherdess, which she never liked much in the first place," Joy said impishly. "Camilla looked entirely unrepentant. If anything, she seemed proud of her new vantage point."

"And what of the others?" Freddy asked, heartened by her eagerness.

"Mortimer—the largest of the litter—already fancies himself the king of the drawing room. He lounges atop the sofa, swiping his paws if anyone dares disturb him. Then there is Cecilia, the gentlest, who likes to curl up in one's lap and purr as if she were a little dove." A fond smile touched Joy's lips. "Lord Orville is the most spirited—he is forever knocking over the vases of flowers or chasing after the maids' skirts. I thought you might wish to have him."

Freddy found himself grinning at her animated account. "I must pay them a visit, if only to witness their antics first hand. I suspect he and I should get on famously."

"I should be delighted to have you call," Joy replied, her tone more relaxed than before. "It is growing lonely with all my sisters now wed." She glanced towards the path that led deeper into the garden, where a lantern-lit arch invited them forward. "Shall we walk for a while? The air is mild, and I find I prefer the scent of roses to that of over-perfumed guests."

Freddy offered his arm. "By all means."

They started along the gravel, the rhythmic crunch of their steps mingling with the faint music still audible from the house. The hush of the garden was soothing, yet a part of Freddy could not relinquish his concern. He walked slower than usual, mindful that Joy might not see protruding roots or uneven patches of ground in the dim light. But he strove to do so without appearing patronizing, altering his step subtly so that she would not suspect he was taking care of her.

A ripple of laughter and applause drifted from the house. Glancing back towards the open doors of the ballroom, Freddy caught sight of a figure whirling past—someone in a bright turquoise gown, slender of waist and with dark, glossy hair cascading in a stylish arrangement. Even at this distance, he could discern Lady Maeve's graceful posture as she turned in time with her partner's steps. She was quite striking —one of the beauties of the Season. Her laughter rang out, clear and melodic, as she spun around.

Freddy realized he had paused in his steps, momentarily distracted by the spectacle. A slight pang of guilt slid through him—here he was, determined to assist Joy, and yet he found himself distracted by a vision of feminine beauty. He gave himself a mental shake and resumed walking, casting Joy a sidelong glance to see if she had noticed.

Her expression was indecipherable, but he guessed she had not seen what had caught his attention. Or, if she had, perhaps it was only a swirl of colour and movement. Did Joy feel any sense of loss at no longer being able to appreciate such displays? It must hurt her pride that she could not fully see—but how could he help alleviate that pain?

"Freddy," Joy said quietly, after they had passed the fountain. "I should like to return inside soon. The night air is—well, it is refreshing, but Faith will fret if she discovers me gone for too long."

They retraced their steps towards the terrace, the sounds of revelry growing louder with each passing moment. As they crossed the threshold back into the ballroom, Freddy noted that the dancing was in full swing. The beautiful Maeve caught his eye once more, spinning gracefully with her partner amidst the crowd.

CHAPTER 2

The next morning, Joy and Lady Maeve were off to visit Hatchard's in search of something new to read. Joy had been awaiting Keats's new book of poetry, and Maeve simply liked any outing. Joy had been grateful that she had taken to Lord Carew's sister so she had someone to experience the Season with, even if Lady Maeve was much more suited to Society. She was beautiful in an elegant, graceful way befitting a lady. She loved the newness of London and everything to be found in a city.

They entered the shop, and Joy stopped to inhale the beautiful smell of leather and paper. She looked around, but it was difficult to make out any detail.

"Do you realize you close one eye when you're looking far away?" Maeve asked quietly beside her.

"No. Do I?" She had never noticed such a habit. Perhaps she truly did need spectacles.

"You should not frown like that," her friend then scolded.

Joy did not wish to discuss her problems. It had been bad enough that she had confessed to Freddy last night. Hopefully, he had forgotten after a night's repose—he tended not to dwell on serious matters overmuch, which was part of what she liked in him.

"I will go and see if my book is available," Joy remarked rather than retort something unkind.

"I see Lady Edith. I will be over there." Maeve pointed in the general direction across the room, where people had gathered on sofas.

Joy was not sure how she felt about Lady Edith, but Maeve seemed to enjoy her company.

"Good morning, Miss Whitford," the clerk greeted her. "I have something for you."

He knew her well. He searched on a counter behind him and produced a lovely burgundy leather-bound volume of Keats's latest poems. The letters swam before her, so she did not try too hard to read them, lest someone else discover her disability. Either it was getting worse, or rather was her ability to disguise it.

She accepted the book and thanked the clerk. When she turned and walked in the general direction Maeve had indicated, she found her friend with not only Lady Edith, but also several other young ladies who were making their debut. They were giggling and whispering behind their gloved hands.

When Joy was close enough to make out their faces, Maeve's cheeks were pink and she looked upset. She knew at once they had been gossiping about her. Joy did not trouble to greet any of them but diverted her steps and made her way to the door.

Maeve soon found her on a bench outside.

"Joy," Maeve said apologetically.

Joy did not particularly wish to have this discussion. "You do not need to say anything. I can surmise quite well what happened. It is human nature to gossip. I would expect no less from those girls."

"But you assume I was participating."

Joy lifted an unladylike shoulder to feign indifference. "I will send the carriage back for you if you wish to stay with them."

"That will never do, Joy. We will go take our walk through the park as we intended, and you will hold your head high. The Dowager would be appalled to find her charges had lost all sense of propriety and abandoned her."

Joy wanted to shout what she really thought about propriety, but she suppressed the urge. She knew very well what would happen if she took the carriage and went anywhere alone.

She stood up and followed, not yet trusting herself to speak. They found the Dowager, who had stopped at the modiste's around the corner to request a change to an order.

"I was just about to come and find you," the Dowager said. "This saves me the trouble. Do you still wish to stroll through the park? I believe I saw Lady Ingram going that way, and I wish to speak with her."

"Indeed, a walk would be just the thing," Lady Maeve replied.

Joy was still brooding. She had to discover a way to convince Faith to let her return to the country. She was not suited to this.

As they walked towards the park, Joy clutched her new volume of Keats against her side. She would have liked nothing better than to return home at once and hide away in her chamber, reading lines of verse until the words danced into her heart. Yet Lady Maeve had a determined set to her mouth—one that brooked no argument—and so Joy found herself stepping into the bright midday sunshine, her eyes instantly watering from the glare.

Across the street, an elegant barouche passed by, its occupants bedecked in the very height of fashion. Joy recognized one of the ladies—tall and stately, with a plume in her bonnet that bobbed precariously—though the details grew hazy after a moment's glance. Feeling a pang of frustration, Joy blinked and looked down at the pavement instead.

They set out along the bustling street. Flower sellers called out their wares, and the occasional horse-drawn cart clattered by. Joy tried to keep her mind from the vexations of the morning, but her thoughts strayed, unbidden, to the whispers that had greeted her. It was one thing to bear gossip about oneself—quite another to see one's friend caught in the middle.

She stole a glance at Maeve. "Was it about me?" she asked softly, scarcely wanting to hear the answer. "You need not spare my feelings."

With a sigh, Maeve nodded. "They were discussing your…mishaps on the ballroom floor." A rueful smile crossed her face. "They mentioned your fondness for animals, which is not a bad thing."

A sharp pang twisted in Joy's chest. She looked down at her reticule, twisting the strings with nervous fingers. She did not care if people called her unrefined—indeed, her own sisters implied as much, albeit more gently—but she despised the idea that Maeve should be tainted by association.

"I am sorry," Joy murmured, voice tight.

Maeve's eyes flashed. "Do not apologize. I am quite capable of deciding what company I keep. And if they disapprove, that is their affair."

Joy's heart softened with gratitude, though she still wrestled with an urge to retreat from London entirely. She hardly had the fortitude to face both her failing sight and the censure of gossipy debutantes. Biting back her frustration, she reminded herself that not everyone was so cruel. Maeve was proof of that, and so was Freddy—even if he did tend to treat life as one grand jest.

They soon arrived at the gates of the park, where a gentle breeze rustled the leaves, and the air carried a faint scent of cherry blossoms. Groups of fashionables sauntered along the paths, nodding politely or, in the case of those more given to chatter, stopping to exchange pleasantries.

The Dowager was already ahead, speaking animatedly to Lady Ingram. The older ladies beckoned for Maeve to join them. Joy escaped, but still within sight. As she made her way down the slightly sloping path, she clutched the Keats volume like a talisman. If only her eyes would allow her to savour each verse properly, she might lose herself in the poet's lines and forget the clamour of her own mind. No, she would save her troubles for the privacy of her chambers.

Reaching the edge of the pond, she paused to admire the sunlight dancing upon the water's surface—though 'admire' was perhaps too strong a word. The brilliance of the sun's reflection hurt her eyes, and the shifting patterns soon blurred into indistinct shapes. Shielding her gaze with one hand, she inhaled, trying to quell the swirl of dismay in her stomach.

She yearned for the comfort of wide green fields where no one cared if she squinted or stumbled. She longed for the carefree rides with Freddy, who never chided her about propriety. Indeed, he was the one person whose presence felt like an escape from the constraints of Society.

Yet the recollection of his concerned gaze the previous evening made her cheeks burn. She had confided in him—spoken of her deteriorating sight—and though he had been nothing but kind, she felt horribly exposed. Even now, she wished she could retract her confession, return to a simpler day when her eyes were merely tired from reading too late at night, not failing her altogether.

A sudden swell of voices caught her attention. She turned, peering through the haze of sunlight, and discerned Maeve's figure among a small coterie of ladies talking to the Dowager. The conversation grew merry, punctuated by dainty laughter. None of them beckoned to Joy, for which she was grateful. She had no desire to hear the newest gossip from the *ton*.

Stepping onto the grass, she approached an ancient oak that spread its branches like a protective canopy. A wooden bench rested in its shade, unoccupied, and she gratefully sat down. Opening the Keats volume, she attempted to decipher the swirling letters, but they refused to come into focus. That old gnawing fear stirred in her belly, and she bit her lip to stave off tears.

How would she endure an entire Season when each day her vision wavered, threatening to expose her secret at any moment? If merely stepping into Hatchard's had revealed that she squinted and frowned in an unladylike manner, how could she pass muster in ballrooms packed with onlookers? One misstep, and the rumour mill would churn with talk of the Whitford girl who could not see and yet dared to dance.

The breeze rustled the leaves overhead, and a single shaft of golden sunlight broke through, illuminating her page. She looked down again, willing her eyes to behave. She managed two lines:

Upon a time, before the faery broods
Drove Nymph and Satyr from the prosperous woods

—before the letters blurred again. With a frustrated sigh, she closed the book. How she longed to be able to read more than a few words again without struggle.

If only she could return to her guardian's country estate, where the world was quiet, and her responsibilities did not include feigning perfect health for the benefit of prying eyes. Perhaps her family would grant her leave if she pleaded her case, though she dreaded their disappointment.

At length, she composed herself and rose. Gathering her courage, she made her way back along the path to rejoin Lady Maeve, who was still in conversation. The Dowager glanced at Joy's face and gave a slight frown, but said nothing. Perhaps her expression betrayed her distress, or perhaps the older woman simply wished to reprimand them both for wandering. Either way, Joy resolved to endure with what grace she could muster.

"You look tired." Lady Maeve cast a concerned glance at Joy. "Shall we return to the carriage?"

"Yes," Joy said quietly. "I should like that."

And so they moved on, the city's bustling noise reasserting itself the moment they passed the park's grand gates. Another day in London, another round of constraints and carefully composed smiles. Yet, pressed against Joy's side, the book of poetry served as a small, comforting reminder of a world beyond the glare and hustle—a world of verse and longing, where perhaps she could escape. If only her eyes and her courage would hold out a little longer so the pleasure of the written word would not be lost to her.

FREDDY REFLECTED that he had been blessed indeed when it came to his family. His father, Viscount Gresham, was more of an amiable country squire than a London lord. He rarely fussed at anyone so long as they stayed out of trouble, preferring his kennel of hounds and his wide expanse of fields to the glitter of Society. His mother, Lady Gresham, was still considered a very handsome woman—so much so that, in her youth, she had been courted by dukes, marquesses, and earls. Yet she had fallen in love with the then Mr. Cunningham instead, and from all Freddy could see, she was perfectly content with her choice, embracing her role as wife, mother, and a leading figure in local church charities, though she did enjoy the Season in Town.

Freddy's sister, Vivienne, had likewise enjoyed good fortune. She had made a good match with Lord Montford, the heir to an earldom and one of Freddy's closest friends. Their marriage was a happy one, despite Vivienne having been expected to marry Lord Rotham from birth. Freddy had often marvelled at how seamlessly that union had come about with little effort on his part.

He'd resumed his carefree life in London, albeit seeking out entertainments with those he had less acquaintance with since his friends had all wed.

With such idyll, Freddy had never anticipated any severe blow from his easy-going relations. Therefore, when the summons arrived before he had breakfasted, he was wholly unprepared for the conversation that would follow. It was only a single note, penned in his mother's flowing script, but its brevity said much: *Come to us at once at Gresham House. Your father and I would have a word.*

His parents were in Town? What the devil?

He read it twice before he found himself dressing with care—whatever it was could wait until he was properly rigged—then made his way to the town house his mother inhabited only for the Season. He arrived to find his parents waiting in the drawing room, both wearing expressions he did not often see—the sort that signalled something truly significant was afoot.

"Has someone died?" he stopped at the threshold and asked before even greeting his beloved parents.

His mother, in a graceful gown of dove-grey silk, was seated upon a settee, hands folded primly in her lap. His father stood by the fireplace, a sheaf of news clippings in one hand. The lines of his usually genial face were set in an expression of stern resolve.

"What kind of greeting is that, son?" his father scolded. Freddy forbade to mention the curt summons he'd received less than an hour ago at an hour when he'd barely raised his head from the pillow. "The Season is set to begin and with it your mother's annual garden party."

Freddy supposed the Season had started last night. He closed the door behind him and dipped his head in respectful greeting. "Father, Mother," he said. "You wished to see me?"

They bade him approach, and as soon as he drew near, his father fanned out the clippings on a nearby table. Freddy recognized the ink and column headings of certain London newspapers, though he could not read the details from where he stood. Still, the small glimpses he caught—words like *race, Melton, scandal, and opera dancer*—were enough to make his stomach twist.

"Freddy," his mother began, her voice formal, "your father and I have grown concerned about your…activities…of late."

His father cleared his throat. "The race you participated in near Epsom was not well-received in certain circles," he stated. "We gather from this article—" He tapped one of the clippings, "—that you were cutting a swath through Melton as though you fancied yourself some Corinthian daredevil. Now, while I have no objection to sport, you must understand that Society is less tolerant of certain extremes."

Freddy knew precisely which incident they referred to. He had, along with a few jovial acquaintances, decided to see whose mount could clear the greatest obstacles in a single gallop—fences, hedges, and even the occasional low stone wall. It had been exhilarating at the time.

He attempted a light quip. "But, Father, you have always said that a Cunningham should know how to handle a horse under any circumstance."

Unfortunately, his humour fell flat. His father frowned, and his mother pressed a hand to her bosom as though she had taken offence. His father continued, voice grim: "The matter would not be so pressing if it were your only caper, but it seems we have a regular pattern here. Another article mentions an opera dancer—some woman known for her flamboyant costumes. Care to explain?"

Freddy blushed, hardly wishing to expound on such a matter in front of his mother. "She is a friend of a friend," he prevaricated. "I did attend the performance, but I fail to see how that alone constitutes—"

His mother cut him off, waving a hand in mild exasperation. "We have been more than patient, allowing you to sow your oats, as it were. But, Freddy, when does it end? We understand you must feel adrift since all of your closest friends have recently married."

Freddy opened his mouth, then closed it, deciding it was best to remain silent. His father took a step closer, folding his arms over his broad chest. "It is time to settle yourself, Freddy. We have indulged you, hoping you would take a sensible step on your own, but it has become clear that you need a firmer hand."

A hush fell over the drawing room, broken only by the sounds from the street outside. Freddy swallowed hard. This was the confrontation he had scarcely imagined would come. Yes, he was nearing his thirtieth year, but he had never thought his father would issue such an ultimatum, not when the elder Cunningham had always seemed content with Freddy's easy-going ways.

His father's brow furrowed. "Have you nothing to say for yourself? Do you not question why we must take these measures?"

Freddy mustered what dignity he could. "What, precisely, do you wish for me to do?" he asked.

At that, his mother threw up her hands as if in a silent appeal to Heaven. She rose from her seat and paced a small circle before turning back to him. "Settling yourself, Frederick," she declared, "means behaving like an adult, choosing a wife, establishing a household, and attending to your lands and tenants."

The last phrase caught Freddy off guard. "My lands and tenants?" he repeated carefully. He glanced at his father, whose eyes gleamed with some unspoken plan. "Are you suggesting something is amiss at Gresham Park? Are you ailing, Father? Do you need for me to come home and take the reins?"

To Freddy's surprise, his father let out a hearty laugh that shook his shoulders. "Nothing is wrong, son, not a whit. As far as I know, I remain in excellent health, but that does not change the reality that I cannot manage everything forever. And, more importantly, you must think of your future. Our line extends beyond me. You are the next head of the family, and it is time you acted in such a manner."

His mother added in a softer tone, "We are concerned for your happiness, Freddy. We want to see you established, with a good woman at your side. A man of your station cannot drift aimlessly, nor can he remain a bachelor forever."

Freddy felt his jaw tighten. *Drifting aimlessly.* That was how they perceived him, then. Perhaps there was truth in it, for his days had passed pleasantly enough in a whirl of sporting events, dinners, and mild flirtations. He had never considered himself irresponsible or reckless, though he now realized that from his parents' perspective, his escapades might appear exactly so.

"I see." He swallowed, aware of a dryness in his throat. "And how do you propose we rectify this perceived aimlessness?"

His father's gaze sharpened. "I shall settle your grandmother's Kent estate upon you when you marry. Then you shall take charge of that estate and learn to live off its revenues. As from six months hence, I will no longer support you in the manner to which you have grown accustomed. That is a fair amount of time, I believe, for you to choose a wife as the Season is in full swing."

Freddy's stomach dropped. He managed to keep his voice steady, though inside he was reeling. "Six months?"

His mother nodded. "That should bring us just beyond the end of the Season. I shall remain in Town to oversee the details of your engagement, once you declare yourself. You may rely on my assistance in selecting an appropriate match.

Lord Gresham set his hand on the table, palm flat. "By the close of the Season, I shall be looking to return to London for your engagement ball. Am I understood, son?"

Freddy attempted to speak, but the words lodged in his throat. It would not do to argue that he knew many others who behaved with far less circumspection. With some effort, he managed to choke out, "Yes, sir."

An uncomfortable hush followed. He could tell from his mother's pinched expression that the matter weighed upon her heart. His father, though gruff, had not made the decision lightly. They genuinely believed this step necessary.

Freddy, on the other hand, felt as though the floor had shifted beneath him. He had never intentionally avoided matrimony—he merely enjoyed the freedom of his bachelor state, and none of the ladies he had encountered had inspired him to relinquish it. Indeed, many of his friends had already succumbed to wedded life. Lord Montford, his own brother-in-law, seemed blissfully content with Vivienne. Another great friend, Lord Westwood, hailed the transition as the best decision of his life. Freddy did not begrudge them their happiness. He simply had never found the impetus to follow suit.

Now, he was being pushed into that very step. *Six months*, he thought again, the words echoing in his mind. In half a year, he would either be affianced or cut off from the paternal purse. No more comfortable allowances to spend on horses, travel, or the occasional flirtation of any sort.

His father dismissed him with a grave nod. "Off with you, then," he said, though not unkindly. "Use your time wisely, Freddy. Prove to us that you are capable of managing your life, and I shall happily establish you as master of your own estate."

Freddy inclined his head in a semblance of deference, murmured farewells to his mother, and exited the drawing room. In a daze, he crossed the threshold into the bright midday sunlight, blinking as though he had woken from a dream.

CHAPTER 3

Of course, Joy would be forced to suffer tea at Lady Abernathy's house the day after her humiliation with Lord Abernathy. She closed her eyes and drew in a long, steadying breath. Of all the trials London could inflict upon a reluctant débutante, being obliged to go there might well rank among the most dreaded. That woman had the memory of an elephant and the social tact of a goose. The very thought of stepping over Lady Abernathy's threshold caused Joy's stomach to twist in anxious protest.

Alas, there was no escape. Lady Maeve had seized upon the invitation and insisted that Joy accompany her and would brook no excuses to cry off. The Dowager—whom would chaperone Joy and Maeve—had further decreed that the call must be made, for Lady Abernathy was 'a woman of significant standing in Society, and it would be a monstrous breach of decorum to snub her.' Such were the Dowager's exact words, in addition to, 'You must face this with your chin up, or 'twill only feed more gossip.'

Thus, Joy found herself in the plush carriage rattling its way towards Charles Street. She fiddled with a ruffle on her jonquil sprigged muslin gown, which was rather more decorative than she preferred. Lady Maeve sat beside her, wearing a striped lawn dress of pale green and pink. The Dowager and Faith sat opposite.

"Lady Abernathy will doubtless give me a wide berth," Joy quipped, though her pulse fluttered in anticipation of the dreaded meeting.

Faith replied, "I am certain she hardly recalls that silly mishap from last year."

The Dowager waved a hand. "Of course she does not remember it," she declared, in the lofty tone that only a venerable matron of the *ton* could manage. "There is no point expecting the worst."

Joy raised an eyebrow, wishing she shared the Dowager's optimism. Last year's 'little mishap' involved Joy tripping over her own skirts during a country fête. The older lady had not been shy in voicing her shock—and, if Joy recalled correctly, had cast many dramatic remarks on the impropriety of young ladies who galloped about as though they were stable boys. Joy's cheeks warmed at the memory, and she realized she was clutching the fabric at her knee a bit too tightly.

The carriage jolted to a stop, and the footman opened the door with a swift bow. Charles Street was lined with elegant façades of town houses, each boasting prim windows and iron railings. Joy stepped down, taking in the sight of Lady Abernathy's imposing residence, with its marble steps and polished knocker shaped like a lion's head. If the outside was any indication, the inside would be a veritable hazard of stiff upholstery, fragile porcelain, and sharp-eyed matrons.

They were ushered inside by the butler, who led them to a large drawing room, all pastel wallpaper and gilt. The group exchanged the usual pleasantries with Lady Abernathy, who sat in a high-backed chair near the hearth, wearing what looked to be enough lace to outfit an entire modiste's shop. Joy's heart sank at the sight of her hostess's triumphant smile.

They were seated amongst a few other ladies who had already arrived. Joy was hoping someone else would distract Lady Abernathy from noticing Joy again.

"Miss Whitford," Lady Abernathy greeted her, voice echoing in the lofty space, "I am so delighted you could join us. I do hope you suffered no ill effects from your mishap last evening?"

Maeve sucked in a breath. Joy schooled her features into what she hoped was a polite expression, though she could feel her jaw tightening. The Dowager gave a slight shake of her head, as though pleading silently for Joy to keep her composure.

"Oh, no, my lady," Joy managed, forcing a laugh that sounded hollow to her own ears. "I scarcely recall it."

"Indeed?" Lady Abernathy's eyes glimmered with mischief. "Well, I recall it very well. Quite the tumble you took, my dear. It was all my poor Alistair could do to rush forward and catch you." She paused, then let out a syrupy laugh. "Ah, how charming these young ladies are—so prone to little swoons. I do not blame you at all, Miss Whitford. Seeing my dear son can have that effect on young maidens."

Joy nearly choked on air. The mortification of that moment threatened to spill out as a burst of wild laughter, for the notion that she had tumbled due to some tendre for Alistair Abernathy was absurd. She could not imagine a man she'd less like to be 'shackled to for life,' as she privately termed it. The alliteration of 'Alistair Abernathy' alone set her teeth on edge; the memory of his tittering laugh did not help matters.

She darted a look at Maeve, who was staring down into her tea cup, lips twitching in silent mirth. That only made Joy's struggle for composure more difficult. She had to clamp her lips tightly to prevent a gale of laughter from escaping. Faith's elbow discreetly nudged Joy's side—clearly urging restraint.

"That must have been it, my lady," Joy managed at last.

Lady Abernathy, pleased with the attention, lifted her own cup in a regal gesture. "And you blush so prettily!" she cried, glancing around the circle as though inviting all present to admire the shade of Joy's cheeks. "Is it not charming, how overcome she is?"

Overcome, indeed. Joy felt a keen urge to bolt. In her mind's eye, she pictured herself vaulting over the settee and sprinting out of the door, shocking every last guest. Of course, that would only confirm

Lady Abernathy's claims of Joy's unsuitably rash behaviour, so Joy forced herself to remain rooted in her chair.

The Dowager, sensing Joy's agitation, cleared her throat loudly. "I have heard that your garden is particularly fine this year, Judith. Perhaps you might share with us how you have managed to coax such blooms in our unpredictable spring?"

The hostess blinked, momentarily diverted by her own horticultural accomplishments. "Ah, yes, the garden. My head gardener is quite skilled, you see, and we have put in new rose varieties." She launched into a detailed explanation of fertilizers and pruning strategies, during which Joy managed to inch her chair back from the centre of attention.

Faith, who sat beside Joy, shot her an apologetic glance. Faith was well aware of Joy's dislike for these sorts of gatherings. But Faith was also pinned by conversation with Mrs. Huntington, who was expounding upon the benefits of a sugared ginger drink for digestion.

Meanwhile, Lady Maeve had turned her attentions to another corner of the room, where the Duchess of Thornhill was holding court. Joy could see Maeve's eyes alight with interest. She was as clever as she was charming, and the challenge of enticing the young, handsome Duke was her particular goal for the Season. Unfortunately, the Duchess was rumoured to have a low opinion of Irish titles, and Lady Maeve happened to be the daughter of an Irish lord. Joy glanced at the scene with mild sympathy. Poor Maeve. The Duchess looked as though she'd swallowed a lemon whole.

Joy sipped her tea, grateful that the inquisition into her clumsiness had passed. One could only manage so many mortifications in an afternoon. If only she could slip away for a nice, hard ride. In fact, the more she considered it, the more attractive the notion became. She could practically taste the country air, hear the rustle of leaves, and smell the comforting aroma of fresh grass and horse.

She nearly sighed aloud at the daydream but caught herself in time. The last thing she wanted was to invite more remarks from Lady Abernathy about her apparently romantic daydreams of Alistair. Heaven forbid. No, the only gentleman whose company she truly missed was Freddy Cunningham, who had been her closest friend for as long as she could remember. He would understand her longing for open fields and dusty roads. If they could slip away for a gallop, she might regain her sense of balance and clarity.

Her reverie was shattered when Lady Abernathy's voice rose again. "Would you care for another pastry, Miss Whitford?" She held out a plate stacked high with confections. "I recommend the cream puffs. My dear Alistair finds them quite delightful."

No doubt they are as puffed up as he, Joy reflected grimly. She pinned a polite smile to her lips. "Who could refuse a cream puff?"

Joy carefully selected the smallest puff available, solely to avoid giving offence. She could sense Maeve watching her from across the room, lips twitching in suppressed laughter. It was all Joy could do not to mirror her amusement. She was certain Alistair would much rather engage in a debate on the best arrangement of a neckcloth or brag about his riding boots than dance attendance on any lady. That was the impression he had given her last Season, at least—endlessly preening and turning this way and that to show off some new ensemble or fob.

Meanwhile, Maeve continued her foray into the territory of the Duchess, ploughing on with fearless charm. Joy caught scraps of conversation drifting across the room.

"...my father is Lord Donnellan," Maeve answered the Duchess's query.

"Is that not an Irish title?" came the Duchess's rather cold reply.

"Indeed. The estate is the most beautiful land and castle overlooking the sea. You should visit one day, your Grace," Maeve chirped, undeterred.

Joy took another sip of tea, letting her eyes wander over the assembled guests. Several ladies in attendance were entirely engrossed in their own chatter—comparing notes on the latest ball, or lamenting the gloom that sometimes clung to London's weather. A pair of elderly aunts clucked disapprovingly in one corner of the room, casting glances every so often at Joy's party, perhaps in search of new fodder for gossip.

The conversation was a whirl of inconsequence. She might go mad if she could not spend some time in the country soon, even if it was just a jaunt to Richmond for the day. Mayhap Freddy would go with her. He was always game for a gallop. She would send her groom over to ask him. Frankly, she thought that another ridiculous rule: that she could not call upon Freddy or send him a note. It was not as if he was a suitor. He was as close to a brother as Westwood, Rotham, Stuart, or Carew, for goodness' sake.

Maeve returned to Joy's side, having apparently retreated from the Duchess's domain. She took a seat beside Joy with a feigned look of calm. "The Duchess is rather high in the instep," she whispered. "I fear my Irish blood does not impress her. Nor does she seem enthralled with my conversation on the picturesque beauties of Killarney. I can hardly imagine why."

Joy smothered a grin. "That is truly a mystery. She must be blind indeed."

Maeve shrugged. "She is not the first to have her nose in the air. We shall see if the Duke himself has any independent thought in that handsome head of his." Then, noticing the remains of Lady Abernathy's persistent chatter, Maeve added in an undertone, "Could she boast more of dear Alistair's trifling accomplishments? I believe we have heard about his mastery of archery, lawn tennis, and whist in the span of half an hour."

Joy nearly choked on her tea again. "This time, it is the violin. Next we will be subjected to him screeching out a concerto."

Maeve hid her amusement behind a gracious smile. "Lord have mercy on our ears."

Lady Abernathy, catching wind of their whispers, beamed in their direction. "Ah, Miss Whitford, Lady Maeve, what do you think of my new tea service?" She gestured to the service of porcelain cups and saucers before them. "Imported from China, you know."

The two friends dutifully inspected their cups, with Joy commenting on the delicate floral pattern as best she could. Trapped in an endless parade of teacups. But she would survive. The thought of a future ride in the countryside kept her spirits from sinking entirely.

At last, when the Dowager deemed they had stayed a polite length of time, and the party made their way out, Joy felt relief wash over her.

Once they were settled back in the carriage, Joy let out a quiet groan. "If I were forced to listen to another word about Alistair's many graces, I might have used that new tea service as a weapon."

The Dowager pursed her lips in disapproval but could not hide a hint of amusement. "Lady Abernathy is a forceful character, I grant you, but she means well…however, it would not do to offend any of the matrons. If you think Lady Abernathy insufferable, you will not withstand the real dragons. You must be more attentive."

Faith, sitting alongside them, patted Joy's hand. "You endured admirably, my dear. I thought you might bolt when she mentioned your blushing."

Joy pulled a face. "The thought did occur to me." And as soon as she was back in the house, she sent a groom off to beg Freddy to go riding at his earliest convenience, then went to find the kittens for solace.

FREDDY TRUDGED along the London streets with a mind as muddled as an untrained pup. He could have hailed a hackney, but the brisk walk, he told himself, would jar his wits into a more useful shape—though he rather suspected his wits were beyond saving at present. Carriages rumbled past, fruit sellers bellowed at passers-by, someone's small lapdog yapped indignantly when nearly trodden upon—but Freddy registered little more than a hazy swirl of noise and colour. The predicament in which he found himself cast overshadowed everything else.

By the time he reached White's, a slight perspiration dotted his brow. Inside, the foyer bustled with gentlemen in various stages of leisure—some lingering about, discussing the latest wagers, others drifting upstairs to the reading rooms. Freddy scanned the faces for any sign of his friends Westwood, Rotham, or Montford but no such luck. Only casual acquaintances, men he knew more for their tall tales than for any genuine intimacy, drifted by to offer half-smiles and nods. He slipped into one of the smaller rooms off the main hall, where a handful of armchairs and a crackling fire provided a semblance of calm. He slumped into a chair by the fire, wondering how to explain his plight without sounding completely hapless.

He had just run a hand through his windswept hair, when the door opened to admit Westwood—looking perfectly pressed in a tailored coat, his expression warm with quiet amusement. Freddy nearly leapt from the chair in relief.

"Good Lord, Cunningham, you appear as though you've run the length of Bond Street," Westwood greeted him, doffing his hat before setting it on a nearby table. "I did not expect to find you brooding by the fire in the middle of the day."

Freddy managed a faint grin. "I might prefer a run if it would solve my problems. But alas, I fear I must burden you with them first." Westwood's eyebrows rose in gentle mockery. "Burden away. I assure you, I have endured worse."

Freddy was just about to launch into the tale when a second figure strolled in—Rotham, the picture of dark, handsome elegance. He nodded to them both. "Why, Cunningham, you look as though you've seen a ghost. Care to enlighten us?"

Freddy gave a dismal shrug. "I wish I could say all was well. In truth, my parents have made it clear that my bachelor days are done. They threaten to revoke my allowance if I am not engaged by the end of the Season." He expelled a long breath. "In short, I must find a bride or starve."

Westwood gave a soft whistle. "That is quite the ultimatum. And here I thought your father was all good cheer and easy indulgence."

"He was," Freddy said, gesturing helplessly. "But he has evidently run out of patience with my…ah…lack of direction."

"Lack of direction," repeated Rotham, lips curving. "Is that what enjoying one's freedom is called these days?"

Freddy let out a humourless chuckle. "He may have used terms like reckless, aimless, and heedless, but I did not care to retain the full list. Suffice it to say, I have six months to secure a match—or I am cut off. Even then, I am to run an estate for funds."

Westwood tugged thoughtfully at his cravat. "The good news is, six months is a fair span if you set your mind to it."

"Ha," Freddy said, scrubbing a hand over his face. "If I set my mind to it. My mind, Westwood, is not the deepest lagoon."

"If not your mind," Rotham put in with a sly grin, "then your charm may suffice. You have no shortage of that. Start combing through the throng of débutantes. Dance with them. Make conversation about the weather, ribbons, whatever it is their fancy to discuss. Then narrow down the list to who does not bore you silly."

"And if that fails," Westwood added, "you can always let Montford parade you about. He is sure to babble on about how marriage to your sister has improved him in every conceivable manner. Ladies do love a successful romance."

Freddy, who had been half-smiling in spite of himself, gave a rueful shrug. "If you consider nauseating happiness success a good thing. Though I fear that being forced into marital bliss is hardly the same as leaping into it of one's own accord." Freddy's shoulders sagged. "I see the logic of it, truly. I simply dislike being forced. Marriage should be about…I do not know, something more pleasant than 'choose or lose,' if you take my meaning."

"That is how many in our set find themselves betrothed," Westwood pointed out, settling into a chair opposite Freddy. "Parental edicts are quite effective, if unromantic. Could be worse."

Rotham snorted, perhaps recalling his own parental edict. "One must count blessings where one can." He sobered, then regarded Freddy with a thoughtful tilt of his head. "But, truly, do you have any lady in mind? Have you yet surveyed the new crop?"

Freddy hesitated. His mind flitted to the beautiful Lady Maeve and then for some reason to Joy—his best friend, though why she would appear in his thoughts he did not care to explore. He suspected that path was riddled with more hazards than he could undertake just now. "Well," he said at last, "there may be a face or two, but no one I have had a chance to properly know. I suppose I need to go into Polite Society more. I went to the ball last night solely for Joy. I will have to attend every devilish music recital and soirée and—heaven help me—make afternoon calls."

Westwood patted his arm consolingly. "Doing the pretty is a small price to pay for salvation from penury, my friend."

A footman sidled into the room just then, delivering a tray of refreshments. Freddy seized a glass of brandy and downed the whole. Rotham and Westwood exchanged an amused glance.

"What about your father's other requirement—about living off the land?" Rotham asked, once the servant had discreetly departed. "He wants you to take charge of an estate?"

Freddy grimaced. "Yes, indeed. My father believes a wife and an estate will bring me to heel in short order."

Westwood set down his glass, leaning forward with a conspiratorial grin. "Between you and me, I have known men forced into less palatable circumstances. Managing an estate is not all tedium. You can keep horses and dogs, hunt...and if your wife is lovely and good-tempered, you might find yourself quite content."

"It is the 'if' in that sentence that sets me trembling," Freddy said in earnest. "Still, I see no alternative. I shall cast my net wide, as you suggest—perhaps fate will throw me a lifeline."

"Exactly," Rotham agreed. "Leave no tea undrunk, no garden party unattended. Smile until your jaw aches. Compliment every bonnet in sight—and all the matchmaking mamas will sniff out your intentions before you walk through the door."

Freddy groaned, though a hint of laughter escaped him despite his gloom. He recalled, not so long ago, when Rotham fought his own forced betrothal tooth and nail. "I suppose I can manage to compliment a bonnet or two—if I must."

"You always did have an eye for fashion," Westwood teased as he looked at his perfectly tied neckcloth and exquisite waistcoat. "You are halfway to joining the rest of us in blessed matrimony."

Freddy tried his best to listen, though his thoughts wandered. Was it really so pressing for him to find a wife? He wasn't opposed to marriage, but he found the idea unnerving. Adult responsibilities, an estate to manage—he could hardly picture himself as a sober country gentleman, overseeing harvests and tenant disputes. Yet he could not deny that his father's ultimatum had left him little choice.

At length, Westwood finished recounting which families might be in attendance at each event. He peered at Freddy expectantly, as though waiting for him to select a path forward.

Freddy swallowed another mouthful of brandy, trying to calm the knot of anxiety in his belly. "Very well," he said at last. "I shall go where you tell me, meet whom you recommend, and attempt to conduct myself with all the charm I can muster. If, in six months' time, I have failed to find a bride, then at least I will have done my best."

They chatted on a while longer, adding more amusing strategies for Freddy's forced courtship: from creating a list of potential heiresses to bribing hostesses for invitations to exclusive gatherings. By the time the conversation drew to a close, Freddy's shoulders felt no lighter. His friends had found love matches. They couldn't understand his predicament.

When at last they decided to depart, Freddy stood with them, pushing aside the residual dread that threatened to clamp down again. "Shall we find Montford and see if he can sing the praises of matrimony until I am suitably convinced?" he suggested, half-rueful, half-humorous.

"Unfortunately, we are promised to dine with family." Rotham and Westwood were now family. "Come, we will give you a ride."

Westwood, hat back in hand, grinned. "Be warned, once Montford starts talking about your sister's perfections, you may never hear the end of it."

Freddy settled into the carriage, a swirl of uneasy excitement dancing in his gut. Six months. Such a finite span, and yet it could change his life irrevocably. He pictured a quiet manor house of his own, a wife who might greet him each morning with a smile—or a scowl, if he chose ill. It was a risk, certainly, but he could not avoid it any longer.

Freddy only half listened, his mind drifting in and out of the conversation. The weight of so many changes pressed upon him, and he could almost feel the turning of fate in the warm breeze that drifted through the open window.

Yet amidst the swirl of apprehension, he clung to the faintest spark of hope. Perhaps, by some stroke of luck, he would meet a lady whom he found intriguing—someone who would laugh at his jokes, be a bruising rider, and not expect him to sit in her pocket. If such a match lay before him, then maybe his father's ultimatum was more of a push in the right direction than the dreaded sentence it felt like now.

He shook his head at his own wandering thoughts and gave his full attention to his companions. Westwood was describing Lady Ingram's penchant for elaborate musical entertainments as a place for Freddy to survey options, while Rotham mentioned how Miss Hargrave—a distant cousin, apparently—was quite clever and pretty, if a bit reserved.

Freddy nodded along, determining to keep an open mind, no matter the introductions. If he was to succeed, he would have to cast aside his usual ambivalence and embrace every opportunity.

Westwood caught Freddy's eye as they stepped down from the carriage. "Take heart," he said kindly. "You are not such a lost cause as you think. You are a genial fellow, well-bred and reasonably handsome." Rotham snorted at that. "A little effort, and you shall have half the Season's débutantes fluttering their fans at you."

Freddy chuckled at that. "Reasonably handsome, am I? You flatter me, sir."

He knew his friends did not truly understand. All of them were married now and happy to be led around on a lead. He needed to discuss this with Joy. She would understand.

CHAPTER 4

~~~

Joy was enjoying a rare moment of quiet in the Westwood town house's garden. On this particular morning, the Dowager Lady Westwood had gone to an exhibition with Patience, Faith, and Lady Maeve. Joy, pleading a headache, had remained behind, savouring the lull that descended on the otherwise bustling household.

As kittens tumbled about her feet, she strolled through the neat rows of box hedges, pausing to admire the early roses that clustered along the wall. Their pastel petals shone under the late spring sun, their fragrance much nicer in its natural habitat than when used as perfume.

Here, in the hush of the garden, she could imagine herself at the family's country estate, free from the prying eyes of London Society. Her responsibilities as a young lady in her first Season felt far away. Here there was no pressing need to smile and curtsy at the next tedious event or to feign pleasure at yet another prospective suitor whose conversation she could hardly endure.

The sound of the back gate's latch clicking broke her reverie. She turned, expecting perhaps a footman, bringing a message, or a gardener in search of tools. Instead, she saw Freddy slip through the gate from the mews. The sight of him brought an immediate, uncomplicated joy to her heart. Since they'd come to London, Freddy had been the one constant, friendly presence in her life—brotherly, comforting, and wholly unconcerned with propriety when it came to climbing trees or galloping across fields.

No one in Society looked askance at their familiarity, for they were viewed more as siblings than potential sweethearts. He was practically family, and Joy had never shown the slightest inclination to swoon in his presence (nor he in hers). It was an arrangement Joy had always cherished: the closeness of a companion without the weighty expectations that haunted so many other young ladies.

But as she watched him cross the garden, she noticed something peculiar in his stride—an anxious energy, as though he bore unwelcome tidings. He did not greet her with his usual teasing quip or lively wave. Instead, he approached more slowly, his gaze fixed on the gravel path.

"Freddy?" Joy called gently. "Whatever is the matter? You look as though you have just lost a race."

He glanced up, wearing an uncharacteristic grimace. "Only the race to escape my future, perhaps."

She frowned at the cryptic remark. "Explain."

Without further invitation, Freddy slumped onto a marble bench beneath a beech, letting out a heavy sigh. Joy scooped up Lord Orville, then seated herself beside him.

"Until now, my parents have not seemed inclined to curb my freedoms." His lips tightened. Joy's eyes widened. "Surely they have not banished you to the colonies or something dreadful of that sort?"

"Worse, in some ways." Freddy let out a shaky laugh. "They have decreed that I must marry and take charge of an estate." He paused, raking a hand through his blonde curls. "I am not entirely sure which estate it is—my father has a property he has threatened to bestow upon me for years—but the important point is that he refuses any longer to humour my bachelor ways. I am to be wed by the close of this Season, if possible." He leaned closer, dropping his voice in mock calamity. "It is my thirtieth year, you know."

"How awful!" Joy gasped. She stroked the kitten's ears, cogitating upon this development. "I…I do not think I will like it when you marry, Freddy. We will not be able to stay friends as we are now."

At that, Freddy's distress seemed to heighten. "You see? It is a noose around my neck, Joy!" he exclaimed, pressing a theatrical hand to his chest. "No more carefree races. No more walking side by side without a chaperone scolding us." His face twisted in exaggerated dread. "I will be forced into a staid, responsible figure, looking after tenants and sheep, and hosting dull dinners for my neighbours. Does that not sound like something out of a nightmare?"

Joy was torn between sympathy and amusement. Freddy so rarely displayed genuine alarm. Even in the face of mild scandal, he normally offered a quip and a smile. Now, though, he seemed sincerely troubled—and she found herself longing to comfort him, even as she shared some measure of his dismay. If Freddy married, her most steadfast companion would be transformed into someone else's husband. Their easy camaraderie, once taken for granted, might slip away.

She inhaled, searching for a constructive suggestion, and studied him for a moment, trying to imagine Freddy married. It was not something she desired for herself, and she did not wish it upon him either. Her heart softened with sympathy, and a kernel of an idea formed.

"Perhaps," she said carefully, "there is a way for us to remain friends whilst also satisfying your family's demands." She tapped her chin, eyes alight with mischief. "Let me think…how best to ensure we continue to see one another?"

Freddy perked up a little. "Yes, go on. I am desperate for any plan to keep life tolerable."

"Well," Joy began, "maybe we should marry each other's friends—assuming we can find suitable candidates—so that we might remain in the same social sphere, free to visit without raising eyebrows. If I married your friend, and you married mine, we would all be a cosy group, do you not see? Attending dinners together, going on outings. We would be forced into the same circles."

At this, he let out a short bark of laughter. "Except, might I remind you, most of my close friends are already wed. The ones who remain unmarried are older than I—some well into their fourth decade." He pulled a face. "Old codgers, all."

Joy made a dismissive gesture. "You do not act old, Freddy."

Freddy grimaced. "Precisely. I may be on the cusp of thirty, but my spirit is that of a man ten years younger. Some of my acquaintances—take Westwood or Rotham, for instance—have grown as serious as clergymen since their respective marriages. Or Montford, who is so happily married to my sister that all he does is extol the virtues of wedded life. The rest are no better. Even Carew is smitten. My set has deserted me in droves."

Joy tapped her foot against the gravel, pondering the predicament. "Well, then our grand scheme to marry each other's friends cannot succeed unless you discover new, unmarried companions. Meanwhile, I suppose I will scour my circle for a lady who might suit you whom I can also tolerate." She offered him a playful smile. "Any ideas?"

He narrowed his eyes, serious in thought. When he produced no answer, she tried a different approach.

"What qualities do you seek in a wife?"

For a moment she watched him in silent contemplation. It felt oddly comforting—and yet a tinge of sadness flickered through Joy's heart, for she knew that once Freddy truly stepped into the realm of matrimony, the easy, unguarded nature of their friendship would change.

Abruptly, Freddy stood up and paced across the pebbled path.

"If you are to be forced into an estate and a wife, we must ensure it is at least tolerable. Shall I take a guess? Let me see...do I know any lady possessed of good humour, not a prosing bluestocking, and a willingness to let you chase foxes across muddy fields?"

Freddy raised an eyebrow. "A short list, I suspect."

She tapped a finger to her lips, thinking aloud. "Lady Celia Linton is newly come to Town, said to be quite lively. Then there is Miss Ariana Porter—a bit shy, but rumoured to love horses. Perhaps I should contrive invitations to some small gatherings and see which lady you take a fancy to, although I can only claim one true friend, and that is Lady Maeve."

He perked up at that name. "She is quite bonny."

"Indeed, but has her sights set on a duke. Nevertheless, she is my friend and perhaps we can convince her of your finer qualities."

He stopped and wrinkled his brow. "A duke, you say?" Lord Orville jumped from Joy's lap and rubbed himself against Freddy's legs.

"Thornhill," Joy confirmed.

"We are acquainted since Eton, though he has not been much in Town. Any chance you could distract him while I court Lady Maeve?"

"Does he like animals?"

"I do not see why he would not. He was fond of horses when I knew him."

"Then I shall try my best." Though Joy could not think her beauty comparable and she possessed no feminine wiles to speak of.

"Capital! I shall invite him to ride out to Richmond on the morrow, if that suits you?"

"I will talk to Maeve and send word."

Thus, a plan hatched, they began walking slowly along the garden's edge, gathering the kittens and discussing possible events where Freddy might cultivate new candidates. Joy promised to keep her eyes open for any young ladies whose temperament aligned with Freddy's, while he offered to do the same for her. Whilst she faced no parental ultimatum, she knew her own family harboured hopes of seeing her settled—and she very much feared she would lose Freddy if this plan did not work.

∼

FREDDY HAD ALWAYS CONSIDERED himself an uncomplicated, easy-going sort of fellow, fond of friendly company and boisterous outings rather than the delicate niceties demanded by London's drawing rooms. So when Joy suggested a riding excursion to Richmond, while also surveying a future wife, he seized upon it with gusto.

He found himself mounting his chestnut gelding in front of Westwood House, shading his eyes against the bright sun as he surveyed his little party.

Joy, astride her spirited mare, Nightingale, offered him a wry smile. She wore a riding habit of deep green wool, cut in a flattering yet practical fashion, with a short fitted jacket buttoned neatly over a cream waistcoat and a matching skirt that draped elegantly to one side of the saddle. A jaunty velvet hat, trimmed with a modest ribbon, sat upon her wind tossed curls. In the bright sunlight, she seemed every inch the lively country miss rather than the weary débutante he often saw in stuffy drawing rooms. The mischievous gleam in her eyes told him she was just as eager to be free of London's constraints as he was.

Lady Maeve sat upon a sleek grey mare, all but glowing with excitement as she fiddled with her reins. Her riding attire displayed a touch more flair—a blue-grey habit with delicate ivory piping, complemented by ribbons of pale blue that flowed from her hat. She had chosen gloves of the same shade, creating a pleasing ensemble that displayed to advantage her dark hair and bright complexion. And then there was His Grace, the Duke of Thornhill—the quintessential tall, dark, and handsome gentleman, and a quietly magnetic presence that had already sparked a buzz in the *ton*. He would be a worthy opponent if ever there was a contest for Maeve's hand.

Freddy had known Thornhill long before he became the Duke. Thornhill was somewhat reclusive, dashing, and reputedly with a fortune the size of Derbyshire—traits that made him an object of fascination and frequent speculation. A young, single duke did not come along often, but Freddy worried not. He knew he was a great favourite with the ladies as well.

In Freddy's mind, this ride was a stroke of genius. He, Joy, Maeve, and Thornhill—all friends, with similar interests. A chaperone was not required for such an excursion as this, as Freddy and Joy were as brother and sister. If it just so happened that Freddy could orchestrate a small romance for Lady Maeve and himself, well, that was making the best of the situation.

"Shall we be off?" he called, waving the riding whip he had been tapping against his boot.

The three others nodded, and with a chorus of gentle clucks and a flurry of hooves, the party set forth from Mayfair towards Richmond.

Before long, Joy spurred her mare forward, drawing level with Freddy. "Is this not the perfect day for a ride?" she said, her cheeks flushed with exhilaration, looking quite pretty. Funny he had never noted that about her before.

They began by winding through the bustling streets of central London. Even at this early hour, the thoroughfares were lively with carts rumbling towards market stalls, flower sellers hawking their wares, and carriages carrying gentlemen into the city. Freddy could hardly wait to leave behind the clamour of vendors and the press of foot traffic. As they progressed westward, the cramped buildings gave way to wider avenues lined by elegant residences with small, tidy gardens. The tang of smoke from countless chimneys gradually diminished, replaced by air that felt fresher, though still touched with the city's lingering haze.

Once they reached the outskirts, the scenery transformed. Narrow lanes meandered between open fields, dotted here and there with grazing sheep or a rustic windmill. The road wove beneath canopies of elm and beech, the sunlight filtering through leaves to create dappled patterns on the ground. Indeed, the entire scene felt worlds away from the grand ballrooms and whispering gossips of the *ton*. Freddy inhaled deeply, revelling in the sense of freedom.

Thornhill and Lady Maeve rode beside each other, while Freddy and Joy naturally fell in alongside one another.

Richmond Park itself—once they entered—offered sweeping vistas of rolling grassland, ancient oaks, and the distant sparkle of the Thames. Deer grazed quietly amid tall ferns, lifting their heads in mild curiosity as the riders passed. Freddy had the distinct impression that here, under broad skies and among gentle slopes, one's thoughts could roam as freely as the wind. No wonder Joy had clamoured to come. She practically glowed as she guided her mare along a winding path.

"This is heaven. If I had been forced to endure one more tea party discussing gowns, or watch the Dowager fuss over seating arrangements for some dreary dinner, I might have run away entirely."

Freddy smothered a laugh. Joy's candour always amused him, though he knew she was not entirely jesting. "We cannot have you running off, my dear Joy. Who would keep me on my toes otherwise?"

Her eyes narrowed in mock exasperation. "You would manage. Yet I should hate to see you roam the salons unchecked. It would be far too easy for you to flatter your way into half a dozen young ladies' good graces."

"Flattery? Me?" He feigned shock. "I prefer to call it 'polite conversation,' but if you must be uncharitable—"

"Oh, hush." She elbowed him lightly, earning a playful snort from his gelding. "Better you than those stiff-necked bores who can talk of nothing but the latest parliamentary debates."

Freddy saw Thornhill and Lady Maeve riding side by side a short distance ahead, their figures silhouetted against a backdrop of rolling green. He leaned closer to Joy. "What do you think?"

Joy followed his gaze. "It is hard to say. Lady Maeve is all smiles, but the Duke's countenance is rather unreadable. I think there is hope for friendship amongst us all."

"Excellent," Freddy murmured. He'd privately hoped to observe Maeve without signalling any preference, leaving the path clear for him to stake his own claim if the inclination took him. But in truth, he wasn't entirely certain whether his interest in Lady Maeve was genuine beyond her pleasing face and countenance. Marriage was for a lifetime.

Joy, apparently reading his thoughts, nudged him. "You do intend to speak more than two words to Lady Maeve today, do you not? I thought you were—well, not fixated, but at least curious?"

Freddy's mouth twisted. "I am curious, indeed. However, there is ample time for conversation once we find a suitable spot to rest the horses. For now, let Thornhill amuse her."

Joy gave him a long-suffering look. "Very well. Just do not let the entire day pass before you so much as enquire after her wellbeing."

"And the same goes for you."

They continued in this vein for some time, bickering with the ease of siblings, trading witty barbs about each other's riding style, the kittens, and what other diversions they could plan to further Freddy's cause. So engrossed were they in their chatter that they scarcely noted how far they had ridden until Lady Maeve called back to suggest exploring an ornamental maze said to be tucked away near a grove of old yews.

"Come along," Maeve urged. "I heard rumour there is even a carved wooden bench at its heart, for those who find it."

"That sounds diverting," Thornhill agreed in his low, even tone. "A challenge for the mind as well as the legs."

They dismounted at the maze's entrance, a low hedge forming the perimeter. Tethering the horses to a sturdy post, the quartet set off on foot, wending their way along narrow paths hemmed in by high shrubbery. Joy took the lead with characteristic boldness, claiming she could find the centre without error. Freddy followed closely, indulging her confidence yet fully expecting to become lost at least twice. Thornhill and Maeve brought up the rear, Lady Maeve for some reason eagerly comparing English gardens with Irish ones. A dead bore, if you asked Freddy.

Within moments, the group's banter grew lively as they encountered closed ends and looped paths. Joy, her cheeks aglow from fresh air and excitement, let out a cry of triumph when she discovered a hidden plaque that pointed left. Freddy teased her that she'd misread it, only to find himself at an impassable hedge. Their laughter echoed among the hedgerows, and though they wandered in circles, no one seemed to mind.

At last, they stumbled upon the maze's centre, where a neatly trimmed alcove contained a carved wooden bench, just as rumoured. Freed from the confines of the narrow paths, they paused to catch their breath and share their successes—or lack thereof. Thornhill, it turned out, had deduced a pattern of turns to reach the heart more swiftly, while Maeve had happily tagged along, proclaiming that she preferred the scenic route anyway.

Freddy surveyed the cheerful group with satisfaction. What a capital plan this was, he congratulated himself. A day in the country, good company, and the glimmer of friendship blossoming. He and Joy bantered so naturally that one might suspect they were indeed siblings, though occasionally a small pang reminded him that Joy also needed to find a mate.

They lingered in the maze's centre for a while, swapping jokes about the many times they had nearly walked directly into a hedge. Eventually, a low rumble from Freddy's stomach broke through the merriment. He winced, pressing a hand over his midsection. "It appears our expedition has left me quite famished. Did we not discuss a picnic?"

Joy's face fell in exaggerated dismay. "Alas, no."

Lady Maeve and Thornhill exchanged chagrined glances.

Freddy held up his hands. "No matter. Thornhill and I shall hunt down provisions. There is a tavern just over the hill. Joy, Lady Maeve—why not wait nearby with the horses or stroll the grounds for a short time? We shall return with sustenance soon."

They retraced their steps out of the maze, collected their mounts, and set off along a narrow lane that looked promising. Sure enough, within minutes they came upon a small tavern nestled in a wooded copse, its sign bearing the faded image of a fox. Within, the air was warm with the smell of roasted meats and fresh bread. Freddy, stepping inside, found a lively crowd of local folk—field hands, travellers, an elderly man playing a fiddle in the corner. The landlord greeted them politely enough, though he appeared mildly taken aback by the presence of gentlemen in full riding regalia.

Thornhill, unassuming despite his lofty status, spoke in a quiet, respectful tone. "We should be obliged if you could supply us with a few bread loaves, some cold meats, and perhaps a flask of ale. We have ladies to feed, and we have neglected to bring a hamper."

The landlord, swiftly recovering from his astonishment, nodded. "At once, your lordships."

Freddy pressed several coins into the man's hand, adding, "And some cheese, if you have any." The man bobbed his head eagerly, then disappeared into the kitchen to gather the requested items. Within minutes, the two gentlemen had a motley assortment of foodstuffs wrapped in cloth parcels.

They returned to find Joy and Maeve waiting under a grand oak near the edge of the park, the horses grazing contentedly. Maeve clapped her hands in delight at the sight of provisions, while Joy laughed at the hodgepodge nature of their 'picnic'. Soon, they had spread a borrowed horse blanket beneath the oak's shade and were passing around bread, ham, cheese, and ale with the kind of camaraderie that arises when hunger meets simple fare.

Freddy found himself seated beside Joy, watching as Thornhill tore off a chunk of bread and offered it gallantly to Maeve, who rewarded him with a dimpled smile. The two conversed softly, occasionally glancing in Freddy's direction as though to include him in the talk.

When at last they finished their makeshift meal, the sun had shifted westward, lengthening shadows over the grass. They mounted up and began the journey back towards London, lingering at a leisurely pace until the outskirts of the city beckoned them into narrower roads and heavier traffic. Freddy took the lead, ensuring they navigated the busy thoroughfares without mishap—though Joy joked that she had never seen him so dutiful, teasing that perhaps fatherhood would be his next accomplishment.

It was only when they reached the familiar London streets, their horses weaving between carriages, that Freddy felt a sharp jolt of realization. He'd spent the entire day bickering with Joy and arranging amusements, and hardly spoke a word to Lady Maeve to forward the notion of courting her. He cast a quick look in Maeve's direction. She seemed content, chatting quietly with Thornhill about some detail about a garden party next week.

Freddy inwardly groaned. Had his day's enjoyment blinded him to his own objectives? Perhaps so. And yet, as he watched Thornhill's warm smile and Maeve's answering laughter, a curious pang of both regret and genuine gladness stirred in Freddy's chest.

He reined in his horse outside Westwood House, assisting Joy in dismounting while Thornhill assisted Lady Maeve. They exchanged polite farewells, with Thornhill pressing Lady Maeve's hand a fraction longer than etiquette dictated. Joy eyed Freddy quizzically, as though reading the confusion in his mind. But all he could manage was a shrug and a lopsided grin, murmuring that he had been "very pleased with the day."

As the Duke took his leave, Freddy remained at Joy's side, his chestnut gelding snorting impatiently. Joy cleared her throat and rubbed at her temples. "I do hope you enjoyed yourself, Freddy. Even though you forgot something important."

"I did not notice you make any effort to engage Thornhill," he retorted to her scolding.

"We both failed."

"Yes," he admitted, lowering his gaze to the cobblestones. "Yes, I rather think we both did."

CHAPTER 5

*J*oy sat cross-legged on the floor of the Whitford sisters' sitting room, while Camilla, the marmalade kitten, pawed at a ribbon she dangled. The bright afternoon sunshine streamed through the tall windows, illuminating the comfortable space with a warm glow. Scattered about were baskets lined with cushions, a spindly-legged tea table, and a few embroidered footstools which had become playgrounds and scratching posts for the kittens.

Maeve, perched on a low ottoman near the hearth, clapped her hands as Mortimer—a grey tabby with a mischievous glint—pounced on a stray tassel that dangled from the stool. "Oh, Joy, just look at them!" she cried. "I cannot decide which is more charming, Lord Orville or Mortimer. Come here, you little rascal. I should not have let Grace keep Evalina." Maeve scooped up Mortimer, who offered a half-hearted squeak of protest before settling into her lap. "I vow, if the Duke—"

She paused, flushing slightly, then let out a high-pitched laugh. "Oh dear, listen to me. I cannot go a moment without mentioning him, can I?"

Joy gave a dry little smile. "The Duke does feature rather heavily in your conversation these days, I must admit."

"He is everything a girl could wish for," Maeve declared, hugging the kitten a little tighter. "Undeniably handsome, and possessed of impeccable manners. It is no wonder half the ladies in the *ton* are scheming for a chance of his attention." Her eyes shone with excitement.

Joy was certain it had nothing to do with his illustrious title, and felt disappointment for her plan with Freddy already going awry.

"And I—I alone—may boast of having walked in the park on his arm, receiving fresh lilies from him the very next morning. Is that not the height of romance?"

"Lilies?" Joy repeated with forced enthusiasm. "How thoughtful. I recall you prefer violets, though."

"Oh, hush. The gesture was beautiful, lilies or not." Maeve traced small circles on Mortimer's back. "Truly, Joy, you cannot imagine how it felt to stand beside him in the Row, all eyes upon us, people whispering, 'Who is that with his Grace?' It was glorious."

Joy's mouth tightened briefly, but she exhaled, offering a nod. "I am glad for you," she said, meaning it in her own half-hearted way. She paused to stroke Camilla, who cuffed her sleeve. "I think I should hate being so conspicuous, myself—everyone gawping at me, gossiping about every look or word. I do not know why anyone would long to be a duchess, with all the scrutiny it brings." She found what she said was true. Not that she ever truly thought she could attract Thornhill anyway. Besides, he was far too high in the instep for the likes of her.

Maeve shrugged, an unabashed smile curving her lips. "Ah, but being a duchess also brings an estate, a grand household, influence in Society—why, you could do so much good if you wished to. And for some of us, that sense of accomplishment is appealing. I was brought up to the life, after all, with all its demands and benefits."

Joy bowed her head, her hair falling forward to hide a small frown. She could not help recalling how her elder sister, Hope, had always dreamed of grandeur: fancy titles, glittering jewels, a court presentation. Joy, in contrast, felt stifled just imagining the endless obligations.

Even as she listened to Maeve's excited ramblings, a flicker of jealousy stirred within Joy—not that she envied Maeve the Duke, exactly, but a restlessness tugged at her. She had half-hoped that her close friend Freddy might find his own spark of interest in Maeve. After all, she reminded herself, Freddy had spoken of courting Lady Maeve. Yet now, here was Maeve, daydreaming about the Duke, having fallen under his spell of lofty titles and quiet magnetism. Joy felt a small pang for Freddy.

Mortimer suddenly tumbled off Maeve's lap and landed on his feet with a mutinous squeak. Maeve giggled, lifting him up again. "Oh, Joy, if only you could see Thornhill as I do. He is not stuffy at all, once you coax him from behind his reserve. Why, just the other evening, he told me a ridiculous anecdote about a parrot in the Duchess's drawing room that nearly scandalized a visiting bishop by squawking out a most unrepeatable phrase—"

The door to the sitting room opened, interrupting Maeve's narrative. A footman cleared his throat. "Mr. Cunningham to see Miss Whitford."

Maeve raised her brows in delight, setting Mortimer gently down. "Well, that is opportune timing," she teased, tossing Joy a sidelong glance. "He is come for a diversion, perhaps?"

Joy felt an inexplicable swell of relief. "I should see what he wants," she said, rising to her feet. The kittens mewed in protest at the sudden removal of their plaything, but Joy left them to Maeve's cooing attempts to draw their attention back.

She stepped into the hall, adjusting her pale blue morning gown and smoothing any stray wisps of hair that might have escaped her pins. Her hair was always escaping. Freddy stood in the entry, hat in hand, wearing a broad grin. He looked positively smug.

"What mischief are you planning?" Joy asked, eyeing him with mock suspicion.

Freddy put on an expression of wounded innocence. "Must it be mischief every time? Perhaps I have come to carry you off to a delightful surprise—entirely respectable and above board."

"Your respectable surprises have been known to involve orchard walls and torn petticoats," she quipped lightly, though her eyes sparkled at the prospect of leaving the town house.

He gave a theatrical sigh. "I resent that insinuation. Come, I have my curricle outside. The weather is splendid, and I promise you something truly beneficial—though you may not thank me at once."

Curiosity piqued, Joy asked Hartley to inform Maeve and the Dowager she was leaving, then allowed him to lead her out. As they crossed the threshold, she threw a parting glance to where Maeve waved from the doorway, a kitten perched on her shoulder like a small, furry parrot. Joy tried not to dwell on how her friend might be daydreaming about the Duke, picturing an elegant wedding, or perhaps receiving more lilies. *Oh, Freddy, you really are letting our plan slip through your fingers.* It had not occurred to her that she should have furthered Maeve's suit with Freddy by having her accompany them.

⁓

FREDDY TOOK up the reins of his curricle with a flourish, a pleasant hum of anticipation thrumming through him. A crisp breeze caressed his cheeks, carrying the faint scent of fresh straw drifting from a nearby hay cart. He rather liked this time of day, when the sun sat high enough to warm the streets, yet the press of London's traffic had not reached its peak. He glanced aside to make certain Joy was comfortably settled on the seat beside him, then he urged the horses forward.

They set off at a brisk trot, the vehicle rolling smoothly over the cobble-stones. Joy possessed a natural demeanour that soothed him, and though she was neither simpering nor flirtatious, he had always appreciated her company. Not for the first time, he thought how simple life could be if all ladies were as unaffected as Joy. But of course, that thought immediately summoned an image of Lady Maeve and of Freddy's half-hearted—if he was frank with himself—vow to court her.

It wasn't long before Joy turned to him with a look he knew all too well: arched brow, a hint of challenge in her eyes. Bracing himself for whatever was about to tumble from her lips, he nonetheless felt a fond amusement tugging at his mouth.

"I must ask," she began, voice lightly laced with admonishment, "do you truly intend to pursue Lady Maeve? Because if so, you are doing a remarkably poor job of it. You have barely spoken to her in days, while the Duke calls upon her regularly, takes her driving in the park, sends her flowers—by the dozen, too. She is quite dazzled."

Freddy pulled a face in mock horror, letting out an exasperated huff. "Flowers? Driving in the park? Is that what I must do to win a lady's hand? Good heavens, Joy, that sounds positively laborious." Deep down, he knew she was right—he had done little to keep pace with Thornhill's gallant gestures. Yet he balked at the very idea of following the same mundane approach.

Joy's snort of disbelief made him smile despite himself. "You need not be so dramatic. Maeve is a lovely friend, and you once claimed to be interested in her, but for a week you have not so much as enquired after her health. Instead, you dawdle about with me, complaining about your father's demands."

At that, he gave a playful shrug and cracked the slightest grin. "Well, in my defence, you are infinitely more entertaining than a formal call. Maeve is sweet and a beauty, I grant you, but a man can only handle so many fluttering glances and parlour visits before he loses his wits."

He felt the words come out more sharply than intended, but it was true enough. The thought of a meticulously planned courtship made him inwardly cringe. He had no wish to spend hours engaged in tiresome small talk, always on his best behaviour, always mindful of a thousand unspoken rules. There was a thrill in spontaneity with his chums—a thrill he found more readily with Joy than with half the ladies in London combined.

"So you concede the field to the Duke?" she pressed, arching that brow again.

Freddy gave another shrug. "I suppose so. He clearly excels at the gentlemanly arts of courtship—all that polite fuss. I doubt I can match him if that is what Maeve truly wants." And there, plain as day, was his truth. If wooing Maeve required elaborate gestures he found stultifying, perhaps it was never a good match. He straightened in the driver's seat, eager to change the subject. "Nor is my future title so lofty. But never mind that. We are nearly at our destination."

He caught the fleeting expression of puzzlement that crossed Joy's face as she looked around. They were on a quieter street, lined with orderly shop fronts and tidy windows. He knew she would notice soon enough that this was no typical social call or scenic route. A sign with gold lettering announced the shop he sought: *Optician*. He felt his heart quicken with a twinge of concern, hoping Joy would accept his plan with minimal distress.

"Freddy…why are we—?" she began, a note of apprehension colouring her tone.

He offered her a sidelong glance, injecting a gentleness into his voice. "I promised I would help you with this, Joy. You mentioned that your eyes trouble you—particularly the one—and the very thought of spectacles made you anxious, but you cannot continue stumbling in ballrooms and tripping over lords. I have found a discreet optician who can help." He mustered a small, reassuring smile. "No one else need know for now, if that is your worry. At least you can see what he thinks and discover if spectacles would even help."

Her cheeks flushed, and Freddy could see the conflict flickering in her eyes. She was proud, no doubt, but also practical in many respects. He suppressed the urge to drape a protective arm over her shoulder.

Joy's voice wavered slightly as she murmured, "I—I do not relish the idea of looking like a bespectacled bluestocking."

Freddy knew there was more to it than her looks. She hadn't seemed to mind the scar, which at the time had been much more evident than glasses would be. He responded with a teasing wink, hoping to lift her spirits. "What if you do? If it helps you see without worry, why care about a few stares? I think you will look smart even with them."

She snorted.

"What about a quizzing glass?"

"You would have me look like a dandy or a dowager?"

"Is it not better to see than to worry over such trivialities?"

Watching her bite her lip, Freddy felt a surge of sympathy. He was not oblivious to how difficult it must be for her to confront the reality of poor eyesight. Joy prided herself on her independence; to admit she needed spectacles was an unwelcome reminder of her vulnerability. Still, he guided the curricle to a halt outside the modest little shop, handed the reins to his tiger, then hopped down to assist her from the seat.

The moment they entered, Freddy was greeted by the cosy hush of the place—a world apart from London's clamour. Shelves lined the walls, replete with frames and glass lenses glinting in the light. A bespectacled gentleman approached, bowing politely.

"Mr. Cunningham, I presume?" he said in a respectful voice. "And this must be Miss Whitford? Jeremiah Dempsey at your service."

Freddy cleared his throat, willing confidence into his tone. "A pleasure, sir. We come seeking your expertise." Then, with a sideways glance at Joy, he noticed her stiff posture, as though she expected the floor to swallow her whole. He smiled encouragingly.

Mr. Dempsey ushered them into a small examining area behind draped curtains. Freddy let Joy take the chair while he stood a discreet step behind her, resting a hand on her shoulder in silent encouragement. He felt her tense at the question about reading letters on a chart, and his heart ached at the discomfort he sensed roiling inside her.

She tried reading the chart, faltering as the lines shrank. Freddy watched with a mixture of pity and determination. When Mr. Dempsey moved on to different lenses, Freddy forced himself to stay silent, though he wanted to praise her for each correct letter. Instead, he simply squeezed her arm lightly now and then, hoping to communicate his unwavering support.

Mr. Dempsey was methodical, making notes, humming as he tested Joy's left eye, then the right. Freddy heard the optician's sympathetic tone as he enquired about the accident, and Joy's halting explanation about falling from a horse two years ago. Freddy recalled that day vaguely—he had not been present, but he remembered the gossip that followed. How typically Joy it was to brush aside a grave injury as "just a bit of dizziness and occasional headaches."

When the time came to inspect frames, Freddy practically leapt at the chance to lighten the mood. "Could you perhaps show us frames that might suit a lady's taste? Something discreet yet sturdy?" he asked, stepping to the display counter. He watched Joy's face as she tried her first pair, sensing her mixture of fascination and dread.

"You look rather dashing, Joy!" he proclaimed in earnest. "In fact, you appear like a very dignified scholar who might soon lecture me on some classical text." He felt a little proud of that line, pleased that she gave a shaky laugh instead of frowning.

As Joy tested different sized frames, Freddy offered murmurs of approval or suggestions. He caught Mr. Dempsey's discreet nod when Joy found a pair that provided a good fit. The relief flickering across Joy's face—just for an instant—seemed to validate every bit of trouble he'd gone through to arrange this meeting.

The man bowed and assured them the frames would be ready soon. Freddy, feeling a pleasurable sense of accomplishment, guided Joy back outside.

He assisted her into the curricle, then climbed up to settle beside her, taking the reins. "I hope you are not at outs with me for springing this upon you," he said quietly, flicking the horses into motion with his whip. He cast her a sidelong look, trying to gauge if her face revealed any lingering resentment, but her expression was thoughtful, even peaceful.

"No. I…think I am grateful," she replied softly, her gaze on the passing shop fronts. "I can scarcely remember the last time I saw letters so clearly. To read again without headache or humiliation—heaven knows I miss burying my nose in a novel—but I do not know if I am ready to sport them at a ball."

"One step at a time. Maybe next you will confess to your sisters?"

"Perhaps."

He could only hope.

"Now, you truly must not forget your vow to woo a lady next time. I shall not let you wriggle free so easily."

He feigned a groan. "Joy, must you remind me of my father's edict? Are flowers and calls, all that nonsense, truly necessary?"

"Yes, indeed," she countered, one brow arched imperiously. "Most ladies expect it."

"But not you, Joy."

"No, not me. Do not be ridiculous, Freddy."

CHAPTER 6

About the only thing worse than a ball was a garden party to draw attention to one's incompetence at being a lady. Balls, at least, involved movement. One could dance, or make a well-timed escape behind a potted palm. But garden parties? The main entertainment was idle chit-chat and the ever popular game of who-was-wearing-what and who was matching with whom. Tête-à-têtes with strangers Joy had no desire to know, forced smiles and compliments on hats—it was too much to be borne. If only someone would seat her with the gentlemen and let her debate bloodlines of horses or the merits of different harnesses, she'd be much obliged. But no. Ladies must speak of fabric swatches, and how scandalously low the line of Lady Findley's neck had plunged at the opera.

Still, the Cunningham garden was one of the finest in London. If one must be miserable, it helped that one could do so under a clear sky and surrounded by lilacs. Everything was in bloom. Even Joy could make out the brightness of the roses across the lawn.

Tables were placed about the central fountain, each set with frothy lace cloths and small towers of pastries, tarts, and lemon cakes—her main reason for not fleeing. The punch glittered in the sunlight like rubies. There was a silver lining, after all.

Her sisters were scattered amongst the guests, all fluttering fans and silken skirts—all except Grace, who was still off with Lord Carew, no doubt enjoying some wondrous ruin or windswept cliff on their wedding trip to Greece. The thought made something small and wistful stir inside Joy. Grace had always been her closest companion, her co-conspirator in all things—though Grace was more often the silent partner. Without her, Joy felt a bit like a puzzle missing a vital piece.

She looked over the crowd and sighed. Everyone else looked so polished, so perfectly content. Joy smoothed her skirt and tried not to fidget.

"How are things, Joy?" Hope asked, appearing beside her like an apparition of maternal concern. "I have scarcely seen you since the ball."

Joy resisted the urge to shrug. "Well enough, I suppose. Freddy and I went with Lady Maeve and the Duke of Thornhill to Richmond."

"If you wish to find a beau, Joy," Hope said pointedly, "you might need to stop sitting in Freddy's pocket and vice versa."

"Everyone knows they are as brother and sister." Patience waved a hand, coming upon them from nowhere. "They do not think of each other in that way."

"Be that as it may," Faith added, joining them. "Suitors can certainly gather the wrong impression."

"That is partially on purpose," Joy muttered into her punch.

Three sets of sisterly eyes fastened on her like bees to honey.

"Pray tell," Patience demanded.

Joy took a bite of tart for fortification. "We thought to find spouses together, Freddy and I. Ones who were friends of ours so we might all still be friends."

"Oh, dear," Hope murmured, as though Joy had confessed to running off with a circus.

"I have heard about the edict from Mr. Cunningham's parents," Faith said. "Have you discovered any prospects yet?"

Joy craned her neck, locating Maeve, currently laughing at something the Duke had said. The man looked positively enchanted.

Freddy stood nearby, being talked at by some young miss, looking rather like a man who had brought his best hound to a fair only to watch it run off with the prized pheasant.

"Freddy thought perhaps Maeve," Joy admitted, "but he may have been too slow."

All eyes shifted to the laughing couple.

"I hope there is an alternative plan," Patience murmured. "Surely you were not thinking about the Duke for yourself?"

"Can you imagine me as a duchess?" Joy scoffed.

Mercifully, they refrained from comment.

"Freddy is going to introduce me to some of his friends, and I shall make mine known to him," Joy continued. "Though Maeve was my only candidate thus far."

A footman appeared with punch, and Joy gratefully seized a glass as if it might ward off further discussion.

As Faith and Hope launched into stories of teething and nap times, Joy allowed her gaze to wander, sweeping across the other débutantes gathered. If she was to help Freddy find a bride, she'd best begin sorting the likely from the hopeless. She attempted a casual assessment.

Miss Marigold Henley laughed just then, a high, tinkling sound like a tea kettle on the verge of scalding. Joy winced. Imagine listening to that across the breakfast table every morning.

Then there was Miss Beatrice Plumb—very pretty, but discussed French silks with religious fervour. Freddy—and Joy—would be bored silly.

Miss Eugenia Franks was bookish, which Joy generally appreciated, but not when the lady in question believed novels to be frivolous nonsense.

Lady Lucinda Biddleton had sneezed precisely three times in succession every time she was within ten feet of the kitten Joy had had with her in the park one day.

One by one, Joy mentally eliminated them all. Things were looking grimmer by the moment.

The way matters were proceeding, she might need to throw in her lot with Freddy, and they could simply become a pair of eccentric, lifelong companions surrounded by a menagerie of horses, hounds, and cats. Joy dismissed the ridiculous notion.

Across the fountain, Patience waved, trying to entice Joy into a group that included Lord Montford and a pair of earnest clergymen. She shook her head. The last thing she desired was a conversation of sermons and moralizing. Instead she edged towards a marble bench half-hidden by lilac branches, grateful for the spicy scent that drifted from each lavender cone. When she sat down, her eyes adjusted to a fresh perspective: she could see the sweep of the lawns without being seen, a hodge-podge of parasols, hats, and swirling ribbons. She began sorting them mentally—potential allies (Rotham, who seemed stern but wasn't really), certain foes (Lady Partridge, who was a terrifying meddler), and the undecided middle faction.

Ten yards away, Miss Henley had cornered poor Lord Worth and was waving a parasol like a deadly weapon. The man stood as stiff as a ramrod, nodding in terror each time the pointed edge came too close. Joy's lips curved. Worth gambled too much and had quite the reputation, but he did not deserve evisceration by a parasol.

She lifted a pastry from the plate beside her, broke it neatly in half, and flung a crumb in the direction of a nearby pigeon. The bird fluttered in and landed squarely upon Miss Henley's volant-trimmed shoulder. Chaos ensued—gasps, fluttered fans, Lord Worth retreating as though from artillery fire. Joy, satisfied with her work, munched the other half of her pastry and considered the intervention successful.

The commotion drew Letty Partridge, who minced up carrying a lace-edged handkerchief. "I saw what you did."

Joy stared at the girl.

"You have a penchant for trouble, Miss Whitford," she said, though her smile held the faintest suspicion.

"I prefer to think of it as enlivening things," Joy answered, blinking innocently.

Letty's brows climbed. "You will never keep a suitor if you make a spectacle of yourself."

"Perhaps I do not wish to keep one—like a pet in a cage," Joy retorted. "'Tis better to let them fly free and see whether they return of their own accord."

Letty's lips pressed thin. "Some of us have serious expectations."

Joy caught a faint reflection in the fountain's surface—Letty's proud profile intermixed with her own blurred outline. There was something sad in Letty's desperation, but she could not conjure pity for her.

"I wish you luck in your hunt," Joy murmured.

Before Letty could shape an answer, the Dowager's laugh rippled from behind a statue—the unmistakable sound of triumph. Joy knew that note—it usually preceded the unveiling of a Plot Too Grand to Refuse. The Dowager appeared a moment later, cheeks pink, escorting none other than General Archibald Armstrong—hero of Talavera, and, frankly, far too old for any girl just out.

"My dear," the Dowager said, guiding the General forward, "I was just telling General Armstrong that you are the most accomplished horsewoman in Town. He insists he meet such a paragon."

Joy blinked, caught between horror and hilarity. General Armstrong bowed, a spark of amusement in his eyes—he knew exactly what the Dowager was attempting and did not seem to mind one whit.

"May I present Miss Whitford, General? She is one of Westwood's wards."

Joy curtsied.

The General made a gallant bow for someone of his age. "The pleasure is all mine."

Thankfully he was called away before Joy was committed to anything, and she went back to watching the throng.

She sipped her punch and muttered under her breath, "What *would* it be like to marry Freddy?" Again she dismissed the ridiculous idea as a last resort.

"Did you say something, dear?" asked the Dowager, sweeping past in a cloud of lavender silk.

"I was just admiring the roses," Joy said brightly, though the roses in question were now a blur of indeterminate colour.

"Well, try not to admire yourself into a rosebush," she replied with a laugh, patting Joy's arm. "Twice have you nearly toppled into the flowerbeds already."

Joy smiled sweetly. It was not her fault the flowerbeds had leapt into her path.

Somewhere, she heard Freddy laugh. She looked over to see Maeve whisper something to him while the Duke bent closer. They made a picturesque trio. Joy sighed again, heavily. This matchmaking business was trickier than anticipated.

As she turned back to the pastries, Joy came to one conclusion: it was going to be a very long Season indeed. But she would be dashed if Freddy settled for someone who couldn't even abide a kitten.

∼

It did not take long to realize Lady Maeve and the Duke of Thornhill were not far from a match. Freddy may not boast the sharpest of intellects, but even he could see that they had eyes only for each other. When Thornhill giggled—the indignity!—Freddy had had enough. He cast his gaze across the garden, seeking respite from the matrimonial machinations that now surrounded him. He spotted Joy, lounging near the pastry table with her customary air of rebellion and biscuit crumbs. She was the only soul who understood his plight.

Crossing the lawn, he addressed her with an air of tragic resignation. "I knew I should find you near the treacle tart," he said, dropping into the seat beside her without ceremony.

Joy didn't flinch. "You look as if someone tried to foist a bonnet onto your head."

"I feel as though someone did," Freddy replied grimly. "You must save me, Joy. Lady Maeve and Thornhill are all but composing poetry to one another, and every débutante here either simpers like a sick bird or proses on about embroidery."

"Were you lectured about embroidery again?"

"Miss Plumb gave me a twelve minute discourse on her sampler. I now know far more about silks and stitches than any man ought."

Joy sighed dramatically. "Poor lamb. Would you like a tart?"

"Desperately." He reached for one. "Tell me—have you anyone else for me to meet before I offer myself up to the mercy of a vicar's daughter with a claimed fondness for kittens she has never actually met?"

Joy, ever practical, took a sip of her punch and surveyed the blurred garden party like a general reviewing a battlefield. "Well, that one," she pointed discreetly with her chin towards a tall, elegant young lady in violet, "thinks Byron was too restrained."

"Too restrained?"

"I heard her say she writes poetry of her own about stormy emotions and dead flowers."

"Good Lord."

"That one," she gestured again to Miss Henley, "laughs at everything. Even when someone spills tea on her gown. Hysterical, giggling laughter—all the time."

"Is she the one who laughed when the pigeon dived for something?"

"The very one, though I confess I also laughed a little. You remember the hyena we saw at the 'Change?"

Freddy suppressed a shudder.

Joy nodded gravely. "And then there is Miss Franks."

"What is wrong with Miss Franks?"

"She is perfectly lovely, until you realize she has memorized every one of *Fordyce's sermons* and recites them when she is nervous."

"Surely there must be someone with a tolerable sense of humour and an affection for animals?" Freddy asked plaintively.

Joy shook her head. "If there is, she is disguised as shrubbery. Now, do *you* have anyone for *me* to meet?"

Freddy gazed about. None of his new friends were on the hunt for a bride—not that any of them were terribly appropriate. Joy would not mind that so much, but he knew Westwood would be quite particular. Joy was a favourite with all the gentlemen. She was pluck to the backbone, as his friends would describe it, but the problem was it was hard to see Joy as a wife and mother. Well, other than to animals, of course.

"Well...Worth is charming, but he is as poor as a church mouse from gambling debts and is on the hunt for an heiress. Godwin is a devilish boor, and Singleton is hopelessly devoted to a French opera singer."

"So your prospects are no better than mine," Joy concluded with a sigh.

Just then, his mother approached in a swirl of silk and gardenia scent. "Frederick, darling," she cooed, "have you made any progress?"

He looked at her blankly. "Progress?"

"With the eligible young ladies! Lady Constance is hosting a dinner party, and you must attend. Joy, you too, of course. There will be eligible gentlemen present."

Joy opened her mouth to reply, but his mother had already swept away with the regal determination of a mama with a singular purpose.

Freddy turned to Joy with a dramatic shudder. "Eligible young ladies."

Joy pulled a face. "Eligible young gentlemen."

"I cannot think of more damning words."

"Except perhaps, 'suitable match.'"

"Or 'decorous behaviour.'"

"Or 'Fancy a stroll in the garden, Miss Joy?'"

He winced. "That happened to you?"

"At the ball."

"Who is the blackguard? I shall call him out."

Joy smiled and patted his arm. "You are a good friend."

"We are castaways on the same remote island."

They exchanged a grin, united in their mutual despair. They sat quietly a moment longer. The party carried on around them—laughter rising and falling, the splash of the fountain punctuating the hum of conversation.

Then he asked, "Do you think we will ever find the right person?"

Joy didn't answer right away. She looked around, at her sisters laughing with their husbands, at the flowering garden filled with people all seeming to enjoy the gathering. Then she turned to Freddy.

"I do not know. The prospects are not promising."

He smiled. "Why must we marry? Why is it criminal to remain a bachelor?"

"The succession, m'dear," she mocked in a parental tone.

"But you do not have to produce an heir," he replied accusingly.

"I do not, do I?" She laughed, and it made him feel, for just a moment, that everything might turn out well in the end.

"Come on," he said, standing and offering her his hand. "Let's walk. I wish to avoid Miss Plumb and her views on curtain tassels."

Joy took it and rose with a smile. "Lead on, Frederick. To freedom and pastries."

"A fine battle cry," Freddy said, guiding Joy down a side path flanked by espaliered pears—cool shade, fewer inquisitive matrons.

"We should have it engraved on our coat of arms—two crossed forks rampant."

He barked a laugh, bending a branch so she would not brush it.

She tipped her head towards the farther end of the garden, where a low stone wall marked the beginning of the orchard proper. Beyond, neat rows of blossoming pear trees met the skyline.

Petals drifted like confetti, catching in her dark curls and in the folds of his coat. They let silence reign for a dozen paces, both of them savouring the reprieve.

"About prospects," Joy said, interrupting his reverie. "Perhaps we should reconsider our approach. If you must wed someone vapid, take one with a hunting-mad brother. At least you would get decent sport out of the bargain."

"Only if she comes with a string in training," Freddy countered. "Otherwise the bargain is dashed poor."

They exchanged wicked grins, allies again. It was time to return before they were missed. As they re-entered the main garden, Freddy spotted his mother assembling a little knot of gentlemen beneath the large cedar tree—Lord Tinmouth, Sir Gregory Pember, and young Denbigh, all of whom fancied themselves connoisseurs of bloodstock.

Joy followed his gaze. "Shall we run the gauntlet?"

"If we must," he murmured, escorting her back.

His mother's eyes lit up. "Frederick, these gentlemen were asking after our hunters for next season. Perhaps you can enlighten them?"

Before Freddy could begin a reply on one of his most favourite topics, Joy stepped in cheerfully. "Gresham's hunters? Why, good bone, steady on their feet, short cannons." She turned to Sir Gregory. "And above all, a back long enough for comfort yet short enough for power."

Tinmouth blinked while Denbigh's jaw unhinged. Joy, warming to her theme, launched into the pedigrees of his hunters—touching on Highflyer, Luna's hock action, and why a dash of Herod blood would settle Denbigh's infamous stallion's inclination to buck. Freddy bit his lip. Lady Gresham paled, torn between pride and panic. The gentlemen did not know whether to be impressed or alarmed.

When Joy finished, silence reigned for three beats. Then Freddy lost the battle. Laughter burst from him.

His mother's head turned. "Frederick!"

He caught his breath but not his grin. "Forgive me, Mama, but she knows our horses as well as I do."

Tinmouth recovered enough to bow stiffly. "Miss Whitford, your…er…insights astonish."

"Delight, surely," Joy returned, eyes dancing.

Lady Gresham cleared her throat with surgical precision. "Indeed. And now, Frederick, perhaps you will escort Miss Whitford for some punch?"

"With pleasure," he said, offering Joy his arm. As they crossed the garden, he whispered, "You realize, do you not, you have slain three prospects in one volley?"

She tilted her head, pleased. "Only three? Next time I shall quote training plans. However, I am afraid your mother was not impressed."

CHAPTER 7

*T*he soft light of spring spilled gently through the lace-curtained windows of the upstairs parlour. Joy sat upon the Aubusson rug, utterly at ease in her dressing gown, with three of the four kittens clambering over her lap like furry buccaneers. The fourth had taken up residence in Maeve's slipper and was gently snoring, much to Maeve's delight.

"Oh, he is the very soul of mischief," Maeve declared, her fingers lightly scratching behind the ears of a grey puffball that had just decided her lap was the optimal location for his morning nap. "Honestly, Joy, I never thought I should find such delight in cats."

Joy smiled wryly, brushing a streak of cream from her sleeve that one of the kittens had left as a gift. "That is the usual effect. They sneak into your heart and wreck your furniture."

Maeve laughed, her eyes sparkling. "Speaking of sneaking into hearts—did I tell you what Thornhill said yesterday? He remarked upon the particular shade of ribbon I was wearing and said it reminded him of the early spring sky in Ireland. Can you imagine?"

"The man is positively poetic," Joy drawled, reaching for another roll. "Has he also compared your eyes to dewdrops and your laugh to birdsong?"

"He has not been quite so florid, thank goodness," Maeve said with a giggle, accepting a cup of chocolate, "but he did offer to send me a book of Irish poetry. I did not know he was so well read!"

Joy grinned at that, tearing off a piece of roll to feed to a kitten that had scaled her knee like a miniature mountaineer. "Beware the literary suitor. They tend to think themselves quite profound."

"You are cynical this morning," Maeve said, arching an elegant brow. "Surely you do not begrudge me a little happiness?"

"Not at all," Joy said sincerely. "I am very pleased for you. I am only mildly amazed you have managed to captivate a duke without once tripping over a potted plant or spilling tea in his lap."

"I am not so inelegant, thank you," Maeve said, tossing a napkin at her friend. "Besides, it is your turn next. I have made a list of prospects for you."

Joy groaned. "Do not say so."

"Only a short list," Maeve assured her. "Lord Meredith—good family, tolerably handsome, rather serious."

"He once asked if cats were safe to keep indoors," Joy replied flatly.

"Very well. What about Mr. Langdon? He sits a horse well."

"But rides like a sack of potatoes."

"Joy," Maeve said, trying not to laugh, "you are impossible."

"Accurate, though," Joy said, her expression unrepentant.

Before Maeve could press the matter further, the clock on the mantel chimed one. Startled, the kittens leapt in various directions, one sliding across the polished floor like a skater.

Maeve rose with a sigh. "It is the Dowager's at-home day. We had better dress before she finds us still in our wrappers and declares us a disgrace."

Joy made a face but complied. "At least there will be pastries."

They dressed quickly, Maeve in a pale blue muslin, and Joy in a soft yellow cambric that made her look younger, despite her maid's protests. By the time they descended to the drawing room, voices could already be heard from the hall.

"Freddy!" Joy exclaimed in surprise as the butler opened the door to admit Mr. Cunningham. He was dressed smartly with his usual easy elegance, a well-fitted coat of blue superfine, buff pantaloons, gleaming Hessian boots, and a touch of irreverence in the tilt of his exquisite neckcloth. If he was not inured to it, Joy would have teased him for being a dandy.

"Ladies," he said with a flourishing bow. "I beg a private word with Miss Joy before I am required to speak of weather and wisteria."

Maeve gave a knowing smile. "I shall go and enquire about the… pastries."

Freddy waited until Maeve had vanished into the next room before turning to Joy and producing a small velvet box from his pocket.

"What is this?" she asked warily.

"A fashion accessory," Freddy said lightly. "Or a tool…depending on your interpretation."

Inside the box were spectacles—delicate, with thin gold rims and clear lenses. Joy stared at them as if they might bite.

"I picked them up on my way here."

"Oh," she said stupidly, her voice faint.

"You might wear them as an affectation," he said, smiling. "Like a dandy. I have half a mind to get a pair myself."

"I think you mean a quizzing glass, Freddy." Joy picked them up with the same expression she might use for a spider that had wandered into her shoe. She perched them on her nose, blinked once —and then blinked again.

"Well?"

"I can see," she said flatly, "but I hate how they feel."

Freddy looked mildly disappointed.

She quickly removed them and stuffed them into her pocket. "But thank you. Truly. 'Twas thoughtful of you."

He brightened. "You will grow accustomed to them. Besides, why care if you can now see?"

"If only that were the only concern," she said dryly, but took his arm.

As they entered the drawing room, they found it already humming with conversation. The Duchess of Thornhill was speaking to Lady

Westwood, and Mrs. Larkspur had cornered the vicar's wife. But Maeve was unmistakably ensconced beside Thornhill himself, her entire expression transformed.

Joy watched them for a long moment. They leaned towards each other as if the air between them held secrets, their smiles private, their conversation low. Maeve looked incandescent. Joy could not imagine ever being so transported.

She folded her arms and muttered, "Why is it I feel most unnatural at everything expected of a lady?"

"Because you are a glorious rebel," Freddy said at her elbow, "and we are all the better for it."

Joy was about to punch him in the arm when a new voice interrupted them.

"Mr. Cunningham!"

Miss Dorothea Larkspur, curls bouncing, fluttered up like a particularly excitable puppy. She was bedecked in ruffles and emanating rose water.

"What a *delight* to see you! I was just telling Letty Partridge what an enchanting gentleman you are. I do hope you are to attend Lady Jersey's musical evening?"

Freddy bowed politely. "Miss Larkspur. How very…sprightly you look this morning."

Joy raised her brows. Sprightly?

Miss Larkspur giggled. "Oh, Mr. Cunningham, you do tease. Do say you will attend."

"I must consult my engagements," he said vaguely, shooting Joy a glance that plainly said *rescue me*. But Joy merely smiled into her punch.

"Miss Whitford, your gown is charming," Miss Larkspur added as an afterthought.

Joy inclined her head. "How kind. Your bonnet is…decorative."

Freddy coughed into his hand.

She gave him a knowing look. Decorative was as good as sprightly.

Miss Larkspur lingered a moment longer, muttered something about her mother, and finally skipped away like a lark indeed.

"She is making a cake of herself," Joy said under her breath.

"With too much icing and marzipan," Freddy murmured.

Joy looked sideways at him. "Is that your type?"

"Lord, no. I prefer my cakes solid and fruity."

She smirked. "Would you call me a fruit cake?"

"Never. A plum tart, perhaps, with just enough spice."

Joy laughed, and Freddy smiled, watching her.

In the corner, Thornhill was whispering something to Maeve that made her blush and fan herself with a smile.

"Well," Joy said, straightening, "I suppose it is time we played the game."

"I thought we were already."

Before Joy could summon a witty retort, the butler appeared with a gentleman trailing in his wake—tall, sun browned, with a roguish dimple and shoulders that would not have looked out of place in cavalry blues.

"Colonel Edward St. John," the butler announced.

Joy's eyes widened ever so slightly. The gentleman bowed with easy grace and offered Freddy a firm handshake. "Cunningham! I did not expect to see you here."

Freddy grinned. "St. John! I thought you were off fighting wars or chasing smugglers."

"Both, if I am fortunate," St. John replied with a gleam of humour in his hazel eyes.

Joy took a moment to appreciate that he looked every inch the sporting gentleman—a fine, athletic frame, strong hands, a sun-kissed jawline, and a smile to warm a girl on a cold day.

"Introduce me," she commanded, straightening her spine and stepping forward.

Freddy blinked, then chuckled. "Colonel St. John, may I present Miss Joy Whitford. Joy, this scoundrel is Colonel St. John, a school friend of mine and an inveterate stirrer of trouble."

"Only the worthwhile kind," St. John said with a bow. "A pleasure, Miss Whitford."

"I should hope so," she said, extending her hand. "If I am to be introduced as a command, I ought to live up to the occasion."

He laughed. "You may consider me duly impressed."

Joy tilted her head, intrigued despite herself. Well, she thought, this morning had taken an unexpected turn for the better.

∽

THE ARRIVAL OF COLONEL ST. John disrupted Freddy's careful sense of order like a rogue gust of wind toppling a neatly laid deck of cards.

From across the room, Freddy observed the newcomer with mild consternation. St. John, with his sun-burnished charm, broad shoulders, and disarming smile, was exactly the sort of man mothers introduced to their daughters while casually pointing out his status as a second son. However, a dashing soldier seemed to overcome any reservations a lady might have—especially a cavalryman who would match Joy's skill on any horse.

And Joy was listening. Not simply hearing, as she did with most people, nodding politely while dreaming of a faster horse or a nap. No, she was *listening*. Raptly.

She tilted her head, laughed—laughed—and even leaned closer when St. John said something Freddy could not hear.

Freddy's stomach did something unusual, a slow twist that felt like regret and indigestion had made an ill-fated pact.

He had no cause to object. None. Joy was free to like whomever she pleased. She'd even been kind enough to ask his opinion on suitors, though he'd spent most of the time inventing faults too ridiculous to speak aloud. One of them, he now recalled, was that a certain gentleman bore the tragic disadvantage of resembling a trout.

He made his way to the refreshment table with more purpose than thirst, pouring himself a glass of lemonade that tasted too tart. He watched Joy from the corner of his eye. St. John had fetched her a pastry.

Pastry fetching? Was this courtship now?

Freddy sipped again and tried to recall if Joy had ever looked at him quite like that—eyes bright, mouth tilted in that wry half-smile. Of course not. They were friends. They had always been friends. She trusted him, confided in him, laughed with him…

…and now someone else was making her laugh.

He sighed and turned to find a young lady at his elbow, fluttering lashes and fan alike.

"Mr. Cunningham, how droll you looked during your waltz last night—as if your partner had stood upon your toe."

"Only lightly," he murmured, struggling to remember the chit's name and unsure whether to smile or bolt.

He escaped to the edge of the room as soon as he could extricate himself, where the air was cooler, and watched as St. John made Joy laugh again. And then again.

It wasn't jealousy, precisely. He didn't want to be the one *always* bringing her pastries or quoting poetry. But he'd always imagined that if someone were to earn her admiration, it would be someone who—well, someone who already knew the names of her kittens.

"You look as if you have swallowed a lemon whole," Maeve said, sidling up beside him.

"I am merely contemplating how swiftly one may become obsolete."

"You? Never," she said cheerfully. "But if you intend to watch like a hawk all afternoon, do try not to moult feathers all over the floor."

Freddy offered a short laugh but said nothing. He looked again at Joy and tried to smile.

Just then, St. John bent towards Joy and said something, apparently in a low voice. Joy laughed, then stood up.

"Shall we take a turn about the park?" he heard St. John say.

Freddy stiffened. Oh, very well then. Driving in the park now, was it?

Before he knew what he was about, Freddy turned on his heel and made straight for Letty Partridge, who had been loitering near the refreshments like a decorative sculpture.

"Miss Partridge," he said brightly, startling her so that her macaroon tumbled to the carpet. "Might I tempt you with a drive through the park?"

Letty blinked. "Why…yes. I would like that very much."

He offered his arm. "Excellent. I find it the perfect cure for over-heated parlours and over-zealous flirtations."

She gave him a puzzled look, but Freddy only smiled. Whatever else the day brought, he would not allow himself to feel left behind.

He called for his curricle to be brought around, just after Joy and St. John had left. After seeking permission from Lady Partridge, they set out, and soon the crisp wind was whistling by them as he hurried along, trying hard not to crane his neck in the most undignified fashion to see how far ahead they were.

They entered Hyde Park nearing its most fashionable hour, and Freddy immediately felt the energy and excitement of the throng around them. Carriages rolled leisurely along the paths, riders trotted elegantly, and pedestrians wandered in lively conversation. It took Freddy a moment to find Joy and St. John among the milling crowd, the Colonel's black curricle blending with the vibrant scene. Joy's bonnet ribbons trailed like pennants, and her laughter carried on the wind.

Freddy narrowed his eyes. Was she—was she driving?

Indeed she was, perched on the seat of St. John's curricle, ribbons flying and curls bouncing, reins confidently in hand. St. John lounged beside her, clearly besotted, offering no protest as Joy handled the reins with a devil-may-care flourish.

"Of course she would be. She is a great gun," Freddy muttered, but noticed she was not wearing her spectacles.

"I beg your pardon?" Letty asked.

"I said this is great fun," he replied quickly. "Capital weather."

But he could not let them have all the attention. Freddy leaned forward and gave the reins a flick. "Shall we see what my greys can do, Miss Partridge? Hold tight."

They flew down Rotten Row, horses stretched, hooves pounding, wheels a blur. Freddy grinned as the wind slapped his cheeks. Up ahead, Joy turned and spotted them.

Never one to back away from a challenge, she gave a delighted whoop and urged her team on. The race was on.

They drew alongside each other, shouts and laughter echoing through the park as startled onlookers leapt aside. Freddy tipped his hat at Joy as their curricles jostled for dominance.

St. John bellowed, "Mad woman!"

Freddy laughed. "Takes one to keep up!"

It was Joy's turn to laugh—wild and wicked, the sound of utter freedom.

But as they reached the far end of the park, a cluster of spectators waved frantically. They slowed, and Freddy recognized the formidable figure of Lady Severn, Countess of Severity, as she was known in private circles.

"Mr. Cunningham! Miss Whitford! This is not Newmarket!"

Freddy winced. Joy's eyes widened.

"We are to be scolded," she muttered.

"Roundly," he agreed as he reined in to greet the Countess. "Lady Severn." He doffed his hat.

Lady Severn's lorgnette snapped open like a guillotine. "Neck-or-nothing galloping in Hyde Park at the fashionable hour—what are you, a pair of circus equestrians?" Her words fell sharply, laced with proper outrage and disappointment.

"My apologies, my lady, we were merely giving the horses a run." Freddy dutifully hung his head, murmuring apologies that he only half meant. Beside him, Joy pressed her lips together, eyes sparkling mischievously even as she meekly inclined her head to the lecture.

"A run?" she huffed. "It looked more like a bid for an undertaker's custom. Miss Whitford, young ladies with marriage prospects do not drive as though chased by Bonaparte."

Joy, still breathless, managed a nod. "I shall endeavour to remember, Lady Severn—though Bonaparte rarely keeps to The Row."

That earned a scandalised gasp from two onlookers and a muffled choke of laughter from Freddy, quickly disguised as a cough.

"See that you *both* remember," the Countess concluded, perfuming the air with disapproval before sweeping away in a rustle of bombazine and censure.

"Yes, my lady."

Freddy glanced sideways at Joy, who was flushed and windswept, laughter still dancing in her eyes.

"It was worth it."

"Entirely," he said.

Once free from the Countess's severe scrutiny, Freddy drew closer to Joy, feeling oddly buoyant. "That was exhilarating," he said, unable to mask his grin.

"Utterly," Joy agreed, laughter bubbling beneath her breath. She glanced at him slyly, her eyes dancing. "Though I suspect we have scandalised half the park."

"Only half? Clearly, we must do better next time."

Joy's laugh, soft and infectious, buoyed him further. Yet just as Freddy basked in their shared camaraderie, St. John leaned forward, his charismatic presence dampening Freddy's high spirits.

"Quite the show," the Colonel said amiably, eyes lingering appreciatively on Joy. "You handle reins better than half my regiment."

"High praise, indeed," Joy replied, cheeks rosy.

Freddy forced a smile. "Perhaps next time, Colonel, you will demonstrate your own expertise."

St. John chuckled warmly. "Gladly. But I fear I may pale beside Miss Whitford's superior skill."

Freddy's heart sank again, realizing that St. John might be the very one to tempt Joy. Should he not be happy that there was someone else to make her laugh?

CHAPTER 8

⚜

Joy was still catching her breath when the great door of Westwood House shut behind her. The sound echoed through the front hall like a sentence passed, but she paid it no heed. Her cheeks remained flushed from the wind, her gloves smelled faintly of leather and spring air, and her heart beat with the proud thrum of victory. She had, after all, outrun Freddy—and not by a little.

It would not last. Of that, she was certain. There would be reproaches, raised eyebrows, perhaps even a letter sent to her guardian, Westwood, who had retreated to the country with Faith. But in this bright, reckless moment, she would not surrender her triumph.

She slipped out of view before the butler could announce her return, her slippers whispering along the carpeted stairs. No one stopped her ascent, and soon she had reached her bedroom, flinging open the door as though storming a castle. The kittens—Freddy the cat and her four remaining offspring—lifted their small heads, blinking sleepily from their nap on the window seat.

"Well, at least someone welcomes me home," Joy declared, dropping to her knees to bury her face into the warm fur. Frederica, the mama cat, rewarded her with a lofty purr as if she had known all along Joy would triumph over that cheeky Freddy Cunningham.

"Tell me, my loves," she murmured, scratching Cecilia beneath the chin, "what is so very wrong with me that I should prefer speed to slippers, wind to waltzes, and freedom to flirtation?"

Cecilia answered with a mewl that sounded suspiciously like concurrence.

Joy kicked off her boots and collapsed onto the window seat, curling her legs beneath her like an overgrown child and tucking Cecilia under her chin. The others arranged themselves along her limbs and lap with a decided air of possession.

She spotted the slim volume of Keats she had purchased but not read, and beside it—those confounded spectacles. They looked innocuous enough now, sitting quietly on her little table, but how she had resisted them! As though a bit of clear glass might proclaim her unfit for Society.

"No one shall see me here," she muttered, slipping them on. The room came into focus so suddenly it was almost alarming. Even the lettering on the page was sharp, no longer prone to wandering into watery confusion. She stared out of the window and across the garden, surprised by how crisp the hedges were, how defined the crocuses peeking out along the walk.

Keats, when she opened the book, made perfect sense. Line after line tumbled out, unmarred by squinting or floating words.

She stood and turned towards the looking glass.

The girl staring back was not ugly, but she was certainly not the delicate ideal her sisters had mastered so effortlessly. Her nose turned up, her mouth never seemed still, and her hair refused to lie obediently under pins. The spectacles made her eyes appear a touch too large.

Still, she tilted her head, studying her reflection this way and that. It was not beauty, perhaps, but it was something.

It was hers. She traced a finger over the scar that was a daily reminder of her grand mistake.

Apparently she would never learn, even though racing a curricle was hardly the same as attempting tricks on the back of a horse.

No, now was not the time to don spectacles in public. Her reputation was in shatters as it was, and the good Lord only knew what would be said of her were she suddenly to wear them. How would she bear the stares and the pity?

That tentative self-assessment was interrupted by the unceremonious entry of Maeve, who swept into the room like a breeze carrying judgement.

"Joy!" she cried, the name stretched out like a reprimand. "Tell me—my eyes must have deceived me—was that truly you racing Mr. Cunningham through the park?"

Joy winced and snatched the spectacles off her face, thrusting them into the pocket of her gown before she turned.

"I cannot deny it," she said, attempting an air of insouciance.

Maeve sank onto the chaise longue with the air of one overcome. "Great heavens, I was *afraid* it was you. Thornhill and I were out walking—he had just shown me the primroses blooming by the Serpentine—and there you were, flying past in a curricle like a highwayman on the run!"

Joy rubbed at her temple. The dull ache had returned, no doubt from the shrieking she'd done during the race.

"It is all anyone is speaking of!" Maeve continued, in a voice tinged with both horror and fascination. "Two matrons nearly swooned. Lady Bexley called you *that girl* with a curl of the lip I have only ever seen used for actresses and Americans."

"I do not think before I do things," Joy said simply.

Maeve fixed her with a knowing look. "Even I know it is not done, Joy."

Joy dropped onto the edge of the bed. "What do you think will happen, besides Westwood returning with a thundercloud stitched between his brows?"

Maeve hesitated, folding her hands in her lap. "They say you are becoming unmanageable."

That caught Joy's attention. *"They* say that?"

"One dowager in particular," Maeve admitted, her tone dropping. "She said, *'If she were mine, I would marry her off as quickly as possible—let her husband take her in hand before she kicks over the traces completely.'*"

Joy gave a snort of laughter that startled the kittens. "And here I thought marriage was meant to be a romantic union of souls. Not the acquisition of a scolded filly."

Maeve did not laugh.

Joy's smile slipped. "You agree with her?"

"No. But I do worry for you. You make it so easy for people to misunderstand you. I daresay there are men who would find your high spirits refreshing—but they are few, and none of them are dukes."

"I do not *want* a duke," Joy retorted. "I want a fast horse and a well-sharpened wit and perhaps a man who does not find either alarming."

"Then you must wait a long while," Maeve murmured, "or else resign yourself to being talked about forever."

Joy turned her face away, blinking at the bookshelf. The Keats lay open, abandoned. "Do you know," she said softly, "when I was younger, I used to wish I were Hope."

Maeve looked surprised. "Hope?"

"She's gentle. Lovely. Everyone always esteemed her. She never frightened the vicar's wife with questions about sea battles or asked to shoot the pistol at the fête. I was forever getting smudges on my gloves and knots in my hair, and Lady Halbury would say, 'Oh, Joy, why can you not be more like your sisters?'"

Maeve gave a small smile. "I never had a sister."

Joy sighed, sinking deeper into the mattress. "But I do not wish it now. I should be so *bored*. And besides, someone has to keep Freddy Cunningham on his toes."

Maeve arched a brow. "Is that what this is?"

Joy did not answer immediately. The room was quiet but for the kittens' steady purring.

"Not in the marrying sort of way. Just…he has never tried to change me. He grumbles, certainly, but he never says I ought to be more demure or less daring. He is maddening at times, but he lets me be *myself*."

"And supposing he does not always?" Maeve asked. "Just suppose, one day, he begins to think like the dowagers?"

"Then I shall race him again," Joy said, "and put him back in his place."

Maeve chuckled. "Good heavens, I do not doubt it. What of the dashing Colonel St. John?"

"He did not seem concerned by my antics." Could she have finally found someone to accept her as she was?

"Perhaps he is worth more consideration," Maeve agreed.

"If he ever comes near again after today."

They sat together a while longer, not speaking, just listening to the rustle of the garden through the window and the occasional bump of a paw on the floorboards.

"I shall go and change before dinner," Maeve said at last, rising with a sigh.

"I suppose I must attempt something with my hair," Joy said. "Though I doubt it shall obey me."

"Try a ribbon," Maeve offered, pausing at the door. "It makes you look less like a governess and more like a wild heroine in a Gothic novel."

Joy laughed. "That is the strangest advice I have ever received."

When Maeve had gone, she drew the spectacles from her pocket and placed them gently on her nose once more. "If Maeve only knew. Governess indeed."

Outside, the garden was sharply green, the sky turning to violet. In the glass, her reflection was unchanged—bold, a little strange, wholly herself.

She rather thought she could live with that.

Westwood did indeed come back to Town, but it was not Joy who was first scolded, but Freddy.

"How could you tempt her to race, Cunningham?" Lord Westwood demanded, stalking across the breakfast room as though he meant to challenge Freddy to pistols at dawn.

Freddy, who had been attempting to butter a crumpet, paused with knife in mid-air and the distinct sensation of being a fox cornered on the hunt.

"I hardly tempted her," he said mildly. "She very nearly *ordered* me to race her. I daresay you could not have stopped her with a regiment of dragoons." Though perhaps it had been he who had sped upon her, after all.

"Don't be flippant," Westwood snapped. "You are the gentleman in this business."

Freddy abandoned the crumpet with a loud sigh. "If you have ever tried to dissuade Miss Joy Whitford from a madcap idea, you would know it requires divine intervention. Or a sedative."

"She is my ward!"

"And a grown woman," Freddy retorted. "Not a porcelain doll."

"No, porcelain dolls do not scandalize the *entire* park by racing through it in a curricle, laughing like a lunatic! I have had three letters already, each more insufferable than the last. Lady Bexley says Joy has 'the constitution of a stable boy and the manners of one as well.'"

Freddy did his utmost not to smile. "Her manners can be quite good."

Westwood's nostrils flared. "You find this *amusing*?"

"Not at all," Freddy lied. "I am properly ashamed. Mortified, even. Deeply repentant."

"You are smirking."

"I am blessed with unfortunate cheekbones. They rest in a smile."

At that moment, the butler cleared his throat in the doorway. "My lord, Lords Rotham and Montford and Major Stuart have arrived."

"Oh, splendid," Freddy muttered. "Let us make this a tribunal."

Westwood pinched the bridge of his nose.

Moments later, Rotham strode in with the easy confidence of a man who would one day be a duke. Montford followed, looking faintly concerned as always, and Stuart brought up the rear with his military bearing.

"Good God," Rotham said, taking in Freddy's expression. "Who died?"

"Apparently, Joy's reputation," Freddy replied. "And I was the assassin."

"Oh, the race," Rotham said, sinking into a chair. "I heard about the bets made. You took Rotten Row by storm."

"Gentlemen, I called you here because I find myself in a rather untenable position." Westwood snapped.

"Yes," Montford said gravely. "You are the guardian of a creature forged of wind and rebellion."

"And kittens," Freddy added.

Westwood growled. He turned to the others. "Her antics are growing wilder. One cannot help but fear what may come next. And now—*now*—I shall have to *increase her dowry.*"

Freddy's head jerked up. "Wait, why?"

"Because gentlemen do not queue up to marry wild mares, that is why! She is beautiful, yes, but she is also untamed. Half the *ton* thinks she is a scandal waiting to happen. The other half thinks she *already has.*"

Freddy coughed delicately. "You say that as if it is a flaw."

Westwood ignored him. "If I am to secure a match befitting her name and station, I must make it worth the gentleman's while."

"She does not need a poor gentleman," Freddy said before he could stop himself. "She needs a gentleman who actually *accepts* her."

Westwood's eyebrows shot up. "We are not discussing a governess or a lapdog! This is Society, Cunningham."

"Forgive me," Freddy said dryly. "I had quite forgotten we are all pawns in a particularly tedious chess game…except all four of you. You were the exception."

Rotham stirred. "Joy is not the sort of girl to be bartered off with a purse and a curtsy. You increase her dowry and she will know it. And then God help the poor devil she is forced to wed."

Montford crossed his boots. "She will make her husband's life hell —if she marries at all, which I doubt."

"It is hard to imagine Joy married," Stuart mused aloud. "Her intended must agree to raise racehorses, adopt stray cats, and allow her to live in the stables."

Freddy found himself oddly defensive. "She is not *so* wild. Not really. She is simply honest about what she likes, which is more than can be said for most young ladies."

Westwood rounded on him. "You sound *suspiciously* admiring."

"I do admire her," Freddy said, folding his arms. "Doesn't everyone?"

"No," said Westwood and Montford simultaneously.

"She is more admired by coachmen and stable lads than Society's matrons," Rotham added, but with a glint in his eyes that suggested he admired her too, in his own way.

"She needs reining in," Westwood declared. "I cannot spend my nights wondering if she has climbed onto a roof or challenged someone to fisticuffs. There must be boundaries."

"Then set them," Freddy said, "but don't try to remake her. There is nothing *wrong* with her, Westwood. She is just not what you expected."

There was a pause.

"She will never marry if she keeps on in this manner," Westwood said finally. "And she will be miserable."

Freddy leaned back. "Or she will find someone who doesn't mind that she is herself."

"Or be a spinster."

"There are worse things," Freddy said lightly. The others chuckled.

"You seem particularly invested in her future, Cunningham," Rotham observed, tilting his head.

Freddy feigned ignorance. "Do I?"

"Yes," Montford said. "You do."

"I am fond of her," Freddy admitted. "In the way one is fond of an unruly hound or a childhood friend who always stole the last biscuit. She is…Joy."

ELIZABETH JOHNS

"That she is," Stuart murmured. "But she cannot stay that way forever. Society does not forgive eccentricity in unmarried women, only in wealthy men."

"And poets," added Montford.

"Which is why I should increase the dowry," Westwood said, with a sigh. "Do you suppose twenty-five thousand pounds should do the trick?"

There was a collective murmur. Even Freddy blinked.

"Well," Rotham said, "that ought to fetch a few offers."

"Yes," Freddy said quietly, "but from the wrong sort of men."

"Joy is an original. Such damsels have succeeded in the past," Rotham recalled.

Westwood did not answer. He walked to the window and looked out over the street. "She deserves better than ridicule. And she deserves better than scandal. I may not know how to help her, but I must try something before she becomes…ruined."

Freddy glanced down at his hands, now clenched on the arms of his chair. He had known, of course, that Joy was a complication. But he had not realized until now how keenly he disliked the idea of her being married off to someone who viewed her as a *burden* to be endured or reshaped.

"She will not be ruined," he said. "Not while we are about."

"Indeed not," Rotham agreed. "So long as we are careful. And so long as no one tempts her further—"

He stopped, giving Freddy a scolding look.

"I did not tempt her," Freddy said slightly too quickly.

"Mm," said Montford.

"Of course not," said Stuart.

"Perhaps you are the one who should be courting her. It would solve all your problems," Rotham added.

Freddy stood. "If we are quite done with casting aspersions upon my problems, I shall go and walk off this shame."

Freddy left his own breakfast room with a frown that did not lift until he was halfway down Park Lane and the breeze caught the edge of his coat.

Joy. Racing down Rotten Row like a Valkyrie, hair streaming, laughter echoing behind her.

He was not courting her. He was merely watching her—and wondering what it would take to find a world large enough for her to belong in, without apology. The worst thing in the world he could imagine was Joy being reformed into a stodgy Society matron. He could not let that happen.

CHAPTER 9

Having been summoned to the drawing room the next morning, Joy was instilled with dread. The sunbeams poured through the windows and illuminated the dust motes that swirled in the air. The chamber itself, with its warm rose damask and tall windows, exuded cosiness despite its elegance. Sunlight fell upon the plush carpet in glowing rectangles, where the mischievous kittens rolled and pounced on a feather Joy dangled from a string.

It was then that her sisters descended in unison—a formidable threesome of determined, loving, and anxious presence, determined to salvage her good name. Joy had expected them to dispatch Lord Westwood to lecture her, but instead they had arrived themselves. Faith, Hope, and Patience each scooped up a kitten at once—thereby offsetting the gravity of their business. At least the Dowager had not joined in the scold.

"Joy, you cannot simply hide," Faith declared, seating herself on the settee with Lord Orville, the grey tabby, purring in her arms. Her voice carried a blend of anxious affection and motherly authority. "We cannot let another day pass without setting all to rights."

Hiding had never occurred to Joy, but she instantly thought it a marvellous idea. "I expected a proper scolding from Westwood."

Hope settled next to Faith. "Westwood went to scold Mr. Cunningham. I think you have the better bargain."

Joy's eyes widened. "He went to scold Freddy?" she repeated, picturing Westwood's stern brow as he delivered a dressing-down to her dearest friend. She failed to see how it solved her current predicament. Freddy's reputation would not be tarnished by their race.

"Indeed," Faith replied, "Along with Rotham, Montford, and Stuart, but they can remedy only so much. They cannot confront every last whisper on your behalf."

Joy sighed. "They ought not confront any of them. It was my misadventure that started all this." She felt a pang of regret over her impulsive race through the park.

At that moment, Hope's kitten wriggled free of her arms and bounded across the carpet to chase a stray thread. "Are you truly keeping all these kittens, Joy?" Patience asked, glancing from the purring bundle in her lap to the others on the floor. "They are darling now, but soon they shall grow and make more kittens."

Reluctantly, Joy admitted, "I suppose I ought to find them new families, but it is difficult when they are so dear." She reached down to ruffle Camilla's tiny ears, eliciting an extra-loud purr.

Faith seized upon this gesture to shift back to the matter at hand. "Your exuberance for life has been misinterpreted with regard to certain social niceties, misleading the *ton* to think you a hoyden. We cannot rely on the gentlemen alone to smooth over any misunderstandings. We are here now to decide how to repair your reputation."

"But I *am* a hoyden," Joy protested.

Hope ignored her remark. "You must attend teas and at-homes for the nonce. If you show them that you can be perfectly demure and contrite, then talk will fade."

Joy frowned, stroking her chosen kitten. "No one will believe me meek," she pointed out quietly. "Why can we not simply retire to the country and remain there? I have no need of marriage. I will devote myself to being the doting auntie to all your children."

Her sisters exchanged glances at her plea, then Faith gently shook her head. "That is an option we would prefer to avoid. You know well enough that eventually you will wish for your own family. Beyond that, you deserve better than to hide away."

"Besides," Hope added, "we cannot have the *ton* thinking we are burying you in the country because of some irreparable scandal. If we do that, your reputation will only grow. You must face Society with confidence."

Patience regarded Joy with a measure of sympathy. "We shall attend every gathering by your side. Whenever you are introduced or greet some formidable dowager, we shall be there to steer the conversation and nudge you if you stray from the path of sweet composure."

Joy gave a snort, laced with exasperation. Sweet composure, indeed. "You speak as though I am a wayward child. But truly, if I stand there nodding and uttering polite words, will that not seem most unnatural?"

Joy studied her sisters, feeling resigned. They meant well, of course, and she was keen to restore peace to the Whitford name, but she wondered if it was really worth all the fuss. "Very well," she relented, "but promise me that if we do all this—attend every tea and soiree—only to find the situation hopeless, we might withdraw to the country."

Faith and Hope exchanged another of their knowing smiles. "We promise," Hope said, and Faith nodded in concurrence. Joy suspected it was but an easy vow to soothe her, though perhaps that would suffice to steady her nerves.

"We already have a list," Hope said briskly. "Lady Bellingham's tea on Tuesday, the Rutherford at-home on Wednesday, Lady Minerva's soiree on Thursday, and the Tarlton garden party next Saturday. Each one has its own measure of importance. You must attend all with a composed countenance and unaffected demeanour."

Joy listened to this parade of engagements with mounting trepidation. "This is impossible!"

Faith waved her protest aside. "All you need to do is smile, curtsy prettily, and exchange a few gracious remarks. Meanwhile, we must do something about your madcap dancing."

Joy murmured an apology, feeling heat climb her cheeks at the remembrance of how badly she had danced. It had not always been so, but she was reluctant to confess about her sight. Yet if not now, then when? Recalling Freddy's response encouraged her. She cleared her throat. "There is something else I must confess," she said. "Part of the trouble is that since my accident, my eyes fail me at times, particularly when I exert myself. The world can become hazy, faces and details slip away. I think—I fear—I need spectacles."

Her sisters' surprise was immediate. Faith looked most taken aback. "Spectacles? You never mentioned such difficulties before."

"I thought it would pass," Joy answered, twisting her fingers together. "At times, in bright daylight, I see tolerably well. Then at assemblies, beneath candlelight, everything becomes a blur. I tried harder, hoping to hide it, but that only led to more blunders. I did not realize how badly I might misjudge distances until…" She paused, remembering how she had trod on Lady Abernathy's gown in mid-dance.

Hope's expression was filled with compassion. "Poor dear Joy, you must remedy this at once. There is no shame in spectacles if your vision requires them."

Faith, on the other hand, wore a thoughtful frown. "Of course, if you need them, you must have them. Without clear sight, you risk further mishaps."

Patience, firmly practical, agreed. "It will be far worse for gossip if you continue stumbling around the dance floor. If spectacles will steady your steps, you should have them. We can engage a dancing master for private instruction so that you can grow accustomed to wearing them, if necessary."

Joy felt a surge of mingled relief and dismay. She had always dreaded appearing in such unfashionable contraptions, fearing that the *ton* would find more fodder for mockery of her. But the thought of further humiliations at dances was worse still. "You do not think it will cause more talk?"

"Mayhap, if it makes you appear more studious, it will soften the hoydenish image." Hope was ever optimistic.

Joy did not mention that the doctor had said her sight might fail further. This was enough for now. For Joy and her sisters.

Patience sat back, still cradling her purring kitten. "No one will expect you to transform entirely, Joy. They simply need to see that you can present yourself in a more measured manner. Especially since we fear your last scrape left the impression that you delight in making a spectacle of yourself. Let them see your warmth, not your recklessness."

Their conversation might have continued indefinitely, but it was at that moment that their butler entered. Hartley bore a look of studied neutrality. "Miss Joy," he said, "there is a delivery for you—"

Before another word could pass his lips, two footmen entered, carrying a most enormous bouquet. The arrangement nearly eclipsed the silver vase beneath it, a riot of colour—roses, lilies, violets—so lush and fragrant that the kittens paused in their play to inspect the intrusion.

The footmen placed the vase on the table and withdrew, leaving Hartley to present Joy with a small folded note.

A hush descended upon the sisters, as though the universe itself paused to witness this unfolding. Joy opened the note, her pulse quickening with curiosity.

Miss Whitford,
You are a breath of fresh air! The most capital time I have had in years!
—St. John

The boldness of the script struck her first, followed by the vivid memory of that gentleman's rakish grin. Her sisters pressed close to catch sight of the note as well, gasping at his boldness.

"She will never reform if he encourages her so," Faith muttered.

"He takes no accountability, I see." Hope frowned.

"Perhaps he desires a hoyden for a wife," Patience said hopefully.

Joy glanced at the vivid bouquet, inhaling the sweet perfume of the roses, lilies, and violets. The sense of possibility stirred her heart. Perhaps it was not so dreadful: the notion that she might salvage her reputation, learn to manage her unwieldy vision, and receive the occasional flattering gesture from a gentleman.

She brushed her fingers over the note once more. Then she tucked the missive away safely, away from curious eyes.

Yes, she wished to be done with the gossips' whisperings, and if demure behaviour would pacify them, she would give it her best attempt. She would not lose her inherent spirit, of course—not forever—but a small display of meekness might serve as a shield against further scandal. After all, even her sisters had said she need only do so for a few weeks.

～

FREDDY HAD ALWAYS FOUND a certain comfort in the measured hush and unchanging traditions of White's. Though the venerable walls of that distinguished gentleman's club could hardly be called quiet—there was ever the low crackle of the fire upon the hearth, the clink of glasses meeting in revelry, and the murmurs of men congratulating, disputing, and occasionally boasting in spirited, undercut tones—this particular evening carried with it a charge most unusual.

At half-past nine, Freddy entered the establishment and handed his hat and coat to the major-domo who hovered near the door, as discreet as any well-trained retainer must be in this sanctum of male discourse. He bowed and disappeared into the gloom of the entry, leaving Freddy to proceed into the main room, where his gaze swept over a scene as familiar to him as the face of a dear old friend.

The morning room boasted tall windows that by daylight afforded a handsome view of St. James's Street. At this hour, heavy curtains had been discreetly pulled, and the flickering sconces cast a discreet glow upon panelled walls. A faint haze of pipe tobacco, with the merest tang of brandy seemed to envelop the room. All about, members reclined upon chairs of worn leather, heads bowed together in conspiratorial chatter or games of cards.

Freddy found his friends in a corner arrangement, surrounding a low table upon which sat half-empty glasses of brandy. Westwood, Rotham, Montford, and Stuart were already gathered, and the hush that fell as he drew near gave testament that their conversation was private.

"Cunningham." Westwood gestured him nearer, beckoning with a hand upon which he wore an old signet ring, scuffed from decades of use. "This is a most timely arrival. We were but just discussing—"

"Miss Joy." Rotham cut in with a certain dryness to his tone. "Though we had not the presence of mind, perhaps, to include you in the initial speculation, Freddy. In truth, we did not think you would care to hear the details of her potential suitors, or so-called suitors."

Freddy sank into an old leather armchair with the weariness of a man who expected trouble from the very start. "Why should I not want to hear about Joy? I gather her name is upon everyone's lips tonight. I have heard enough whispers from the hall to suspect the talk has not subsided. I have yet to look at the betting books, but I do not doubt I will find something to dislike."

Stuart leaned forward, swirling his brandy in an indolent manner. "They say St. John has staked his claim—so brazenly one might think he had purchased a new horse or invested in a shipping concern. One could scarcely step foot in here without hearing the tale. Miss Joy is spoken for, St. John's troth is all but declared, and to top it all there is a rumour about a handsome increase in her dowry. An increase so dramatic, fortune hunters from Land's End to John o' Groats shall come galloping."

"Naturally rumours swirl in the clubs." Freddy waved his hand in dismissal as a fresh glass of brandy was placed before him.

Montford, ignoring Freddy's remark, laced his fingers and offered an opinion. "But are we quite sure Joy welcomes his suit?"

"A fair question, Monty. I can attest to St. John's interest, however. He sent Joy a bouquet the size of my entrance hall, and the sisters were all agog at his note. It was hardly one to discourage his suit. It would surprise me not a whit if he has serious intentions. Unless—" Here Westwood paused, lowering his voice. "He means to amuse himself. Yet if that is so, Joy shall be the chief sufferer, and no gentleman would permit that."

Stuart snorted. "Gentleman? There are but a handful of true

gentlemen in Town, and I fear St. John may not entirely exemplify the breed."

"Do you know ill of him?" Westwood asked.

"He is a soldier," Stuart answered, as if that explained all.

Freddy's jaw tightened at the mere mention of Joy in the same breath as ill use. "If he trifles with her, I shall have something to say about it," he stated, setting his glass down with more force than he intended. The resulting rattle had them all glancing at him in curiosity. Freddy cleared his throat, attempting a measure of composure. "I only mean that if a man intends a passing fancy, he need not fix his fancy upon Miss Joy. She deserves better—a serious suitor, a man who will let her be as she is, not stifle her, nor encourage foolishness which might lead to further scandal."

There was a pause, the other gentlemen studying Freddy with various shades of amusement or puzzlement. He schooled his features so they might not guess the turmoil within. Indeed, Joy was a friend— an especially dear one. He could hardly brook the thought of her name being bandied about the gossip mills of Town as though she were fair game for every rake with a polished boot and a sleek coat.

"In any case," Westwood said at last, "the pressing question is how news of her dowry soared so high. I made but a comment yesterday— yet now the entire membership of White's speaks of nothing else."

Montford shrugged. "One must never underestimate the speed with which gossip travels, Westwood. One may as well attempt to hold water in one's hands as keep a secret from the wags of the *ton*."

Rotham, who was the most cynical of the group, raised a brow. "Servants. It is always the servants, my friends."

Freddy stifled a groan. "A sure enticement for those creatures who call themselves gentlemen but exist solely to chase a fortune. The last thing Joy needs is such fortune-hunting scoundrels on her doorstep, wheedling invitations to tea, pestering her, pressing their hapless suits upon her until she cannot tell one slippery-haired courtier from the next."

Stuart laughed. "I do believe our dear Cunningham is quite riled over this. Is there something you wish to share?"

Had the light in the room been brighter, perhaps they all might have seen Freddy's momentary flush. He swallowed, keeping his voice carefully neutral. "I wish only to see Joy contented in an arrangement of her own choosing. You know I esteem her with the warm regard of a dear friend."

"Of course," Rotham murmured with a knowing arch of his brow. "But come, the matter of St. John remains. Could there be sincerity in his suit beyond amusement?"

"I sincerely hope so," Westwood replied, scowling as he sipped his brandy. "A friend or two I trust well have spoken in St. John's favour—he is not known to be an unrepentant rake. But if he is to encourage her wildness, then…" He left the consequences unspoken.

"Indeed," Freddy said, rather briskly. "St. John may not be a blackguard, but if he is uncertain of his intentions, he could do harm. Joy… is not one to accept caution with grace as she loves the lure of adventure. And if she is led to believe the man thoroughly admires her—then he abandons her at her most vulnerable—" He stopped, the image too disturbing for him to articulate further. He instead took refuge in the warm comfort of brandy, letting the rich taste of it roll over his tongue.

A faint silence fell over them, broken only by the clink of a decanter as a footman refilled glasses. A cluster of gentlemen nearby were reading the betting book, scribbling wagers as though the apocalypse itself could be staved off by a timely bet on the next political scandal or upcoming horse race. Somewhere across the room, a hush of laughter passed in little waves. It was that sort of evening at White's, where half the men seemed to live for wagers and the other half thrived on hearing them.

Westwood leaned forward. "As the person providing Joy's dowry, who is taking bets on it? I wonder if they might list the precise sum, or if they are speculating upon how many hundreds or thousands more she might be worth than previously thought."

Montford snorted a short laugh. "I glimpsed at the betting book as I came in. There are indeed a few lines scribbled there—some wag is offering five to one odds that she surpasses Lady Eugenia Knight's portion, and eight to one that you have settled upon her an estate in Shropshire. Though it is also rumoured that a house in Bath is said to be part of the settlement as well."

Freddy nearly choked on his brandy. "This is absurd. Joy, who would sooner take a horsewhip to Bath than live in that watery city? She cares nothing for the amusements of those mildewed Pump Rooms. Doubtless it is all nonsense."

"Oh, nonsense indeed," Westwood agreed calmly, "because there are no properties in Shropshire or Bath."

"Ah." They liked to tease Freddy, and normally he did not mind, but could not disguise his irritation with Joy being such an object of amusement. "If this turns Joy's Season into a gauntlet of fortune hunters, I shall hold all of you personally responsible." That remark drew a chorus of half-ironic protests.

"Us?" Westwood coughed. "You propose to hold me personally liable for my offhand remark, made quite inadvertently, and quite without intention that it be repeated? Cunningham, you are turned tyrant."

"He is," Montford agreed with a faint grin, "but a well-meaning one, I believe."

Freddy sighed, pinching the bridge of his nose. He had not meant to sound so heated, but anxiety prickled at him in a way he could hardly name. Joy was her own person—vivacious, adventurous, impossible to contain. The notion of her heart being trifled with by a man who might not appreciate all that she was…that notion roused in Freddy an uncomfortable mixture of protectiveness and indignation.

For a moment each gentleman was quiet, turning over the matter in his mind. Only Stuart, who had an adventurous wife himself, ventured a small reflection. "I do believe that Joy's best chance of happiness, if she does not choose St. John, lies with a man who admires her high-spiritedness—who would never scold her for an unladylike impulse. One who might even share her enthusiasm for those pursuits Society deems improper. She is rare, is she not?"

"Hear, hear," they all agreed and raised their glasses to Joy, but leaving Freddy feeling completely unsettled inside.

CHAPTER 10

Joy adjusted her spectacles for the hundredth time since stepping into the carriage, tugging the delicate gold frame as though it had somehow shifted from the last careful adjustment. They were so uncomfortable and she felt as conspicuous as though she had a target painted on her face. Her heart fluttered beneath her bodice, and she drew a long, steadying breath, hoping Faith and Westwood would not notice her agitation. Across from her, Faith sat as serene as ever, her pale blue silk gown shimmering subtly in the dim carriage light. Beside Faith, Westwood lounged in comfortable silence, impeccably tailored and thoroughly unperturbed, as though the evening ahead held nothing more challenging than one of their usual, quiet family dinners.

But for Joy, this evening at Lady Constance Houghton's was nothing of the sort. It would mark the first time she had dared to appear before a full company—gentlemen included—in her spectacles. She had survived a seemingly endless series of teas and visits over the past week, suffering through interminable hours where conversation had rarely risen above whispered admonitions of her recent escapades and faintly pitying commentary on her upbringing. "Her parents died when she was a babe, poor child," one dowager had sighed loudly, as though Joy's hearing were impaired rather than her sight.

"Perhaps her accident damaged the demure part of her head," another had mused in hushed tones, lifting her lorgnette with a pointed glance in Joy's direction. It had taken all her strength of will not to scowl at them, keeping instead a falsely sweet smile firmly pasted upon her face. She had nodded meekly, dutifully sipped weak tea, and endured as best she could their endless scoldings and thinly veiled judgements. She wished her sisters would just send her back to the country, where at least she could roam fields freely rather than be trapped in drawing rooms with women twice her age or more whispering about her as though she were absent—or incapable of understanding their every word.

Tonight would be different. There would be younger people at Lady Constance's dinner, gentlemen among them. And Colonel St. John. She had overheard Faith mention his attendance, though her sister had made a valiant attempt to disguise the revelation beneath casual conversation. Joy was not fooled. Her pulse quickened at the mere thought of facing him across a candlelit dinner table, bespectacled and vulnerable. Would he find her altered? Less charming or witty, her eyes magnified through glass?

Her gown had been chosen with meticulous care, partly to bolster her confidence, partly at Faith's insistence. Pale lilac silk fell in elegant, shimmering folds, embroidered subtly with silver thread in a delicate floral pattern along the hem and sleeves. It was fashionable without being ostentatious, perfectly suited to her age and standing, as Faith had repeatedly assured her. Tiny pearls caught the faint flicker of lantern-light from outside. Her ebony curls had been carefully arranged by the maid's skilful hands into an artful cluster atop her head, secured by pearl-headed pins that matched her gown. The overall effect was pleasing, sophisticated even, though Joy could scarcely believe such words might be applied to her.

As the carriage rumbled along the cobbled streets, Joy clasped her gloved hands tightly in her lap, wishing fervently that Freddy might have been permitted to accompany them. Freddy would have known just what to say to calm her nerves—very likely something irreverent enough to make her laugh and forget her anxieties entirely. But no, Freddy had been forbidden her presence this past week as if he were the very source of her mischief, the catalyst for her recklessness. Absurdity itself! Yet here she was, venturing into the social fray without her closest confidant and ally.

Faith seemed to sense her unease and offered a gentle smile, reaching across to lightly touch Joy's hand. "You look perfectly lovely, Joy. Truly, you have nothing to fear."

Joy attempted a brave smile in return. "Thank you, Faith. But supposing—" She paused, her voice betraying her uncertainty. "—supposing the spectacles make me look utterly foolish? I do not think I can bear to be laughed at again."

"They do nothing to diminish your beauty, Joy," her motherly sister was compelled to say. "Once the newness wears off, no one will even notice them."

Westwood's voice broke in softly, gentle yet firm. "No one would dare laugh, Joy. And if any do, rest assured I shall deal with them most severely." The faintest twinkle in his eyes softened his stern words, as if he would do something so absurd.

"Yes, and I shall help," Faith added with playful resolve. "We shall set them all straight. Spectacles are hardly a crime, and they rather enhance your eyes."

Joy was grateful for their support, though what else could they say? As the carriage slowed before Lady Constance's town house, her stomach tightened anew. Lanterns illuminated the grand entrance, footmen standing in readiness to assist guests down from their conveyances. It was too late now to retreat; there was nothing for it but to face the evening bravely.

She took Westwood's offered hand, stepping carefully down from the carriage into the warm glow of lantern light. Faith adjusted a stray curl atop Joy's head, offering a last, encouraging smile. "Remember, Joy—confidence. Even if you must pretend."

Joy nodded, straightening her shoulders whilst refraining from any retort of how the entire Season was one big farce of pretence.

Inside, the entrance hall was filled with elegant guests mingling beneath ornate chandeliers, their gowns and coats glistening in soft candlelight. Joy felt a familiar pang of dread, her hand drifting unconsciously to adjust her spectacles again. Faith gently intercepted her wrist, whispering softly, "Leave them, dearest."

"Faith! Westwood! And Miss Joy, how charming," Lady Constance greeted them warmly, sweeping forward to take their hands in turn. "And such fetching spectacles, Joy. Quite dashing!"

Joy murmured her thanks, her cheeks burning slightly. Was the compliment genuine, or was Lady Constance merely displaying kindness? Whilst it was better than the alternative, her hopes of them going unnoticed failed.

Her uncertainty deepened as she was escorted further into the drawing room, acutely aware of curious gazes following her, eyes assessing her through jewelled lorgnettes and fans subtly raised to conceal whispering mouths. Then, abruptly, her gaze caught that of Colonel St. John, standing by the mantelpiece in his dress uniform, his own gaze fixed firmly upon her.

As St. John approached, Joy noticed how strikingly dashing he appeared in his Regimentals. His scarlet coat, perfectly tailored and adorned with gold braid and polished buttons, accented his broad shoulders and lean figure. His white breeches and gleaming black boots added to the impressive uniform, drawing appreciative glances from nearly every lady present. His dark hair was combed into the Windswept style and framed his confident face and sparkling eyes.

"Miss Whitford," St. John greeted smoothly, offering her a respectful bow. "I must confess, I hardly recognized you at first with your new adornment."

Joy raised her chin, determined to hold her ground despite the fluttering in her chest. "Adornments? My spectacles, you mean. Do they so drastically change my appearance, Colonel?"

"Only in that they enhance what was already lovely," he replied effortlessly. "I see now your eyes hold even greater depths—perhaps more perilous to gentlemen than ever before."

She raised an eyebrow, suddenly feeling her confidence return. "Perilous? Colonel, you make me sound ridiculous."

"Never ridiculous," he countered warmly, "but certainly intriguing. They are the kind of eyes in which a fellow might happily become lost."

"I should hope, Colonel," she retorted in her straightforward way, "you possess better skills of navigation than to become lost so easily."

St. John chuckled appreciatively. "Alas, I fear I am quite helpless when faced with fathomless blue. You leave me entirely at your mercy, Miss Whitford."

Joy could not help but laugh softly, feeling the evening grow brighter. "Then I suppose it is fortunate indeed that I have chosen clarity over vanity tonight. At least now I may clearly see where I am going astray."

"I am happy to lead you about regardless."

Joy narrowed her gaze. "Are you flirting with me, sir?" she asked boldly yet without guile.

"Ah, Miss Whitford, you charm me to my toes."

"I would not know, I am sure. No one ever flirted with me before."

He laughed with a twinkle in his eye that made her heart skip painfully. And for just a fleeting moment, Joy forgot entirely to worry about her spectacles.

Freddy watched with narrowed eyes as Colonel St. John was announced, appearing every inch the dashing soldier in his striking Regimentals. Scarlet coat ablaze under the gleam of candlelight, gold braiding impeccably arranged upon his broad shoulders, and boots polished to a mirror sheen, he drew the eyes of every lady in the room. Freddy prided himself on his own dashing appearance but could only compare himself to this soldier and feel lacking.

In annoyance, Freddy watched as St. John wasted no time making his way directly to Joy, his smile disarmingly charming.

Freddy shifted uncomfortably, a faint scowl darkening his brow as he observed the easy confidence with which St. John engaged her. He spoke with an ease Freddy begrudgingly admitted was enviable, the man's words apparently witty enough to elicit Joy's laughter—a sound Freddy realized he had always considered exclusively his domain.

"I must say," murmured a familiar voice beside him, "St. John seems rather taken."

Freddy turned sharply, startled from his unpleasant reverie to find Rotham watching the scene with amused detachment. Rotham, always so irritatingly knowing, smiled slightly, a hint of a twinkle in his eye as if he deliberately meant to set Freddy ablaze.

"Rather presumptuous, don't you think?" Freddy grumbled, gesturing vaguely towards St. John. "He scarcely knows Joy."

Rotham raised an elegant brow. "It seems to me he knows her well enough. Or at least he wishes to. He certainly has her attention."

"Attention," Freddy scoffed softly, keeping his voice low. "Joy's attention is easily won and quickly lost."

"True enough," Rotham conceded, smiling indulgently. "But look how she laughs. St. John is doing quite splendidly for himself."

Freddy muttered darkly, shaking his head. "If one enjoys excessive charm and overly polished buttons. I dare say that uniform is the most interesting thing about him."

"Jealous, Freddy?" Rotham's tone teased gently, but the edge of sincerity beneath made Freddy bristle slightly.

"Not in the least," Freddy lied smoothly, forcing his gaze away from the maddening scene, because he was jealous. "Merely cautious. Joy is—well, Joy is impressionable. I would rather she not have her hopes raised over a charming uniform and shallow flattery."

"I see," Rotham replied, still amused. "And your own prospects? Is there any progress worth the mentioning?"

Freddy cast a weary glance around the room. Letty Partridge stood demurely nearby, her appearance pleasing enough in a pale peach gown that flattered her fair complexion and neatly arranged blonde hair. She was perfectly acceptable—exactly the kind of young woman his parents would eagerly usher towards the altar. But Freddy knew well that a single dance or pointed conversation would prompt his mother to have the banns read forthwith.

"Slim pickings," Freddy muttered.

"Nonsense," Rotham countered lightly. "Letty Partridge is an admirable choice."

"Admirable, yes," Freddy admitted grudgingly, thinking *but dull*.

Soon enough, they were summoned into dinner. The dining room glittered in gentle splendour, a long mahogany table stretching elegantly beneath shimmering crystal chandeliers that cast prisms of light against pale, silk-draped walls. Gold candelabra marched regally down the table's length, their flames flickering gracefully, illuminating meticulously polished cutlery and gleaming porcelain plates edged in delicate gold filigree. Bowls overflowing with early summer roses and trailing ivy were artfully placed, their fragrance mingling subtly with the rich aroma of the awaiting meal.

Freddy's spirits sank further upon discovering that he had been strategically placed next to none other than Miss Partridge.

He dutifully offered her his arm, escorted her to the table, and seated himself with a resigned sigh. He knew better than to encourage her excessively.

Conversation proved predictably dreary as a delicate poached salmon garnished with fresh dill and a tangy lemon sauce was set before him. At least his palate had nothing to complain about.

"The weather is exceptionally fine tonight, is it not?" Freddy remarked mildly, prodding his fish with disinterest.

"Oh, yes, exceptionally fine," Letty Partridge echoed enthusiastically, eyes brightening as though he had spoken profound wisdom.

"And Lady Constance always sets a handsome table," he continued, mildly desperate.

"Oh, most handsome indeed," she agreed fervently.

Freddy bit back an exasperated sigh. Was this what his breakfasts would sound like, day after day, year after year? Endless agreements and parroted affirmations? Servants silently removed the fish, swiftly replacing it with tender roast duck, glazed and served with delicate vegetables, each plate arranged as though for a painting.

To his other side sat a young lady fresh from Scotland, Miss Flora MacKenzie, whose girlish enthusiasm manifested itself in frequent blushes and giggles. Yet, her conversation held at least a faint charm of unpredictability.

"Ye're a very bonny lad, Mr. Cunningham," Flora informed him with a blush and a shy giggle. "Aye, quite bonny."

Freddy laughed despite himself, pleasantly relieved by her candid compliment. "Why, thank you, Miss MacKenzie. I assure you, your compliment is gratefully received."

A burst of laughter from Joy and Colonel St. John drew their attention. Freddy found himself glaring instinctively, the humour suddenly distant and mocking. He ought to be the one making her laugh, sitting at her side, teasing and exchanging wit—not Colonel St. John, however handsome his uniform.

Freddy felt his spirits sink even lower as dinner progressed. Each course seemed to drag interminably, punctuated by more banalities from Letty and giggling nonsense from Flora. His thoughts wandered gloomily over his limited prospects, his parents' edict, and his inexplicable dissatisfaction with every eligible lady he encountered.

Another laugh from Joy had Freddy straining to hear a snippet of her conversation with Colonel St. John. "You cannot be serious, Colonel!" She laughed. "You actually mistook your commanding officer's prized hunting dog for a fox?"

St. John's eyes twinkled merrily. "Quite so, Miss Joy. In my defence, it was an exceedingly misty morning and the hound had a terribly fox-like tail. You may imagine the general's fury when he discovered my error."

Joy giggled, delighted. "Oh, I can indeed! Did he banish you from future hunts entirely?"

"Worse," St. John confessed dramatically, "he put me in charge of polishing every pair of boots in the regiment for an entire fortnight."

Their laughter mingled, light and easy, sparking Freddy's envy afresh. The dessert course arrived—delicate fruit tarts and spun sugar confections glittering enticingly.

"Ah, the Whitford sisters. They are all sae verra beautiful," Flora whispered, eyes wide with sincere admiration as she saw where his gaze had landed. "Miss Joy especially. The sight of her makes me wish for me own spectacles!"

Freddy again glanced down the table towards Joy, his heart momentarily catching at the picture she presented. Flora was correct. Joy's spectacles did nothing to diminish her attractiveness. Rather, they enhanced the intelligent sparkle in her eyes—the warmth of her engaging expression. She had truly blossomed into a lovely young woman, and pride mingled unexpectedly with Freddy's irritation.

He considered, with rueful amusement, that perhaps his parents were right. His peers were all married, with their offspring already romping about nurseries. He felt rather elderly himself tonight, especially when paired with such youthful dinner companions. Perhaps it truly was time to settle before he reached a stage too decrepit to father children.

His morose thoughts were interrupted by the ladies withdrawing, leaving the gentlemen to their port and quiet conversation. Freddy's glumness lingered until Sir Reginald Ashton leaned closer, pouring port generously.

"Troubled, Cunningham?" Ashton asked shrewdly, eyes twinkling kindly.

"Nothing of consequence," Freddy murmured evasively.

"Ah, young fellow, I know the look. Women are troubling, are they not?" Ashton smiled knowingly. "Allow an old man a word of advice? Beauty fades, charm dulls. Marry a woman who is your friend first. Friendship outlasts all else."

Freddy regarded Ashton thoughtfully. The older man's words resonated more deeply than expected, touching a truth Freddy had been reluctant to admit. Friendship—perhaps it was precisely what he was overlooking. He nodded slowly, thoughtful silence settling upon him. Could he be friends with Letty Partridge?

CHAPTER 11

Through her spectacles, Joy watched Freddy over the rim of the glass as she sipped some wine. Her head was beginning to throb, and despite her spectacles, her vision in her right eye was waning.

Across the table, Miss Letty Partridge leaned towards Freddy. The movement required a perilous tilt of her chair, and more than once Joy expected to see the feathered confection of Letty's headpiece swept ignominiously into the sauceboat. Freddy, ever good-natured, inclined his head to catch the lady's softly uttered witticisms, smiling with attentive courtesy.

Letty Partridge was shamelessly flirting with Freddy and Joy felt a pain of irritation in her chest at the sight. Perhaps the sensation was jealousy, but surely that was only because Freddy was her best friend? Joy observed it all with a queer tightening in her chest, so foreign a sensation she pressed a palm against her ribcage as though her stays had suddenly shrunk.

She tried to look at the situation objectively, knowing she was not a typical female and capable of such behaviour herself.

St. John had been paying Joy marked attention, that was obvious even to her, but she did not think he was seriously courting her. Men never thought of her in a romantic fashion, hoyden that she was.

She had never planned to be a spinster, though neither had she given serious thought to marriage. Oh, she adored a delicious Gothic romance, but she knew it was just fiction and not reality for her... unless perhaps she made some marriage of convenience where there were no expectations of her. Romantic love was not in her future. However, she wanted more for her best friend. Truly, she did. That meant Joy would have to swallow her spleen when other ladies flirted with Freddy. But could he not pick somebody less insipid than Letty Partridge? Surely he could see how bored he'd be with someone who could not even sit a horse properly!

Freddy deserved a clever, lively partner, not a beauty who squeaked when her horse did more than amble. The notion that Freddy might, in fact, prefer a delicate bloom of femininity over a hoyden well-versed in saddle sores pricked her conscience, and she sipped again to drown the thought. The wine went down the wrong way, eliciting a cough she muffled in her napkin. Letty Partridge tittered at something Freddy said; Joy stiffened. How could she be so foolish?

Colonel St. John bent nearer. "Are you unwell, Miss Whitford? I fear wine can be a sly devil."

"I thank you, sir, it is nothing," Joy murmured, arranging her spectacles and finding him somewhat doubled before her eyes. "Merely an errant swallow."

To her mortification he studied her pale brow. "You are in pain. A headache?"

"Not worth remarking," she insisted. "Pray, do not trouble yourself."

He settled back with a look that was half-smile, half-frown. St. John's attention in recent weeks had been—how had Faith phrased it? —marked. How could she help but be flattered? Yet Joy could not discern whether the Colonel's notice tended towards gallantry or simple camaraderie born of shared relish for brisk exercise and unpaved roads. Men never wooed a lady who carried a whip more readily than a fan. Still, the Colonel's hazel eyes held kindness, and when he spoke, his voice possessed that mellow timbre which suggested interest. It was pleasant, undeniably.

At last the courses ended, the gentlemen agreed to forego the ponderous ritual of lingering over port, and the party adjourned to the great saloon, where frivolities suitable to a country house party were already being arranged. Charades was proclaimed by acclamation; *The Frolics of the Sphynx* book of charades was produced. Joy, who loved any amusement, cursed her aching head to perdition, and volunteered at once. Letty Partridge declared herself needing a clever partner and fluttered onto a sofa, summoning Freddy beside her with an arch of perfectly shaped brows. Freddy hesitated, his gaze skating to Joy, who barely suppressed a snort.

She offered him a brisk nod—*go on, rescue your cornered self*. He bowed his mocking thanks and was promptly netted by Letty's shrill laughter.

The teams were drawn, and fortune—or misfortune—placed Joy and Colonel St. John upon the same team. Freddy's lot fell to the opposition, securing him for the evening at Miss Partridge's right hand. Joy, determined to demonstrate how little that circumstance signified, threw herself into the game with unladylike zeal.

"We shall crush them, Colonel," Joy whispered. "Though Mr. Cunningham is quite adroit at these."

"I am all astonishment." Joy ignored his sardonic tone.

The first riddle was Joy's. She drew a number, then read her riddle, voice sparkling:

"My First is eaten with apple or beef;
   If you're my Second I pity your grief;
   My Third owns no colour that stays the same hue."

Freddy, across the table, murmured encouragement to Letty, who looked mystified. Freddy furrowed his brow in concentration, then brightened. "Pie—bald! Pie, because of fruit or meat; bawled for the grief; and a pie-bald horse is mottled."

Letty applauded. "Oh, how clever you are, Mr. Cunningham!"

Letty then chose her number, and read her selection with solemn drama:

"Though to youth oft my first you may safely apply,
   On my next you may rarely it venture to try,
   If you suffer my whole you must fairly admit,
   'Twas your own want of skill, arrangement, and wit."

"Check mate!" Joy shouted without consulting her partner.

"How? It makes no sense. It is unfair that anyone could think so quickly," Letty declared. Joy only smiled, considering the score nicely even—and the entertainment just begun.

Freddy and Joy, whose penchant for charades kept the more knowing away, proceeded to give little chance to their partners to shine.

When, at length, the game was declared concluded, the company dispersed to card tables or to the long windows overlooking moonlit lawns. Joy, her temples throbbing, slipped into an antechamber hung with sombre portraits and attempted to remove her spectacles for a moment's respite. The instant they left her nose, the world tilted: candles became comets, carpet patterns swam. She caught hold of the door-case.

"Steady." Colonel St. John materialized, easing the spectacles from her trembling fingers and replacing them. Vision cleared slightly; pain did not.

"I am a nuisance," she murmured, ashamed. "No, do not contradict me. A lady who cannot bear a trifling headache without drama is precisely that."

"It is not trifling," he said. "Your eyes are unequal." He produced a handkerchief lightly scented with bergamot and pressed the cool linen to her brow. "You ought to lie down."

"Impossible. My sisters would think me overset by a parlour game."

He smiled. "Nonsense." Then, in a tone half teasing, half coaxing: "Will you permit me to tell your chaperone?"

Joy hesitated. St. John's solicitousness was very pleasant. Yet accepting would be to acknowledge weakness, and she had lived her whole life determined not to be thought fragile. She opened her mouth—

"Joy?" Freddy stepped from the larger room, concern plain upon his handsome, slightly flushed features. "Are you unwell?"

"I am perfectly well," she said, too hastily.

Colonel St. John released her hand and straightened. "Miss Whitford may benefit from quieter surroundings. I was about to find her chaperone."

Freddy's eyes flicked to their joined hands and away again. "I will see to it."

St. John's smile held no warmth. "As you wish."

Joy wished the carpet might swallow them all. "I am sure either of you would do, but since Mr Cunningham feels responsible—"

"Thank you," Freddy said, offering his arm with exaggerated gallantry. "Shall we?"

She accepted, aware of St. John's disappointment, though he bowed with impeccable grace. Freddy steered her through the dim corridor, his pace leisurely so that she need not jolt her aching head. When they had gained the foot of the staircase, he paused beneath a lantern and studied her face.

"You are truly in pain." It was not a question.

"Merely fatigued. My right eye rebels, that is all."

"Why did you not tell me at dinner?"

"Because you were occupied with Miss Partridge." The words emerged sharper than intended. She sighed. "Forgive me. I am out of sorts and therefore unjust. Besides, I can never refuse charades."

"Occupied," he repeated, as though testing the taste of it. "Joy, Letty

Partridge is a feather-brained flirt. I would sooner marry my bay gelding."

"That is unkind to Letty." *And a relief I ought not to acknowledge.* "Besides, your gelding cannot play the pianoforte, and you have no other candidates."

"My horse has other merits." Freddy's smile became crooked. Then, more seriously, he said, "I saw St. John take your hand. Did that distress you?"

"I—" She faltered. "No, only surprised me. He...looks at me as though I were not merely an amusing companion but—" Her voice dwindled.

"A woman," Freddy supplied quietly.

"Yes." Silence pressed. "It is—sufficiently odd that I scarcely know how to respond."

Freddy's gaze grew intent. "You need respond only as you feel. If his attention troubles you, I shall speak with him."

"Absolutely not," she cried, then winced at the echo in her skull. Moderating her tone, she added, "I can manage my own affairs."

A flicker of something—hurt, maybe—crossed his face, gone almost before she registered it. "Joy," he said, taking her hand, his voice rougher than usual, "you are—not merely adequate, or capable, or my dearest friend. You are extraordinary and need not settle where your heart is not affected." He released her as though daring her to dispute him.

Speech deserted her. Heat rose from her collarbones to her hairline. The throbbing in her skull battered a rhythm equal to horses' hooves. When at last she managed to breathe, she found her reply woefully feeble. "Thank you."

He offered his arm once more. "Come. Let us find Lady Westwood to see you to your pillow before the household concludes you have eloped with the Colonel."

She managed a laugh and allowed him to guide her to a quiet place to await her escort home. Pain notwithstanding, her heart felt strangely buoyant, as though she had stepped from solid earth onto a craft of which the destination remained undecided. Freddy's steady presence at her side, the remembered heat of St. John's fingers, the lingering hiss of Letty Partridge's laughter—all blurred together into something new and unsettling. She did not know whether she liked it, only that she was vividly, terribly awake.

As Westwood and Faith joined them to see her home, Freddy returned to wish her goodnight. "Rest, Joy. Promise me?"

"I promise." She hesitated, then rose on tiptoe to press a swift kiss to his cheek—nothing more than any sister might bestow. "Good night, Freddy."

He touched the spot lightly, as though surprised to find it still warm. "Good night."

When they had entered the carriage she leaned against the wall, spectacles askew, head pounding yet spirit oddly light. Through the drumming in her temples rang one incontrovertible truth: whatever course her future followed—spinster, convenient marriage, or something unimagined—life had grown more complicated this night. And complications hurt her head.

∽

FREDDY MEANDERED into his dining parlour at half-past noon, the hour to which he clung on mornings following a particularly late night. Dobson, the invaluable valet-and-major-domo who presided over his bachelor establishment, intercepted his languid progress with a bow just shy of reproachful and deposited a steaming cup of coffee upon the small rosewood table by the south window. The porcelain was hot enough to warm his hand, the aroma sharp enough to cut through the last vestiges of a headache. Beside it lay Freddy's paper, ironed as flat as any neckcloth and folded so that the leading articles could be surveyed with the least exertion.

He took an appreciative sip, accepted a slice of lightly buttered toast, and unfurled first the *Morning Post's* Society sheet. It was his invariable habit to skim first the turf results—of which there were none fresh, to his mild disappointment—and then the gossip columns, that he might be forearmed against any pronouncements likely to disturb the parental temper. Lord Gresham, though fond of his only son, held decided views on decorum; Lady Gresham, though indulgent, possessed an imagination apt to magnify the vaguest rumour into a catastrophe.

Half the column was the usual tittle-tattle concerning heiresses, hothouse lilies, and naval promotions. But the next paragraph commanded his entire attention:

IT IS WHISPERED that Colonel SJ—of His Majesty's Life Guards and a decided favourite in certain drawing rooms—appears earnestly to be courting Miss J—— W——, who, to universal astonishment, donned a pair of spectacles at Lady Constance Houghton's dinner last evening. May this be the true cause of her well-acknowledged clumsiness upon the dance floor? The next ball shall surely tell. We enquire further whether said infirmity likewise explains her notorious curricle race in Hyde Park. Perhaps it was instead a runaway pair? Will the lady's accessory start a new fashion —or is her newly enhanced dowry the lodestone attracting so gallant a suitor?

THE PRINT BLURRED. Freddy lowered the sheet so sharply that the edge caught the rim of his coffee cup, catapulting a scalding torrent across the tablecloth and—worse—onto his favourite waistcoat of indigo silk with silver embroidery. A curse erupted, vehement and wholly unlike. Dobson, who at the first tremor of the cup had sprung forward with a cloth, silently blotted the tidal wave before it reached the carpet, then produced a second napkin for Freddy's aching fingers.

"Another cup, sir?" Dobson asked, as though gentlemen overturned their breakfast beverages for sport.

"Another cup—and the devil take the *Post*," Freddy muttered, dabbing at the waistcoat. He flung himself into the armchair and glared at the offending column once more. How dare they make sport of Joy's spectacles, which he'd had a devil of a time convincing her to wear! And this wretched scribbler presumed to attribute St. John's attentions solely to her fortune! If he ever discovered who wrote these columns, he would gladly wring their neck!

He wadded up the paper and thrust it aside. If there lay a true attachment, Freddy desired nothing more fervently than Joy's happiness. He knew her merits, her kindness, her ungovernable delight in life. But if St. John's motives extended no further than purse and consequence, then Frederick George Marshall Cunningham would find the means—quiet or otherwise—to frustrate them. Joy Whitford might be clumsy, headstrong, and, in his private estimation, the most bewitching female presence in London, but she should never be another man's prey.

A brisk ride through the park dissipated some of his ill humour, though the thud of hooves upon Rotten Row invited recollections of that infamous race—Joy's laughter on the wind, the Colonel's approving smile, the sudden throb of fear that she might overturn her curricle. By the time Freddy had winded his gelding and set off towards Berkeley Square, he had persuaded himself into a semblance of equanimity. He would observe; he would weigh; he would not, heaven help him, behave like a jealous schoolboy.

The Square, with its plane trees and sober brick façades, looked serenely indifferent to his inner tumult. Yet a splash of colour betrayed the presence he sought. Outside Gunter's fashionable confectioner's clustered a small tableau: Joy Whitford, in a gown of sprigged muslin that fluttered about her ankles, Colonel St. John, immaculate in bottle-green coat, and two kittens—no longer the minuscule mites Freddy recalled but half-grown adventurers—twining about the lady's boots. Joy balanced a dish of ice in one hand, spectacles perched upon her nose, while she attempted—with mixed success—to allocate morsels of sponge cake between Cecilia and Mortimer.

Freddy slackened his pace, content a moment to watch unseen. There was animation in her gestures: the deft bend to rescue a fallen spoon, the quick smile offered to a passing child, the rueful shake of the head when St. John proffered his own pocket handkerchief to stem dripping ice. A curl escaped her bonnet and brushed her cheek.

He knew precisely how soft that curl would feel. He had once teased her that it smelled of sunshine and horsehair ribbons. She had threatened him with a riding crop.

Cecilia, meanwhile, launched herself upon Mortimer, who retaliated with all the swashbuckling dignity of a young lion. In an instant, the pair were a rolling tumble of claws and exuberant tails, darting beneath the hooped skirts of a lady descending from her barouche. The shriek Freddy anticipated never came. Instead, Lady Marchmont —renowned for an appetite for scandal surpassed only by her love of exotic pets—uttered a delighted trill.

"Kittens!" she exclaimed, gathering the voluminous folds of her lemon-coloured silk and stooping with surprising grace. Joy started forward, clearly mortified as St. John made an abortive reach, but Lady Marchmont had already emerged, holding Mortimer aloft like a trophy while Cecilia clung to the flounce of her gown.

"My dear Miss Whitford, these are splendid creatures. Do tell me they are in want of a good home?"

Joy, recovering from her blush, laughed, even though Freddy knew she'd had no real thought of parting with any of her precious darlings. "Indeed, my lady, they grow daily more mischievous, and Lord Westwood vows the house cannot contain them much longer."

"Then I must have them—oh, yes, I insist. Sir Percival—" She referred to her long-suffering pug who stood at the door of her carriage wheezing. "—will adore the company."

Freddy chose that moment to approach, doffing his hat. "Lady Marchmont, you are all charity. May I assist by disentangling Miss Cecilia from your—ah—ruffles?"

"Mr. Cunningham! Please do." Her ladyship beamed, evidently pleased to have widened the audience for her benevolence.

Freddy effected the rescue, receiving only a modest scratch, and surrendered the wriggling tabby into Lady Marchmont's arms. Introductions followed, during which Joy's eyes—bright behind the spectacles—met Freddy's with a sparkle of relief and something warmer he dared not name.

St. John greeted him too, courteously enough, though the lines about the Colonel's mouth hinted at vexation. Freddy returned the salutation with equal civility, noting the faint smudge of raspberry ice upon the fellow's cuff and feeling absurdly gratified.

Lady Marchmont soon rolled away in her carriage, promising dispatch of her footman and a basket presently. The trio left behind watched the barouche roll away. Joy exhaled sadly.

"Westwood will thank the heavens," she said. "Six kittens were… rather a bounty."

"Four now have homes?" Freddy asked.

"Yes, Lord Orville and Camilla remain, though Camilla shows every sign of adopting Lord Rotham whether he likes it or not."

"Rotham will capitulate. He only pretends to be a tyrant. Speaking of tyrants," Freddy said lightly, "may I hope Miss Whitford is tyrannized by no headache today?"

The question was innocent; the look he gave her was not. Joy coloured. "I am perfectly restored, thank you. A twelve hour respite from shining chandeliers works wonders."

"And how are the spectacles?"

She touched the gold rims. "I have reconciled myself to their necessity. I find the world altogether clearer, though whether Society will forgive the eccentricity remains to be seen."

"Society," Freddy declared, "must learn to value clear sight above the mere appearance of it."

St. John regarded him with an expression too bland to be trusted. "Miss Whitford's appearance would never be dimmed by such."

St. John seemed amused rather than repulsed by Joy's antics. Freddy reminded himself that was a good thing.

"Have you plans for the afternoon, Miss Whitford? I thought to exercise Banbury and might prevail upon you and Nightingale to join us."

St. John accepted this request with equanimity. "Alas, duty calls me to the Horse Guards, else I would enjoy watching her put the horse through its paces. Miss Whitford's company is ever a pleasure."

"Then you will excuse us," Freddy said, offering Joy his arm, "I will escort her home."

She thanked the Colonel prettily and permitted Freddy to accompany her, though he felt the tension in her silence.

"Am I guilty of abduction?" he asked, when distance made confidences safe.

"Not at all. I only happened upon him here with Faith, and she left me in his charge."

"I should tell you," he said, keeping his eyes ahead, "that the *Post* makes ignoble sport of you this morning."

"I guessed as much by your expression when you first approached. Does it wound your pride that my foibles supply the scandal sheets?"

"It wounds nothing so much as my faith in mankind's discretion." He hesitated. "They speculate upon your dowry."

Her shoulders lifted, then fell. "I cannot help what tongues wag. If St. John courts me because I am suddenly worth another ten thousand, better I learn it before sentiment complicates matters."

"Has sentiment," he ventured, "begun to do so?" Freddy felt as though his heart paused while he awaited her answer.

She was quiet for several beats, the sounds around them muted. At last she answered in a low voice: "I admire him. He is kind, attentive, and does not scold when I do something wrong. But is that enough? I am not certain."

A curious lightness bloomed in his chest. "Then give yourself time. The Colonel is a man of consequence, yes, but also of ambition. Ensure his affection is constant."

She turned to him. "What of you, Freddy? Has any particular lady tested the steadiness of your heart?"

"I daily surrender it," he said, daring a grin, "to whichever filly runs swiftest."

"That," she replied, laughing, "is not what I meant."

He sobered. "When I find the person who renders the rest of the world dull by comparison, I shall know."

Her gloved hand settled on his sleeve, a light pressure, yet it sent awareness skimming to his fingertips. "Whoever she is," Joy said softly, "she will be fortunate indeed."

He had vowed to protect Joy's happiness at any cost. He could not yet discern whether that cost might be his own.

CHAPTER 12

Joy had never regarded a drawing room with such mixed emotions as she did that mild spring afternoon when Grace—newly Lady Carew, glowing with Greecian sunshine and wedded bliss—returned to Westwood House. The doors stood open upon the terrace, letting in a breeze. Yet the air inside teemed not with serenity but with the whirl of sisters. Faith, Hope, and Patience already occupied the chairs about the low mahogany table. Kittens—two of the original six—prowled between skirts, intent upon crumbs of seed cake.

Grace burst through the door in a dove-grey pelisse, carrying a basket which she deposited on the floor. "My dears!" she cried, and was immediately engulfed by embraces, exclamations, and the inevitable pleasant chaos of family reunited. Joy received a hug smelling faintly of lemons, and, for a moment, forgot every recent perplexity—St. John's unfathomable attentions, the still-stinging tattles of the *Post*, even the spectacles that had refused to stay perched upon her nose that morning.

No sooner had Grace deposited the wicker basket upon the Axminster than its lid gave a most determined wobble. In the next instant Theo's nose appeared, followed smartly by Evalina's mewl.

They scrabbled over the rim, tumbled in a flurry of paws to the carpet, and scampered, pell-mell, across the drawing room towards the others. Frederica lifted her head from the hearthrug, uttered a low, welcoming chirrup, and in a trice both truants were nuzzling beneath her whiskered chin. Lord Orville arched his back in pleasure and bestowed upon his sister Camilla a conspiratorial swat, whereupon the pair bounded forward to join the reunion. In that harmonious circle of purrs and gentle head-butts, the five felines formed a tableau of domestic felicity.

"Where are the others?" Grace asked, looking around.

"Lady Marchmont has adopted Mortimer and Cecilia," Patience answered.

"Ah, I suppose it would be impossible to keep so many." Grace's face evidenced the sadness Joy felt as well.

"We miss Mortimer's antics dreadfully," Patience said, handing out cups of tea.

"Lady Marchmont sent a note this morning—he mastered Sir Percival's trick of begging within an hour and is the darling of her Thursday salons," Joy felt compelled to tell them as well as reminding herself.

"And she says that Cecilia," Joy added with a soft sigh, "has taken to the Marchmont nursery as though born to sovereignty. I dare say the children are her grateful subjects."

Grace's smile held both pride and a hint of melancholy. "Then the little ruffians will want for nothing." She stroked Freddy behind the ears.

Joy, whose lap was presently occupied, managed a rueful grin. "We were never destined to keep a whole litter. Seven cats in Town would have overturned even Westwood's benevolence. Still, the house feels empty without all of them."

A sympathetic murmur circled the table. Then Hope leaned forward. "You must tell us every particular of Greece, Grace!"

Grace's cheeks coloured prettily and a spark of mischief glimmered in her eyes. "It was quite romantic: a volcano, Mediterranean sunsets, swimming in the warm ocean—"

"'Tis the stuff of novels," Joy snorted.

"Or catastrophes," Patience remarked with practical serenity. "I trust no lava was involved?"

"Sadly, no. Only in tales of antiquity. We confined ourselves to ruins and excellent ices in Athens." Grace lifted her teacup but paused, blue eyes sharpening upon Joy.

"Speaking of ices, what is this I hear about Gunter's?" Hope asked.

Every neck turned towards Joy. She felt Camilla knead her skirt as though applauding the change of topic. "Colonel St. John encountered me whilst I was purchasing raspberry ices," she said, affecting nonchalance she did not entirely feel. "It was a happy accident, nothing more."

Grace, however, was not so easily diverted. "Accidents seldom prompt gossip columns to speculate upon dowries and courtships," she observed, her tone gently concerned.

"You saw that, did you?"

"Carew did. Tell me, sister—are you tempted to follow the drum?"

Joy opened her mouth, found no sufficient answer, and closed it again. The mere thought of a soldier's itinerant life—camp chests, foreign billets, the ceaseless rumble of movement—thrilled and terrified her by equal measure. She had no doubt she could ride with the baggage train, mend tackle, harness, or saddlery, and brew coffee over a campfire; but she could less easily picture herself as the dignified officer's lady who charmed provincial governors' wives at parade dinners. And beyond all: was St. John even serious?

Patience, recognizing Joy's fluster, interposed. "Grace, let her breathe for a moment. She has endured interrogations enough these past weeks."

But Hope bristled on Joy's behalf. "If the Colonel dangles without intention, he deserves a set-down. Our sister is not a pastime."

Joy mustered a small laugh. "He cannot toy with me if my affections are not engaged, can he? It is nothing more than the flirtations people discuss so drearily in drawing rooms."

Faith's eyes, always sternest where decorum was endangered,

flashed. "Young ladies do not engage in flirtations, Joy. They accept addresses." She pronounced the verbs as though reciting gospel.

"Why will none of you believe that, in my case, marriage is no imperious duty?" Joy asked, exasperation pricking like pins beneath her stays. She pressed a hand to her chest. "You wish me a different creature—docile, soft-voiced, content to stitch chemises and practise quadrilles—but I am not so formed."

Her declaration cast a hush over the room. Even Camilla froze mid-purr, tail curling about her feet in feline sympathy. Grace set down her cup with a click. "Joy, dearest goose, no one wishes you remade—merely content."

"You wish me to be content," Joy echoed, "but you define contentment as wedded life because it suits you all." She gestured, one sweep of her arm encompassing Faith and Hope's new motherhood, Patience and Grace's newly wedded glow, before continuing: "Whereas my imagination shrivels at the notion of housekeeping lists and social obligations."

Hope bit her lip, searching for diplomacy. "We do not ask you to pretend, only to remain open if a worthy gentleman appears."

"And if he does," Joy allowed, a dimple smothered beneath earnestness, "he must value me precisely as I am—spectacles, curricle races, Gothic novels, and an unladylike aptitude for fouling a hem."

Laughter rippled, easing the tension. Faith leaned forward and kissed her sister's brow. "We love every outré inch of you, even when you alarm us half to death."

Patience, ever the mediator, tapped the cooling teapot. "Perhaps we may agree upon a truce. Joy will not disclaim the Season altogether. We will cease besieging her with schemes to allure suitors."

"Perhaps," Grace added, slyly arching a brow, "she has found what she seeks in Colonel St. John."

Joy swallowed a retort. "I will not retreat. That would be churlish."

Grace's smile softened. "Tell me, then. What do you admire in him?"

The enquiry, though gently put, required consideration. Joy folded her hands around Camilla. "He treats me as though I were—interesting," she began, feeling heat rise within. "He listens when I speak of stallions' bloodlines. He does not flinch if I misstep a quadrille; he only steadies me. And though he has a soldier's polish, he does not feign superiority."

"A promising catalogue," Patience conceded. "Yet does friendship bloom into something warmer?"

Joy gazed out at the gardens where shadows danced across clipped yew hedges. "I do not know," she admitted softly. "When he looks at me, my stomach performs inconvenient somersaults, but I cannot decide whether those belong to affection—or alarm."

Hope's grin was wicked. "The line is exasperatingly fine."

Grace reached to squeeze Joy's hand. "Trust your instincts. Like riding a horse."

Joy recalled the race that had set so many whispers afloat, and her face heated.

The door creaked. Hartley entered, bearing an envelope upon a salver. "A note for Miss Whitford," he announced.

Four pairs of sisterly eyes converged upon Joy. She accepted the letter, breaking the seal with a tremor she hoped escaped notice. Colonel St. John's hand was bold, confident, slanting.

Dear Miss Whitford,
Will you honour me with a ride tomorrow at ten? The tulips are in full bloom along the Long Walk, and I would show them to you before they fade.
Your servant, St. John

Silence thickened while Joy read, folded, and tucked the sheet into her pocket. She met Grace's questioning glance.

"He asks to ride in the Park." Her voice sounded inadequately steady.

"Well, will you?" Hope breathed.

Joy's thoughts scattered—morning sun through new leaves, the sure rhythm of hooves, a gentleman's smile as warm as June—she might as well see where things led. She cleared her throat. "I...believe I shall."

Approval, relief, and excitement mingled in her sisters' expressions. Faith clapped once; Hope smiled in relief; Patience nodded as though tallying favourable odds. Only Grace remained pensive.

"Joy," she began, her tone pitched solely for younger-sister ears, "remember you need never accept someone you cannot abide. A ride is not an engagement. Admiration is not possession."

"I know." Joy's answering smile felt wobbly. "But I must also remember fear is not wisdom."

Grace squeezed her hand. "Well said."

Tea resumed—plates of seed cake passed about; kittens indulged with judicious saucers of milk. Talk flowed to lighter topics: new gowns, Greek cuisine, and teething babies. Yet beneath the chatter, Joy sensed a quiet shift, like the tide turning.

Joy had declared indifference to husbands, but perhaps the greater truth was uncertainty.

Should Colonel St. John's admiration prove shallow, if any fortune-hunting glint surfaced in his fine hazel eyes, Freddy would be the first to sense her heartbreak. And she would not, must not, break. Whether spinster or bride, Joy Whitford would step forward with head high, spectacles shining, unashamed.

∼

FREDDY SUBMITTED with outward docility to the careful strokes of Dobson's razor. In his mind, he rode again yesterday's hack with Joy, reliving every jolt of the quarrel that had followed. Westwood, hoping to silence London's whisperers, had insisted Joy take a groom to ride ten paces behind for propriety's sake, which made her bristle from the start. Immediately she began interrogating him.

How progressed his search for a bride? Had he settled his mind at last? Freddy, nettled by the implication that he dithered, answered that Miss Letty Partridge would do as well as any. "Do?" Joy had repeated, blue eyes sparking behind the hated spectacles. Did he mean to be bored to tears for an entire lifetime? The accusation stung—worse, it lodged. He retaliated with a jibe of his own. Would she like to be abandoned while Colonel St. John gallivanted with the army?

"That would suit me perfectly," she had snapped. Then, with exasperating calm, she had dispensed advice. Introduce Miss Partridge to the pursuits he himself loved—Ascot, Henley, any field where a pulse might rise—and observe her response. A sober suggestion, delivered with military precision. But the sting lingered. A man did not relish being characterized as a fellow who settled.

Now, Freddy admitted a flaw in the scheme. Ascot lay weeks away, Henley more distant, and he had little time to spare. In the meantime, he must contrive some demonstration of gallantry. And there, Fortune (in the form of Joy) had placed an opportunity squarely in his path. Lord Orville, the kitten destined for his future ownership. "Does not everyone love kittens?" Joy had remarked, handing the creature into his arms the evening she had proclaimed its custody.

It seemed a plan of simplicity for Freddy's simple mind. A gentleman presents his adorable feline; the lady's affections soften; admiration for the gentleman blooms. Certainly this would enable original conversation with the pretty Letty. With this agreeable prospect, Freddy submitted to Dobson's ministrations, chose a waistcoat unexceptionable in pattern, and set out for Westwood House to collect the ambassador of his courtship.

Westwood's butler ushered him into the smaller morning room where the kittens loved to bask in the sun. Hartley informed Freddy that Joy and the ladies were out on morning calls, but he knew Joy wouldn't mind if he took the little fellow. Within, Lord Orville reposed like a sultan upon a chaise longue, pale eyes narrowing in suspicion as his tail whisked slowly.

"Come along, your lordship," Freddy coaxed, gathering the kitten. "You must help me woo." The kitten offered a plaintive mewl as Freddy lowered him into a wicker basket, but no claws yet pierced the wicker. Encouraged, Freddy tucked the basket beneath his arm, thanked the butler, and descended the steps.

The curricle awaited. The tiger—an imp of twelve years and infinite curiosity—secured the basket by a strap in the seat next to him. Not two furlongs along Brook Street the first hint of rebellion emerged. A faint scrabbling, then the distinct pop of loosened wicker. Freddy spared a glance, and four white paws protruded through the lattice.

"None of that!" he urged with a tap. The paws withdrew. Peace lasted until the corner of Bond Street, whereupon Lord Orville executed an escape worthy of a seasoned picklock. He erupted onto Freddy's lap, tail lashing, and fixed luminous orbs upon the passing thoroughfare as though debating a launch.

The curricle swerved. Shoppers scattered. "Confound it, sir," Freddy muttered, wresting the reins with one hand while the other tried to cradle a wriggling bundle intent on scaling his perfectly tied Mathematical. By prodigious luck they arrived without collision at the Partridge town house in Grosvenor Square, though more than one jarvey shook a fist at the reckless driving.

Lord Orville seemed content to be on Freddy's person. So be it.

He handed the reins to his tiger, then proceeded up the steps to the Partridge front door.

Freddy was shown in, and though the butler's eyes had fixed upon Lord Orville, he refrained from comment.

In the lemon-striped drawing room Letty looked every inch the genteel idyll, pale curls arranged round a heart-shaped face, and an embroidery hoop poised in her hands. Her mama, installed on a rosewood settee, surveyed Freddy with canny pleasure giving him a sense of distaste at his errand.

"I wondered," he began, mindful of Joy's inclinations, "whether you might enjoy to meet my small friend." He indicated Lord Orville on his shoulder.

Lord Orville performed his entrance with theatrical finesse. A leap to Letty's lap, a half-spin, and a squeaking purr pitched for universal delight. Letty gave a delicate gasp, and Freddy exhaled. Success. Or so he reckoned until the kitten discovered embroidery thread—the very skein currently attached to the fichu near Letty's needle.

A flurry of claws, a shriek, and the fichu unravelled like a cavalry charge. The kitten flailed, tangled in silk, and scampered—unfortunately—up Letty's sleeve. Freddy, heart plummeting, darted forward, but silk tore with an especially expressive ripping sound. Lady Partridge swooned whilst the butler fetched a servant armed with pruning gloves, and Letty's composure dissolved into high treble.

The rescue, once effected, left Freddy and the servant clutching a quivering kitten swaddled in a tea towel and Letty dabbing tears (of mortification rather than injury). The fichu was beyond salvation, the sleeve in want of repair, and Lady Partridge's earlier approval cooled to a polite frost.

When, at length, order reasserted itself, Lady Partridge spoke with brittle composure. "You do not intend to keep that creature, do you? Cats belong in the barn or, at the very least, in the kitchen. Perhaps, Mr Cunningham, the kitten would prefer—open air?"

The translation was plain enough for Freddy: retreat, regroup, preferably elsewhere.

Freddy bowed, murmured apologies, reclaimed the culprit—who emitted an indignant chirrup—and allowed the butler to escort him out.

Driving back towards Berkley Square he attempted stoicism. Kittens, apparently, were not a universal passport to feminine favour. Lord Orville, exhausted by his exertions, curled upon Freddy's lap, tiny paws flexing in dreams. Freddy slowed the vehicle to an amble and considered alternatives. A vision flashed in his mind's eye of Joy herself, laughing as the curricle raced the wind, arguing between leaps, bonnet ribbons trailing. Freddy's heart performed an unhelpful skip. She would have adored Lord Orville's escapade. He smiled and turned a corner. He hoped she was now home so he could tell her the tales!

"A slight contretemps?" Hartley enquired, eyeing the silk threads still clinging to Lord Orville's claws.

"A massacre," Freddy admitted.

"Miss Whitford has returned, sir, and is in the ladies' parlour."

"I will show myself up, Hartley."

"Very good, sir."

He found Joy attempting to teach Camilla to retrieve a paper ball. At the sound of his step she looked up; the kitten abandoned him and streaked beneath the sofa.

"You look as though Trafalgar has been re-fought upon your person," she observed, taking in the destroyed neckcloth and a suspicious rent in his sleeve.

"Only feline antics," Freddy said, depositing himself on the nearby settee. "Your protégé distinguished himself."

Joy crouched, gathering the kitten, who immediately purred like the angel he was not. "What mischief?"

"Invasion, occupation, and the wholesale destruction of Miss Partridge's embroidery, fichu, and sleeve. I arrived bearing him like a peace offering, yet I departed like Bonaparte from Moscow."

Laughter burst from her—bright, unrestrained, deliciously improper for a lady. Freddy felt the tension of the day melt as she fell back with ungirded laughter, tears of mirth glazing her eyes.

"Tell me everything," she commanded, seating herself on the hearthrug. He obeyed and recited first the escape from the basket, then his lordship deciding Freddy's neckcloth was where he ought to perch, then on to the fichu massacre. With each fresh calamity, Joy's amusement grew. By the time he described nearly crawling beneath the sofa while Letty squealed and her mama swooned, she was quite helpless, pressing a hand to her ribs.

"Oh, Freddy," she gasped, "if only I had been there to watch!"

"You would have joined Lord Orville in climbing inside her sleeves."

"Undoubtedly." She wiped her eyes, still smiling. "So, the experiment in the universal charm of kittens has failed?"

"Spectacularly." He studied her upturned face—cheeks flushed, eyes dancing behind their lenses—and felt a queer warmth expand beneath his ribs. "But you were right on one point: the creature is an incomparable judge of character. He spotted a room devoid of adventure and remedied the want in under a minute."

Joy laid her cheek against the kitten's head, dimples deepening. "He is your perfect accomplice, then."

Freddy sobered. "How do I retrench and regroup now? I have two knocks against me."

"Do not lose heart yet, Freddy." She furrowed her brow, considering his question. "Perhaps a house party, Freddy, where you can see if she suits away from Society."

He sighed heavily, not wishing to force the issue or show partiality, but he was becoming desperate. "I will speak to my parents. You will come, will you not?"

"Anything to go to the country," she retorted. "However, I know just the thing to lift your spirits."

"Are you going to tell me?" he asked impatiently.

"We have been invited to Ascot!"

Freddy perked up at the word. "By whom?"

"Thornhill's Banquet is racing!"

"Whyever is Thornhill inviting you to Ascot?"

Joy looked heavenward so he must be doing something daft again. "Not me, all of us. Carew, Grace, Maeve, Ashley, and Patience—it is to be a party."

"Then why did you not say so from the beginning?"

"I thought it was obvious that Thornhill is taken with Maeve. The rest of us make it respectable."

"Well, as you know, I am always game for a race!"

CHAPTER 13

Joy awoke well before the maid tapped at her door, buoyed by a delighted certainty that, for at least one day, London's stuffy drawing rooms lay far behind. By seven o'clock, two travelling carriages waited in Westwood's forecourt. Lord Carew, Grace, and Maeve were to ride in the first, Patience and Ashley with Joy in the second. Freddy had gone down the previous afternoon with Thornhill in the curricle, so the gentlemen might see to his thoroughbred, Banquet, which would face the favourite, T.A. Fraser's Champignon, in the The Gold Cup. To complete the party, Thornhill had generously offered places in his booth to Miss Letty Partridge and Miss Arabella Finch, a merry dark-haired girl fresh from the schoolroom. The extra guests, Grace assured Joy, would remove any hint of preference from one particular lady.

Joy privately doubted whether preference could be disguised when Freddy spent half his waking hours dangling after Letty like sugar plums before a child at Christmas. Still, Ascot was horses and the country. She resolved to enjoy every moment, even if it meant sharing the vantage with Miss Partridge's insipid sighs.

By the time Ascot Heath shimmered on the horizon, Joy was near to bursting. Carriages four abreast jammed the approach;

grooms shouted; footmen established impromptu hierarchies of precedence; gentlemen in morning coats and beaver hats swarmed in the middle distance as the Grand Stand towered over a sea of parasols.

Their party alighted near Selwood Park, where a liveried steward ushered them towards the towering booth Thornhill had had built for the occasion. Joy, trailing after the others, felt her pulse quicken as she took it all in: a famous jockey weighing out, someone haggling over odds with a dapper bookmaker, a merry band blaring, vendors hawking souvenirs, and the smell of crushed turf mingling with roasted meat.

Inside the booth the view commanded the whole straight run to the winning post. Joy dashed to the railing, spectacles catching sunlight, and drank in the scene—shimmering rails, horses in colours, green-coated officials clearing the track, the expectant roar of thousands of spectators.

Miss Partridge soon joined them, a vision in palest jonquil muslin, escorted by her mama. "How delightfully energetic it all seems!" she cooed, executing a curtsy of studied delicacy for Freddy.

Freddy bowed low. "The exact tint of your gown matches the June sun, Miss Partridge—who could ask the weather for better company?"

Letty's eyelashes fluttered whilst Joy tried not to laugh.

Barely had the party adjusted its formation before Miss Arabella Finch bounded up like a spring tide, curls escaping a chip-straw bonnet festooned with pink flowers. "I declare I am giddy with anticipation of trumpets and the thunder of hooves!" she cried, nearly tripping over her sprigged muslin. Trumpets? Without ceremony the girl linked arms with Joy—whom she had met but once—and confided that she had placed a shilling on Banquet.

Below, Thornhill's bay circled, his coat gleaming like new mahogany. Joy seized the field glasses and whistled. "He moves like Pegasus, missing only wings."

"You must not lean so perilously," Letty fussed, edging closer. Freddy produced a programme, pointing out the rival colours—Thornhill's scarlet-and-white; Petersfield's purple-and-gold—and bent to explain the odds, his shoulder almost brushing Joy's. She pretended not to notice the small prickle between her ribs.

Thornhill arrived, wreathed in confidence. "Back him at five to one, Cunningham, and I shall double your stake myself."

Joy laid a modest wager, causing Letty to gasp, "Ladies never wager!" but, coaxed by Freddy's low assurances that it was only chicken stakes, surrendered a half-crown to him. Miss Finch flourished her shilling like a banner.

While Joy was absorbing everything, she noticed Colonel St. John in the throng below. She made to wave at him, but he slipped between two booths, and merged with a stranger whose dark coat and slouched hat obscured his face. Their heads bent close—heated words, perhaps? The exchange ended inside a minute. St. John emerged, felt Joy's stare, and waved with airy cheer before making for the stairs. Unease tingled along Joy's spine, but she kept her own counsel.

St. John then made an appearance, immaculate in blue superfine and buff breeches, his boots scarcely dusted by the turf. He mounted the steps to pay his respects, offered Joy a bow and congratulated Thornhill on the "fine goer" his Banquet was. Yet even as he spoke his gaze roamed the crowd, searching. After exchanging the barest pleasantries with those present, he excused himself on the pretext of finding an acquaintance and slipped away down the stairs, vanishing into the press of onlookers and bookmakers before anyone could force him to stay.

Then all was forgotten as a bell rang and horses pranced to the Royal Stand. Joy's heart hammered while Freddy pressed against the rail beside her and grinned like a schoolboy escaped from lessons.

"Look how he settles," Joy breathed as Banquet danced into place. "Head low, ears flicking—he knows."

"Better seat than any," Freddy said of the jockey, nodding his agreement.

Their shoulders touched as they gripped the edge of the balcony.

The starter waved his hand. A thunderclap of hooves tore along the course. Joy forgot decorum and leaned forward, spectacles clenched, the field a blur—scarlet-and-black, purple-and-gold, green, blue. At halfway Banquet lay third. At the wooden distance-post he edged to second alongside Champignon. Joy's pulse matched each stride. Freddy shouted encouragement, waving his hat aloft. Letty squeaked with excitement, and the Grand Stand roared as horses flashed past like coloured lightning.

With three furlongs to run, Banquet's rider slipped an inch of rein. The bay lengthened—a beautiful, loping surge that sent a tremor through the crowd. Champignon clung inside, his jockey low, purple cap bobbing.

"Come on, lad—pick him up!" Freddy yelled, voice raw.

Maeve clasped her gloved hands to her mouth, whilst Miss Finch bounced on her toes. Letty then shrank from the rail, murmuring that the pounding hooves made her faint.

Joy could hear nothing now but wind and thunder. In her left eye the two leaders blended, red sleeve against purple, moving as one. She willed Banquet forward, palms burning on the rail.

Inside the final furlong the duel tightened. Banquet gained a neck then Champignon answered, the great chestnut stretching with killer resolve. Fifty yards out, they were nose to nose. A collective gasp rolled through the booth.

"Touch him with the whip, man!" Thornhill shouted.

The jockey gave Banquet a single flick. The bay flattened—then drifted fractionally towards the rope. In that breath, Champignon seized the gap, thrust his head ahead, and they flashed past the winning post and the judge. A hush, a susurration, then the announcer's bell.

"First—Champignon—by a short head!"

Groans, cheers, the rustle of losing tickets. Joy exhaled a breath she had not known she held. Her knees trembled. Beside her, Freddy closed his eyes, his jaw tight.

"Gallant as St. George, yet beaten," he said.

Joy turned, laying a hand on his sleeve. "A finer race I never saw."

He met her gaze; disappointment warred with admiration. "Nor I. Thornhill's fellow can be proud."

Joy turned to look behind them to where Maeve comforted her

crestfallen beau. Letty fluttered that at least the horses looked very pretty when they ran fast, which earned her a sharp stare from Joy.

Thornhill managed a rueful smile for his friends. "We shall have him at the next one."

Freddy clapped his shoulder. "Good show! He wants only luck—and a post six inches nearer."

Joy felt the crowd's energy shift from tension to convivial chatter. Bets were settled, hampers opened; champagne corks flew in popping salvoes like the King's birthday salute. Yet under the clamour her unease about St. John returned. Twice she scanned the environs but there was no sign of the Colonel or his mysterious companion.

Thornhill's servants poured champagne, though not quite for the celebration they'd hoped. Freddy carried a glass to Letty, bowing with an extravagant flourish. Joy watched, an unfamiliar throb tugging beneath her breastbone. Letty's answering simper set her teeth on edge.

Turning away, she fixed her attention on Banquet walking back, sweat darkening his shining coat. "You will win next time, brave fellow," she murmured.

Freddy rejoined her while the others picked over strawberries and lobster patties. For a moment they stood alone, looking onto the course where Champignon once again paraded past the Royal Stand.

"There is no thrill like it," Freddy said, his voice pitched low for her ears alone.

"None," Joy agreed, daring a sidelong glance. His profile looked stern, almost wistful.

Before the conversation could take shape, a footman appeared to inform Freddy that Miss Partridge desired Mr. Cunningham's presence. Freddy glanced at Joy, apology in his eyes, and went.

Letty, all dimples and batting lashes, flirted shamelessly, and took possession of his arm while Freddy obliged with impeccable courtesy. Joy's annoyance rekindled. Why could Freddy not see the emptiness behind those wide blue eyes? What had happened to their agreement to choose friends? Colonel St. John appeared at the back of the booth just as the party lifted glasses in consolation for Banquet's razor-thin loss. His manner was oddly watchful as he offered courteous congratulations to Thornhill on "the finest second I have ever witnessed," bowed to the ladies—lingering a heartbeat over Joy with a murmured hope of her continued good health—then, almost before anyone could frame a reply, excused himself and slipped down the stairway, vanishing once more into the milling throng.

Joy scanned the crowd but saw no further sign of Colonel St. John.

***

Freddy had spent the last two hours pretending to listen to Thornhill's rapturous account of Banquet's race while his mind rehearsed a far more troubling question: Why, in the name of common sense, did Joy appear so taken with Colonel St. John? He was handsome, yes, being broad-shouldered, with a cavalryman's skill in the saddle. But when Freddy considered the man coolly, something didn't ring true: a faint stiffness about the smile, a guardedness in the gaze. It was a thought difficult to voice in mixed company, but circumstance spared him from immediate confession. After the exciting day at the races, the party removed to Thornhill Lodge—a rambling Tudor place. The ladies retired, citing fatigue, and at last, in that satisfied hush peculiar to country houses late on a successful sporting day, the gentlemen gathered in Thornhill's study.

Freddy followed Carew, Stuart, and Thornhill into a room that proclaimed a man's domain. Stag antlers bestrode the mantel, and two vast leather sofas sprawled across Turkish carpets patterned in imperial reds and golds. Above the hearth hung a portrait of a snorting chestnut—no doubt an ancestral winner—whilst between two windows glinted twin cavalry sabres crossed in silent salute. Thornhill's bulldog snored in a basket by the fire.

Thornhill passed around balloon-bellied glasses of brandy. The amber liquor caught the lamplight in cheerful flames, and for a moment camaraderie exhaled like a contented sigh.

Freddy set his shoulder to the mantelshelf, cradling his glass in one hand. "An incomparable day, Thornhill," he said, nodding towards the bulldog. "Even Charlie has dreamt himself into victory."

"To the next race," Thornhill toasted, administering the dog a triumphant thump. "Banquet will make the rest look like coach horses."

"He will prevail in the next Cup," Carew put in, seated at a low table strewn with newspapers and betting lists.

Talk drifted through pedigrees and training regimens until Freddy's patience frayed. He lifted his glass, let lamplight flicker against the oily surface, and cleared his throat. "Gentlemen," he began, striving for casualness, "did any of you happen to observe Colonel St. John's…negotiations…this afternoon?"

Stuart lifted sleek brows. "I wondered which of us would breach the subject first."

Thornhill's merriment dimmed. "Negotiations?"

"Bookmaking," Freddy clarified. "I saw him under the Grand Stand with a fellow who would make you cross the street and dart into an alley to avoid."

"I saw as well," Carew admitted, fingers drumming a muted cadence on blotter leather. "And I have laid enough wagers in my time to know there was nothing respectable about that bookmaker."

Stuart swirled his brandy, watching the eddies. "From a distance the Colonel appeared in some agitation—no scandal there, most men flutter when money stands to vanish. Yet he returned to Miss Whitford smiling as though angels sang. The contrast intrigues."

Thornhill bristled. "Do you suspect the man of being badly dipped, Cunningham?"

Freddy exhaled. "That is precisely the dread that nips me. I have never heard St. John boast of deep pockets. Rather the contrary: second son, older brother firmly installed in the country seat."

"He served with honour," Stuart conceded. "That much I know from the dispatches."

"Honour seldom pays promissory notes."

Stuart set down his glass. "Well. I can look into him. Military records are not inviolate." He glanced round the circle, eyes sharpening. "If today's venture went badly, he may grow desperate—better that we learn how deep he stands before matters progress."

"Has she formed an attachment?"

Freddy angled his head in thought. "Joy—?" He broke off, searching for accuracy. "It is hard to say. She enjoys the attentions—who would not?—but I have heard no talk of affection. Flattery perhaps; no more is my guess."

Carew drank, then set down his glass with a bark of decision. "If St. John is a hardened gambler drowning in debt, he must be kept beyond Joy's reach."

"That may prove difficult," Thornhill said quietly from his perch by the window. "A man on the edge clings to any lifeline—especially a dowry rumoured to be as handsome as Miss Whitford's."

"Curse my brother for voicing that aloud." Stuart scowled.

Carew's eyes narrowed. "Does the Colonel possess any solid prospects?"

Freddy shook his head. "Not that I am aware."

"I will look into that as well. I am surprised my brother has not done so," Stuart admitted. "He seems much too old for her."

"Twelve years, the same as me," Freddy remarked.

"But he has been to war," Stuart pointed out. It did not need to be said what war could do to a man.

"True," Freddy admitted, "and I have not spent nine of those twelve campaigning in Spain and France."

"War alters a man. Joy's innocence is easy to covet."

The bulldog snorted, and for a heartbeat only the ticking of a clock intruded on thought.

Carew tapped the arm of the chair. "We must determine two points: the state of the Colonel's purse and the sincerity of his suit. The first Stuart undertakes; the second…Cunningham, you know Joy best."

"So you would have me interrogate her?" Freddy gave a half laugh.

Stuart's smile was thin. "'Twould be better to approach through her sisters. I will ask Patience. She, in particular, is quite shrewd."

Freddy acknowledged the stratagem. "I shall attempt gentle

enquiry. If Joy nurtures only mild interest we may yet avert entanglement."

Carew folded his arms across his broad chest. "All of us will keep watch on St. John henceforth. Gamblers undone today may double their stakes tomorrow. If he loses again, his desperation will surface. I have some connections in the industry I can call upon. If he is under the hatches, they will find out."

Freddy nodded and tossed off the last of his brandy. Heat chased doubt down his throat. "He will not drag Joy into ruin. That much I swear."

They all agreed on that point. Carew leaned back and trained that too-perceptive gaze upon Freddy. "And what of your own campaign, Cunningham? London wagers a tidy sum on the moment you cry off your bachelor's freedom in favour of Miss Partridge's blue eyes." Thornhill chuckled, while Stuart raised a brow.

Freddy found himself swirling the dregs of his brandy. "'Campaign' gives the matter a military grandeur it does not deserve. I have paid court, danced attendance, fetched shawls, and taken her driving…yet every time prudence urges me to advance to the sticking point, the words turn to dust." He managed a rueful smile. "Miss Partridge is amiable, certainly, but when I picture a lifetime of conversation I hear only polite weather and agreement with my opinion. I fear a lifetime of no other topic."

Thornhill gave a bark of laughter, and Stuart's expression softened to a shade approaching sympathy. Carew said simply, "Then do not propose." The simple advice settled in the room like a verdict, and Freddy felt its truth root deep.

When at last Freddy took himself off to bed, his candle flame danced, casting long bough shadows upon timbered walls. Freddy paused outside a mullioned window that overlooked the lawn sloping towards Ascot Heath. Under a crescent moon the course shimmered faint silver.

Why should Joy's admiration for St. John vex him so? Friendship, he told himself wishfully, but jealousy, raw and unvarnished, was the crux of it. He had spent weeks pretending Letty Partridge's docility pleased him. One fichu-wrecking kitten had proved the futility of that experiment. Instead, Joy, with her spectacles and frank opinions, gales of laughter, and untamed heart, had twined herself around his thoughts. And now a soldier with polished boots and empty pockets threatened his dearest Joy. Freddy dared not delude himself that St. John would tolerate Joy's and his friendship. Though, if St. John left on campaign, he would not be there to object, would he? one devil in his head reasoned. But your own wife might not tolerate Joy having free run of the house, as it were, the devil continued his unwanted commentary.

Freddy set his brow to the cool pane. If St. John truly needed money, Joy's dowry would beckon like harbour light to a storm-tossed sailor. The Colonel's war-forged charm might lure even a wary girl, but Joy was not cunning in subterfuge. If someone like him asked for her hand, she might accept, believing it an adventure. And afterward—he flinched at the possibilities: creditors knocking at Westwood's door, years alone while the Colonel's regiment campaigned, Joy's bright spirit dulled by disillusion. Though St. John did seem taken with Joy. Did he, perhaps, do the man a disservice?

Freddy straightened, resolve forming firm as stone. Tomorrow he would watch and listen, and, if need be, act. Friendship sanctioned it, but something deeper demanded it. He just couldn't quite put a finger on what that was.

CHAPTER 14

Maeve burst into the sitting room with that unmistakable sparkle of delight which no effort of decorum could entirely subdue, and with Joy, there was no such restraint. In one lithe movement, she swept up Camilla, held the contented creature aloft, and executed a waltz turn fit to set any Almack's patroness nodding approval. The kitten submitted with only a few mewls of protest. Joy felt laughter rise at the sight, but knew some news must be forthcoming to bring such delight to her friend.

"My dearest Joy," Maeve cried, settling Camilla against her shoulder, "Thornhill is to host a ball!"

Joy arched a brow. "And perhaps," she ventured, folding her hands, "a particular announcement is to illuminate the occasion?"

A dimple flashed in Maeve's cheek, then permitted herself a small, irrepressible squeal. Joy felt the certainty bloom—this was no mere dance, but the herald of formal betrothal.

"The Duchess of Thornhill's famed resistance must at last have yielded to the Duke's wishes," Joy remarked.

"Indeed it has! I do believe Carew and Grace may have helped in that quarter."

ELIZABETH JOHNS

Rising, Joy pressed Maeve's free hand. "I am exceedingly pleased for you. Few couples are so handsomely matched."

Maeve's fingers tightened round hers. "And I wish—oh, how fervently I wish—that you should share the very happiness that is mine, Joy!"

Joy smiled—sincere, though tinged with that curious ache which attends a friend's sudden nearness to bliss. "We must hope," she answered lightly, even as Camilla leapt to the floor and Lord Orville pounced on his sister.

"I have been so consumed by my own prospects that I have hardly asked after yours," Maeve said, sinking beside Joy on the brocade sofa. "Tell me everything about Colonel St. John. Thornhill swears the Colonel could scarcely remove his gaze from you through the entirety of Ascot."

Joy traced the brocade's faded vine with a gloved finger, marshalling composure. "That is hardly the truth as he was scarcely in my presence! There have been no declarations, nor even the hint of one. His attentions, while flattering, have advanced no further than compliments, occasional waltzes, and more talk of bloodstock than of sentiment whilst we ride or drive."

Maeve's brows arched in polite astonishment. "No declarations? I am all astonishment! I thought gentlemen of the army prided themselves upon decisive action."

"Perhaps he practises the patience of a siege," Joy said, essaying a smile. "In which case I may still escape before the walls collapse."

Maeve laughed, but sobered when she saw Joy's expression. "Do you wish to escape?"

"I wish—" Joy paused, aware of the honesty Maeve's friendship deserved. "I wish to feel certain before I am trapped into certainty. At present I like the Colonel very well, but liking is a slender thread on which to hang a lifetime." Including her freedom.

Maeve nodded. "Then we shall abandon speculation and attend instead to affairs entirely within our command—new ball gowns!" She rose and declared that nothing short of a visit to Madame Clement would do for a diversion.

Joy could not but laugh. "Must we? The French dragon of pins?" She sighed dramatically. "Very well—provided you promise to guard my person."

"You are the most unnatural female, Joy!"

"Yes, I am aware of the sad fact."

"Let us find Grace. She will be the perfect one to accompany us." Maeve clapped her hands, and Joy resigned herself to the enterprise.

Grace, freshly installed in her new role of Lady Carew, greeted the plan with approval. Thus Joy found herself seated opposite Maeve in a deep green barouche. The June sun had spent its warmth at noon, and a thin wind flicked the carriage steps as they halted before Madame Clement's polished windows.

Inside, the shop bustled at the height of the Season with last minute orders. Madame herself advanced to greet Lady Carew, then fashion plates and bolts of satin and silk were presented for their delectation. Maeve drifted from turquoise to blush, dreaming aloud of embroidery that would dance in candlelight. Grace examined a sober sheen of silver tissue. Joy, after dutiful inspection, gravitated towards a bolt of water-blue crêpe, the quiet hue of which pleased her eyes.

"*Parfait pour mademoiselle*," Madame crooned, sweeping Joy onto a small dais while her assistants descended like sparrows. Pins flashed and Joy submitted, schooling her features to indifference even as stays were tugged and seams chalk-marked.

Maeve, meanwhile, discovered a brocade the exact tint of peach at sunrise. She clutched it to her breast. "Thornhill shall expire of delight," she predicted.

"Thornhill would adore you in a burlap sack, my dear," Grace cooed.

Joy looked heavenward, knowing Grace's sentiment was probably accurate.

Then Maeve called across silk-draped chairs, "Joy, you look like a cloud adrift on a June morning!"

Joy tried not to grimace at such effusion so foreign to her own nature, but she did have four elder sisters, after all.

Grace smiled, half-teasing. "When St. John sees you, you will not doubt his admiration." Madame murmured something and tightened a sash.

Just then, Maeve stepped towards the front window. Her hand froze upon the peach brocade. "Who is that man?" she asked, her voice low but vibrating with curiosity. She inclined her head towards the street.

Joy, held fast by Madame's insistence that she remain *absolument immobile*, could turn only a little, yet curiosity tugged at her. She followed Maeve's line of sight past the shop's crystal panes to the pavement beyond. Between a brewer's dray and a gentlemen's curricle, she caught the briefest glimpse. A figure in a drab greatcoat, hat brim drawn so low it obscured his brow. The afternoon light lay flat upon his shoulders. Even at distance Joy sensed a familiarity and the hair on the back of her neck prickled.

Before she could get a closer look, a wagon lurched, blocking the view. When it rattled on, the place was empty.

Maeve turned, brows raised. "He looked as if he were watching the shop rather than passing by."

Joy forced a laugh. "In all likelihood a servant waiting on his mistress." She certainly hoped so, because the alternative was too disturbing.

Grace looked from one to the other. "What is it?"

"Only Maeve's fancy," Joy said, though her heart thumped an irregular tattoo. Maeve opened her mouth, but Joy gave an infinitesimal shake of her head and Maeve allowed the matter to drop.

Madame declared the fittings complete, dismissed Joy to dress, and promised delivery within the week. As the sisters gathered their reticules, Joy could not resist a second look through the window. The crowd flowed unremarked, hackneys jostled, sunlight slanted on a wet gutter stone—but no solitary watcher lingered. It had to be a coincidence. Why would the man from Ascot be following them?

The barouche rolled back to Berkley Square, Grace praising Joy's restraint in selecting so flattering a hue. Joy murmured agreement, her gaze fixed on passing streets, searching every doorway. A hundred nameless Londoners traversed Bond Street. How could she know one shadow from another? Her head ached faintly, and she pressed a palm to her temple.

Maeve caught the motion. "You look unwell."

Grace laughed. "There is nothing in the world so taxing to Joy as the modiste."

"You yourself said I was unnatural." Joy improvised rather than confess what was concerning her. "I shall be sturdy once I have had some tea."

Grace promised to ring for her favourite tarts. Joy thanked her absent-mindedly and allowed the carriage to rock her into temporary calm. Yet the question Maeve had voiced earlier—that little probe into Joy's attachment—now intertwined with a new unease: Had the man from Ascot returned? Was it coincidence that he had appeared or was Joy's imagination weaving pattern from shadow?

Arriving home, Grace shepherded them into the drawing room, where her sisters were already taking tea with the Dowager. Maeve settled onto the sofa, recounting their visit to the modiste and its cause, but Joy drifted to the window and peered into the street. Carriages passed, but nothing stirred that bore resemblance to the stranger.

Hartley brought in more tea, and Grace pressed a plate of honey cake into Joy's hand looking at her with concern. "Is one of your megrims coming on?"

Joy shook herself from her reverie. "'Tis nothing tea will not mend."

She would not trouble Grace with spectres and suspicions.

"I heard Westwood mention this morning that the coronation will not be until August, so it will be longer than usual before we can retire to the country," Faith remarked.

Joy groaned to herself.

"Whyever for?" Patience asked.

"Parliament must be kept sitting to finish the accursed Bill of Pains and Penalties," Faith replied.

"What an odd name for a bill, though quite fitting all the same," Patience muttered. "All because King George is behaving as obstinately as any spoilt schoolboy and must press the Lords to strip poor Caroline of Brunswick of her rank."

"Do not let anyone else hear you say that!" the Dowager gasped.

"'Tis naught but the truth, and it will not gain him any favours with his people."

Joy concurred. Especially not with her.

～

FREDDY ENTERED the coffee room at White's to discover Montford and Rotham already entrenched upon a sofa, brandies in hand, arguing whether the Lords should pass the Pains and Penalties Bill and strip the Queen Consort of her title—or whether, as Rotham contended, the very attempt had made a heroine of the errant consort.

A pile of newspapers littered the table with various headlines: 'Queen Consort accused of adultery,' 'King George Appeals to Parliament for Divorce,' 'Pains and Penalties debated in Lords.' Montford, whose cynicism on domestic politics was usually unshakeable, now thumped each paper as though it were artillery in a siege. Rotham objected that the real mischief was the delay of the coronation until August, thereby forcing every respectable household to remain sweltering in London when they should have taken refuge in the shires. Freddy drank a light ale and listened for ten patient minutes, but his thoughts were inclined to wander. Frankly, he had no head for politics, divorce bills, or the moral fate of Caroline of Brunswick. If the marriage was so distasteful to both parties, then why should it continue? At least King George hadn't beheaded her like Henry the VIII had when he could no longer abide his wives!

A lull occurred when Westwood, Carew, and Stuart arrived. Freddy seized it.

"Have you discovered anything about St. John, Stuart?"

Stuart accepted a drink from the waiter, then answered, "To be fair, my researches show nothing nefarious. Colonel St. John's commission is honourably held. There is no trace of any complaint against him."

The group shifted uncomfortably at this news. Carew set down his glass, shrugged broad shoulders, and said, "And my enquiries revealed no hints of dipping too deep at the tables."

"Debts of honour are not recorded in ledgers," Freddy countered. "A vowel may pass from hand to hand."

Carew gave a shrug. "Perhaps he avoids the gaming hells, which is from whence my sources hail." He took a sip of brandy. "I share your instinct, Cunningham, yet evidence runs thin. Have you anything besides instinct?"

"Nothing beyond seeing the man at Ascot," Freddy admitted. "Though Joy mentioned that a similar man appeared to be watching the modiste the other day. Perhaps there is nothing more than coincidence, but I cannot shake the sensation that something is not right."

Stuart regarded him gravely. "Instinct saved many a soldier in the Peninsula. I would not discount it."

Carew leaned forward. "What do you propose?"

"We could have him followed," Stuart spoke up. "But in the meantime, I have no indication there is any harm in his continued courtship of Joy."

"If that is what it is. He has not spoken to me," Westwood confided.

A silence followed, filled by the hum of conversations around them. Freddy took the brandy set before him yet did not raise it to his lips. "What of St. John's family?"

Stuart shuffled pages from a small leather notebook. "Second son and heir of Earl Trenton. His brother, the Earl, has no male issue, so I imagine this is why St. John now seeks a young wife. My enquiries have revealed he inherited a modest property, one Hathersall Priory in South Yorkshire, which has been let during his time in service to His Majesty."

"Modest," echoed Rotham. "Might be burdened. A let estate may as readily devour rents in repairs as generate income if there are no prosperous farms to support it."

Stuart nodded. "The agent's last report mentions timber blown down in the great gale and a roof needing slate. Nothing ruinous, but nothing to indicate great prosperity either."

"Hence the possible need for an heiress," Montford concluded. "And Joy, with Westwood's guardianship and the dowry, is precisely that."

"Do we fault him? Half the Marriage Mart runs on the same calculation." Rotham was ever practical.

Freddy swallowed the bitter taste uncertainty left on his tongue. "I fault no man for wanting security," he said. "I fault a man only if he trades truth for it."

Carew leaned back, regarding him shrewdly. "You believe his suit lacks sincerity?"

Freddy's fingers tightened round his glass. "I believe it lacks transparency."

Westwood's brows drew together. "You mentioned that Joy described a lurking fellow. Her vision is uncertain."

"With the spectacles her vision is acute enough to distinguish a watcher from a passer-by," Freddy replied coldly, then moderated his tone. He turned to Stuart. "You offered a plan. Put it in motion."

Stuart closed the notebook. "A reliable Bow Street Runner can be engaged by dusk. He will observe St. John's lodgings, track his movements, note all rendezvous. Give me a few days."

Westwood nodded approval. "Do so. Meanwhile we must not alarm Joy."

An ironic smile touched Freddy's mouth. "I doubt much can ruffle Joy. But I shall try to keep mum."

Rotham, who had watched the exchange with mingled amusement, now stretched. "If your Runner digs up nothing, will you concede the gentleman's honour?"

Freddy met his gaze squarely. "If he proves himself honourable I will rejoice, for Joy deserves no less, but until then, I reserve judgement."

With the business temporarily concluded, the circle's attention drifted back to politics. Montford was indignant that anyone would postpone the coronation purely to bully a royal spouse. Westwood argued that public opinion must cool or else stones would fly. Freddy, distracted, let the talk wash over him. If only information could be won about St. John as readily as rumours about the Queen Consort flew about the club.

Yet, what could he do?

Freddy excused himself, then began walking, destination ambiguous. He needed time to clear his head. Something did not feel right about St. John, yet there was nothing to discredit him. Maybe he had dipped too deeply at the races, but that was nothing more than half the *ton* could claim at one time or another. It certainly did not make him unworthy, unless it was something he could not recover from. He was a decorated soldier from a good family. If he made Joy happy, then that mattered above all else.

Freddy knew he should go back to wooing. He could make some afternoon calls and take someone for a drive or walk through the park, yet he soon found himself in Berkley Square.

"Good day, Hartley."

"Good afternoon, Mr. Cunningham. Miss Joy is in the garden with the cats."

"Of course she is. I know the way." Freddy kept his hat since he was going back outside.

"Very good, sir."

Freddy walked through the house and into the gardens and found Joy sitting on a bench near the small fountain. Frederica was sunning herself next to Joy, whilst Camilla and Lord Orville were romping about with each other.

"Why are you not out making calls, young lady?"

"Freddy! I did not hear you come in."

"Is your head bothering you?" He shifted completely to concern, and slid onto the bench beside her.

"I think perhaps I am still adjusting to the spectacles. 'Tis nothing for you to concern yourself with." Frederica rolled over on her back, and Joy began to stroke the cat's stomach.

"You are certain that is all?"

"Freddy, am I erring in some way? There have been no declarations. St. John has not yet spoken to Westwood."

Freddy was glad of it, but he did not say that to Joy. Something inside him twisted with pain that anything would make Joy question herself or her worthiness. Something clawed within—half fury that she should imagine fault, half savage relief that the Colonel was holding his tongue. He watched the wind lift a stray curl from her temple, sunlight glinting off the spectacles' gold rim. She looked very small just then, almost defenceless, as though a change in breeze might tip her doubts into certitude.

"Erring?" he echoed softly. "Joy, you have done everything except ride into Almack's on a charger announcing your dowry. A man who cannot gather the courage to speak when you stand before him is hardly a prize worth fretting over."

She gave a rueful tug at her bonnet strings. "Perhaps he is merely still evaluating me."

"Evaluating is what one does with horseflesh. People require rather more affection." Freddy leaned forward, elbows on knees, forcing himself to sound teasing rather than savage. "Besides, the Season is only half over. There is still time for any number of gentlemen to discover your worth; gentlemen who can complete a sentence without military metaphors—or heroics."

Joy's mouth curved. "It is rather tedious."

His pulse lurched. "I confess I save my heroics for emergencies—runaway curricles, damsels in rivers, that sort of thing."

Joy laughed and the sound loosened a knot beneath his ribs. "What will I do without you to make me laugh, Freddy? Our plan is not meeting with success."

Freddy did not know what to say to that. Part of him wanted to call an end to searching for anyone else, but she deserved to see St. John's courtship through, if that was her desire.

"You will never lose me, Joy."

She thought for a moment and opened her mouth, then closed it as if she decided against whatever she was going to say. "Very well. But if I am to endure more spectacles-induced headaches, I shall require reading aloud—Edgeworth today. Will you oblige?" She plucked the book up off the bench.

"Any time you ask." He took it from her hands.

A warm silence settled as he began to read. Camilla swatted at the tassels on his Hessians whilst Lord Orville settled at Joy's feet for a nap. Freddy watched Joy's smile tilt towards contentment and swore, quietly, that no question of worthiness would reach her ears again—at least, not while he had breath to answer it.

CHAPTER 15

It was a leisurely afternoon—Faith and Hope's children had been brought down from the nursery to play, and the men were in the corner, discussing something or other Joy could not discern. Grace arrived with Carew, as they were all to dress and go to the Thornhill ball together.

Joy could not suppress a groan.

"What happened to the little imp who wanted to convert my ballroom into the Tower of London or the menagerie at the Exchange?" Westwood asked.

"She was knocked in the head and was naïve enough to think she could dance. No one will dance with me willingly now." Joy sounded perilously close to self-pitying.

"You have four brothers-in-law, Freddy, and surely St. John will ask?"

"I dare say he will," she said wearily.

"You do not favour his court?" Westwood now sounded concerned. What had she done?

"I believe you exaggerate if you think he courts me. I have not seen or heard from him since Ascot." And Joy could not but help wonder if she had done something to turn him away.

The gentlemen exchanged glances even Joy did not miss. What were they about?

"Well, you can see now, so once all of the fine gentlemen comprehend you are not truly clumsy, they will be begging for a set. Come now, let us go and dress." Grace prodded Joy from the settee where she'd been most comfortably situated.

"Was that supposed to make me feel better?"

"Where is Maeve?" Grace looked around.

"She wanted to rest before tonight's celebration."

The maids were already in the chambers preparing, and to Joy, it looked like a milliner's stall had taken possession of the apartment. Gowns, gloves, stockings, ribbons, and hair fripperies were everywhere.

She walked over to her gown. It was a creation in blue crêpe, trimmed at the hem with scrolls of white satin appliqué. Tiny seed pearls winked along the empire waist, while a fall of the faintest spider gauze drifted from the short puff sleeves, giving the whole the look of dew sparkling on a fresh web. Joy, regarding it on the counterpane, had confessed herself half afraid to wear the thing for fear of destroying it. Now, as Grace whisked back the curtains to admit the afternoon light, its lustre seemed to grow still more daring. Even Joy was in awe.

Grace would go clad in a silver silk embroidered in silver threads. She turned to Joy with an arch look. "Now, let us have a conversation."

Joy perched at the dressing table while the maid attempted to coil her hair. "Conversation?" she echoed, feigning innocence.

"Do not be provoking, Joy. I refer, as I am sure you are aware, to St. John." Grace dismissed the maid to fetch warm water and closed the door herself. "Tell me truly: if he were to offer for you this very night, would you accept?"

Joy felt the familiar quickening at the Colonel's name—part flattery, part foreboding. She smoothed a fold of gauze to gain a moment's composure. "I am uncertain whether he will offer," she said at last, "so the question may be idle."

Grace waited for her to continue.

Joy traced a pattern on the polished wood. "I like him very well, Grace. He is amiable, handsome, an excellent horseman—"

"And possesses shoulders to make a uniform sigh with gratitude," Grace supplied, twinkling. "Yet something in your tone suggests doubt."

Joy breathed out. "But," she admitted, "I cannot determine if what I feel is admiration or mere relief at being considered worthy. When he speaks, my mind listens; when he rides, my eyes are pleased; and yet when I imagine a life shared—parlours, tours of duty, nursery tales—there is a space where…warmth ought to be."

Grace rested a hand on her shoulder. "You have ever feared being trapped where you could not breathe. Does the prospect of belonging to a gentleman alarm you?"

Joy considered. "Losing my freedom is, of course, worrying, but so is pretending to be what I am not."

While the maid worked pearls into Joy's curls, Grace spoke softly. "Love need not strike like thunder, Joy. Some matches kindle slowly." Much like her own.

"True," Joy murmured, "but candle flame suffices only if one does not recall what it is to stand in sunlight. With St. John I feel a gentle light, but—" She broke off, colour rising.

Grace's hands stilled. "You compare him, perhaps, to another?"

Joy busied herself with the silver brush. "I compare him to…the idea of being wholly myself, and wholly at ease, in another's company. With Colonel St. John I am conscious of my words, my step, the tilt of my spectacles. I do not wish to feel like a schoolgirl."

Grace tied the last ribbon and met her sister's gaze in the mirror. "Is there anyone in whose company you do not feel so?"

The image of Freddy flashed across her mind's eye—mud-splashed curricles, reckless laughter, the steady warmth of his hand in hers when vision faltered. Joy's pulse stumbled. "Freddy, of course," she hedged, "but he is not seeking to marry me. We have the ease of old friends."

Grace's brows arched, but before she could speak the maid returned with the requested warm water. Once Joy was readied and had stepped into the gown, the maid withdrew again. Grace fastened the seed-pearl clasp and spoke in a low tone. "If your heart does not desire the match, Joy, you must heed it—for your sake and for the gentleman's."

Joy managed a sardonic smile. "Tonight, my heart shall whisper only not to stumble or tear a flounce."

Grace bestowed a mocking smile on her as Joy had known she would.

Maeve swept in from her adjoining chamber, her cheeks vivid with happiness.

"The carriage waits—oh! Joy, you are the very breath of spring." She clasped her own hands beneath her chin, then pirouetted so the peach-rose skirts of her new gown billowed like dawn clouds. "Do I look well enough to announce a betrothal?"

"You look sufficiently celestial," Grace assured her, laughing.

The journey to Thornhill Place gleamed with lantern-light, the carriage wheels crunching gravel as stars settled into a velvet dusk. Joy rode with Carew, Grace, and Maeve; the last vibrated with excitement, a single coral rose pinned in her dark hair. Thornhill's great house blazed ahead, windows golden, music already swelling as if the walls themselves breathed a minuet.

Inside, the hum of anticipation trembled through every corridor. The Duke and Dowager Duchess greeted them in the drawing room and then led them into the dining room, where fifty of their closest acquaintances were to dine before the ball.

Dinner was a primer in elegance. The footmen seemed to move with composed precision, the fragrant steam of white soup curling into candlelit air—but an undercurrent of expectancy fluttered round them. Joy, seated between Freddy and Lord Rotham, watched as Maeve's gaze constantly strayed towards the head of the table, where His Grace toyed with a glass of wine more than he drank it.

When the covers were drawn, Thornhill rose. A hush rippled outward; even the footmen seemed to suspend their silent glide. The Duke inclined his dark head towards the Dowager Duchess, then let his eyes rest on Maeve, who sat very straight, looking nervous.

"My friends," he began, his baritone carrying with effortless command, "it is both my honour and pleasure to inform you that Lady Maeve has done me the incomparable honour of consenting to become my wife."

Delight burst forth in a clatter of cutlery and a murmur of congratulation. Joy's own heart gave a little leap—it was one thing to anticipate the announcement and another to hear it spoken, shining and irrevocable. She turned to Maeve, whose cheeks flamed coral-pink beneath the jet of raven hair, and leaned across Freddy to press her friend's gloved hand.

Freddy also murmured felicitations; Thornhill, catching his glance, offered a small bow of thanks. Around them, champagne glasses appeared.

When it was time to move on to the ballroom, Joy's breath caught at the mirrored vista. Couples were already mingling in the ballroom's reflection, flowers scented the air, and a chandelier scattered light like dewdrops. Thornhill's butler announced Colonel St. John, who stepped forward to greet her immediately after greeting the hosts. He bowed deeply. "Miss Whitford—may I say how enchanting you look?"

Joy, never one to appreciate flattery or think it true, merely curtsied. "Thank you, Colonel."

"May I claim your opening dance?"

Joy inclined her head, her pulse hammering. He had come! She felt Grace's gentle push of encouragement as St. John led her to the floor. They waited as Thornhill and Lady Maeve began the first measures together, then his hand, warm through her glove, guided with polished sureness to commence an unusual opening waltz.

St. John's hand guided her waist; they turned. Joy counted beats and let her blue skirts billow like a morning sky. Around them, couples floated; chandeliers glittered; laughter chimed. The Colonel's conversation flowed—touching upon harmless trifles—how Lady Marchmont's kittens fared, the most pleasing weather of late. Joy answered with equal lightness, but somewhere below the exchange her uncertainty coiled tightly. Yet he made no mention of his absence of late, and Joy sensed tension beneath his smooth manner.

The waltz ended. St. John, still breathing evenly, escorted her to Faith. "Miss Whitford," he began, then paused, knuckles tightening on his gloves, "may I secure your assent for supper as well?"

"If you wish it, Colonel."

Relief, unexpected and baffling, washed over her. He was not proposing. He was merely solicitous.

He bowed, evidently satisfied, and withdrew. Joy sank back, her pulse echoing like drums. Why did she feel both spared and disappointed? Because Grace's question still dangled unanswered, or because Freddy—standing across the room now, laughing with Rotham—had looked her way precisely as the Colonel released her hand?

In that moment, Joy discovered clarity: the warmth she wished to feel for a suitor was blazing visibly before her, in Freddy's shining countenance. But was it sufficient, and before it was too late? And could Freddy feel the same?

∼

FREDDY HAD SCARCELY ENTERED the doors of Thornhill's ballroom when Lady Partridge marshalled her way to him like a brigade of well-drilled soldiers. She executed a glide that placed her daughter in his path with military precision. Freddy swallowed the sigh that rose in his throat—there was no avoiding the encounter without visible rudeness—and offered his best bow.

"Mr. Cunningham, what felicity!" the lady sang.

Freddy returned the compliment, enquired after Lady Partridge's health, then turned to the eldest daughter. Letty, adorable in rose satin, bestowed a glance brimming with expectation.

Freddy's heart sank.

"Miss Partridge, may I beg the honour of the next dance?"

A flutter of lashes signified assent. "It will be my pleasure, sir."

Having satisfied propriety, Freddy excused himself to the gentlemen's knot near the card room—Rotham, Montford, and Westwood—only to discover his eyes drifting at once across the floor. The orchestra had begun the set, and St. John, resplendent in red uniform with gold trim, held Joy in the curve of his arm. Her water-blue gown lifted and fell like sunlight on a wave, and the pearls at her waist flashed each time she turned beneath the chandeliers. The pair moved in perfect time, yet Freddy's gaze fixed not on the Colonel's polished elegance but on the glow of delight animating Joy's face. Only yesterday he had sworn to guard her from that very gentleman. Now he found himself standing immobilized, admiration and apprehension wrestling at the pit of his stomach.

Rotham nudged him. "Careful, Cunningham—were jealousy charged by the inch, you would be in debt by dawn."

Freddy disguised a start with a laugh. "Jealous? Only of St. John's ability to pivot without treading upon silk."

"Come, you watch her as a hawk eyes its prey." Rotham's grin took the edge off the jibe. "Dash it, man, why settle on the Partridge chit if Joy sets your pulse dancing?"

"That," Freddy answered, "is a question better unanswered." But the sting of truth lodged in his gullet nevertheless.

The waltz ended. Joy and St. John exchanged the customary quick bow and curtsy, then he led her towards Lady Westwood. Freddy, seized by a sudden resolve, stepped forward—only to be intercepted by Lady Partridge, who delivered Letty for the promised dance. Resignation settled like damp wool. He led her onto the floor and, at the first notes of a country dance, set to the accustomed pattern.

Conversation, however, proceeded with less rhythm.

"What a charming espousal," Letty remarked, referring to the newly publicized match of Maeve and Thornhill. "I do love a courtship that ends well—and the Dowager Duchess appears, so obligingly, to have approved." She giggled behind her fan. "Although I own the bride's friend—Miss Whitford—might have employed her talents more profitably in the drawing room than in the stables."

Freddy blinked. "Miss Whitford's talents are wide, and she is one of my dearest friends, Miss Partridge."

"Oh, certainly, and yet it does seem a pity—such beauty, but she so often behaves like a boy. One would not suppose she had any interest in gowns, were tonight's not exceptional." The remark, delivered in tones of innocent observation, struck Freddy with the force of revelation. It was the most original thought he had ever heard from Letty Partridge—if indeed it had originated with her and not with her mother's constant criticisms.

He executed the chassé, and guided her through a turn, but his focus slipped back to Joy, now standing near the orchestra. Was her beauty wasted? A foolish judgement. He saw now what he had contrived not to see as surely as if a bolt of lightning had struck him: the curve of Joy's cheek, the brightness of her eyes, the grace with which she danced now that she could see again. Blue silk did not transform her; it merely unveiled what friendship's familiarity had veiled.

When the dance released him he escorted Letty to her mama, mumbled something about attending Montford, and retreated to the whist table, where he lost three tricks in swift succession. Rotham laughed while Westwood raked in a modest harvest of counters. All the while Freddy's gaze returned to where Joy now conversed with Grace beneath a spray of moon daisies.

The orchestra announced the next waltz set—his waltz with Joy. Cards abandoned, he crossed the marble like a man seeing clearly after a long mist. Joy greeted him with the warmth of long companionship and placed her gloved hand in his without hesitation.

"It is a relief," he said as they took position, "to claim you after the fencing match of conversation with Miss Partridge."

Joy's eyes sparked. "Fencing? Indeed, I cannot picture Miss Partridge performing a leap of thought."

He chuckled. "She managed a parry—she judged your beauty wasted on a lady who would rather be a boy."

Joy's laugh, bright as chimes, caught several neighbouring couples' attention. "It is not news that I prefer a stable to a drawing room," she said, unoffended.

Music gathered them into motion. Freddy, leading her through the circle, lowered his voice. "Joy—may I confess something without earning your disdain?"

"That depends entirely on the confession."

"I dread offering for her—Letty Partridge, I mean. I cannot bring myself to the sticking point." He managed a half-smile. "I have not called upon her since we returned from Ascot, and the weight of half the Season's wasted effort sits on my shoulders. To start afresh feels impossible, but to proceed feels intolerable."

Joy tilted her head, curls brushing her shoulders. "I am sure Miss Partridge would be delighted to hear your musings. You know I have always thought she would bore you."

"That is precisely why I am in the devil of a fix." He steered them through an elegant turn. "I fear I have raised expectations and cannot honourably back away."

"Perhaps you could consult with your mama? I would never see you in an unhappy marriage, Freddy!"

"Will you be happy with St. John, Joy?"

"I-I…do not know. He is all that is amiable and handsome…"

They both looked miserable as the realization of their predicament came over them.

"What do you want in a husband, Joy?"

"I asked you this before."

"But it has new meaning now."

"I want," she began, smoothing the ribbon at her waist, "a partner who will not scold when I ride too fast, who will laugh when I misquote Shakespeare, and who will not attempt to cage me with embroidery hoops. Someone," she finished with a small shrug, "whose conversation keeps pace with my curiosity."

Freddy's chest tightened. "Then you want much the same as I—a wife who will not expect perpetual doting, who can ride to hounds without swooning, who will turn the dullest day into an adventure."

She glanced up, meeting his eyes—an earnest blue behind their lenses. "We describe each other, Freddy."

He swallowed. "Dash it all, Joy, but you are soon to be betrothed to St. John!"

Joy stuttered in her step, but he corrected the rhythm before onlookers noticed. "Soon?" she echoed. "That is news to me."

His heartbeat hammered against his ribs. "Would you—could you —consider me instead?"

She looked at him with utter shock and almost missed another step.

"Why not? You are my best friend, and you ain't insipid! Life with you would never be dull, and you would not require me to 'do the pretty.'"

Colour blossomed along her cheekbones. "Freddy, I…you would truly consider me?"

"Whyever not?" He managed a crooked grin to mask the quaking inside. "Though, as mentioned, we are in the devil of a fix."

Music drew them through the final revolution. Words faltered, replaced by quiet contemplation. As the last chord faded, he escorted her to the edge of the floor, silence as deep as any chasm between them.

She faced him, still breathless. "It is my deepest wish. I will try to think on what to do. There must be a way, Freddy."

"I am at your mercy."

"Start dancing attendance on several others so she does not seem favoured. Perhaps you could give her a disgust of you, or find her another beau?"

Freddy's brow furrowed as he considered her words. How was he to do that?

"I should go and ask every eligible female to dance this night, and avoid Letty Partridge like the plague!" Joy turned away, and joined Maeve by the refreshment table. Freddy watched her go, every pulse suddenly aware of what he had somehow overlooked for years. Letty Partridge—pretty, pliant, perfectly acceptable—appeared now a painted shell beside the living sparkle of Joy's spirit. And now it might be too late. He sought out the opposite side of the room from Letty and asked the first girl he saw to dance.

CHAPTER 16

Joy awakened the morning after the Thornhill ball with a mind so riotous that even the kittens surrounding her seemed to pounce in sympathetic agitation. Frederica was curled by her head, Lord Orville decided to attack her legs, and Camilla leapt upon the counterpane to pounce on an imaginary thread. The single thought that occupied her entire being was Freddy's remark that he would choose her were circumstances different.

Had it been a casual jest, a friendly gambit in the face of Letty Partridge's desperation? Or had it been a confession he scarcely knew how to frame? The words had been light, yet the earnestness in his eyes had left her tingling from scalp to slipper tips. *Why not?* he had said. *You're my best friend and you ain't insipid!* Joy repeated the phrase now, silently, and warmth flooded her cheeks beneath the bed curtains, knowing it was the highest compliment Freddy could have bestowed.

But then—Letty. Lady Partridge's triumphant cooing at the ball had reached every dowager's ear within minutes. The Dowager claimed that she had overheard Lady Partridge announcing, "The banns are a mere formality, my dear. Mr Cunningham is as good as ours." A formal declaration might not yet have been made, but Society's infallible instinct for matchmaking had drawn its conclusions. Could Freddy extricate himself without incurring the label of jilt?

Joy's conscience pricked. Was it selfish to hope he might try? Had she entertained Freddy's half-avowal too eagerly? All night the question had whirled round her head, stealing sleep and leaving her nerves humming like harp strings. When she rose at last, she found the mirror holding an unaccustomed flush upon her cheekbones, an almost shy brightness in her own eyes. She brushed and plaited her hair with a care she seldom expended outside the stables, and descended to breakfast determined to think clearly.

She found no tranquillity down stairs. Maeve, radiant in a wrapper embroidered with rosebuds, had commandeered the morning room and turned it into a depot of matrimonial strategy. Sheets of parchment, detailing guest lists, overflowed the escritoire; samples of cream satin for altar cushions littered every chair; and Grace, quill poised, presided like an amiable clerk of the rolls.

"Joy," Maeve cried, waving her into the fray, "Thornhill has secured St. George's for the twenty-second of July! And afterwards, the wedding breakfast will be at Thornhill Place."

Joy bestowed dutiful murmurs of pleasure while helping Camilla, who had wedged herself into a basket of thread, to freedom. Amid Maeve's rapture her own disturbance seemed trivial, even selfish, but Grace's perceptive glance soon detected something amiss. When Maeve scurried off to fetch something, Grace caught Joy's sleeve.

"You look pale, yet flushed," she murmured. "Does your head trouble you?"

"My head is clear," Joy replied. "My—my thoughts less so."

Grace opened her mouth, but the footman entered with fresh chocolate and Maeve with a sheaf of more parchment, and the question was postponed. "We will speak later."

Joy retreated behind a cup of chocolate, searching her mind for clarity. Maeve's happiness was pure sunlight and Joy would not cloud it with her own uncertainties.

The midday brought a calling card in Colonel St. John's square, measured hand. He had come to invite her to ride in the Park the next day. Joy stared at the card. Before Freddy's confession the invitation would have been accepted gladly, if with moderate excitement. Now it felt like a test. If he spoke, and she was obliged to answer, what could she say? That her heart was no longer entirely her own, yet still not pledged elsewhere? It would sound like fickleness or folly. Better, perhaps. to deter him gently before any declaration must be refused.

At tea she finally broached the matter with Grace, who possessed a talent for removing the emotion and examining the situation from the reverse. Grace listened and said, "If you suspect his intentions and you cannot return them, openness is kindest, but make quite certain of your own wishes first."

"My own wishes." She admired Colonel St. John—his courtesy, his handsomeness…his seat. Yet when Freddy had asked if she could imagine them as partners, her spirit had flared to life in answer. She could imagine it—laughter over curricle races, debates about horses, quiet evenings warmed by friendship deeper than words. If only Letty Partridge did not stand like a sentinel, barring the gate.

Towards five o'clock, she resolved upon a constitutional round the square to soothe her head. Grace, noting unusual silence, offered to accompany her, but Joy pleaded solitude and a pledge not to stray beyond the square. The day held a promise of summer. She walked with measured step, spectacles glinting when she turned, Frederica accompanying her on a lead.

Halfway round the square, as she paused to watch a hound and its boy romp on the green, a tall figure detached itself from a side street and matched her pace along the pavement. Out of habit she glanced. The man wore a shabby beaver pulled low, a drab greatcoat too large in the shoulders. Heart drumming, Joy quickened. So did he. When she turned at the north-east corner, he halted as if to examine a lamp-post. There could be no mistake: he possessed the same height and stoop she had noted at Hyde Park and again outside Madame Clement's.

Panic threatened, but resentment surged stronger. She covered the short distance to her own gate, signalled the footman, and stepped inside. From the safety of the railings she looked back. The stranger had vanished.

She did not wait for fresh doubt to creep in. She sought the library, where Westwood was reported to be. There she also found Stuart, a letter in his hand. At her arrival they rose, concern etching his brow.

"You are pale. Has something occurred?" Westwood asked.

She told him in quick, quiet sentences. His jaw tightened, and he folded the note and passed it to Westwood. "The Runner has tailed St. John and thus far there is nothing amiss. He attends his duties at the Guards, rides in the Park, visits the Guards Club, and attended the ball. We have yet to discover a connection to your shadow."

Joy shivered. "What can he want?"

"To learn that, we must first capture him," Stuart suggested.

She started to protest, but he lifted a hand. "You trusted me to act—allow me to do so. Have you had any further word from St. John?"

"Only a note begging a ride in the Park tomorrow."

"Refuse tomorrow's ride. Remain here," Stuart advised.

"But is that fair? If you cannot be certain the two matters are linked."

"It is prudent all the same." Westwood spoke, his voice was gentle but brooked no refusal.

"How better to lure him from hiding? Is that not the perfect opportunity to confront him?"

The brothers exchanged glances, and Stuart answered. "Let us discuss it further, Joy. We must have surety that we can protect you."

Joy left them, feeling decidedly irritated that she had had little say in the discussion. She went upstairs and fell into a restless nap. She slept fitfully, dreams twisting between the Colonel's steady gaze and Freddy's knowing smile, between Letty's languid beauty and Lady Partridge's triumphant whisper about banns.

Faith entered, and woke her. "You are late for dinner. Tell me what is disturbing you."

Joy gave her the whole—Freddy's words, the lurking figure, the anonymous warning. Her sister listened in grave silence.

"St. John must be confronted," she said at last. "But not by you alone. Let Westwood—or Ashley—do it. And we will think of something to help Freddy out of his predicament."

Joy sighed, rubbing a temple. "Part of me wishes he would either declare or desist, so that I might be certain of one path."

Faith's smile was kind. "Certainty often hides behind the simplest truth. Ask your heart one question: if Freddy stood before you, free of Letty's net, would you hesitate?"

Joy felt the answer rise swift and sure, and embarrassment tinged her cheeks. "No," she whispered. "I would not."

"Then we must pray he unknots that net quickly," Faith said, kissing her brow. "Meanwhile, you shall make haste to dress for dinner and fret about St. John later."

Joy complied. As she dressed, she wondered why it had taken years, and a single waltz, for both she and Freddy to grasp what now felt inevitable. Perhaps friendship sometimes hid love in plain sight until circumstance turned the colours just so that you could see them.

Whether St. John's suit proved honourable or not, she knew now that her answer must be refusal. Her heart had already chosen its companion for life's road. The real question now was whether Freddy could disentangle himself from Lady Partridge's expectations—and whether he dared speak again, this time without being harassed by other concerns.

∽

FREDDY PRESENTED himself at Gresham House unusually early, the fresh dew still upon the grass and the last of the milk carts rattling away from the servants' entrance. His mother's butler, long inured to her eldest son's vagaries, greeted him. "Her ladyship is in her sitting room, Master Frederick."

Lady Gresham, impeccable in a dove-grey morning gown, occupied a Sheraton chair by the window with her embroidery already in hand. She glanced up as Freddy entered, and one elegant brow ascended a trifle higher than the other.

"My dear boy, you are abroad with the jackdaws," she said, setting

UNENDING JOY

aside a half-finished spray of forget-me-nots. "Should I summon breakfast, or is this visit merely to kiss your mother's cheek?"

"Food is always welcome," Freddy answered, bending to kiss her cheek. "I have come to beg counsel—and, alas, rescue."

Lady Gresham folded her hands in serene readiness. "The Partridge matter, then?"

"You have heard?"

"Lady Amberley sent over a note describing how Lady Partridge was crowing at the ball last night. I should have attended."

He expelled a breath. "I cannot marry Miss Partridge, Mama. Nor can I bear to see her publicly embarrassed, or myself tarred as a jilt."

"Have you spoken to her father?"

"I have not. Nor has any formal understanding been requested. Nevertheless, Society has spun its tale, and I, like a witless fly, have drifted too near the web."

His mother regarded him over the rim of her gold pince-nez. "Then you are not, in the strictest sense, honour-bound to Miss Partridge if affection does not exist, and no promise has been exchanged. However," she added with judicial gravity, "appearances, my dear Frederick, often speak louder than facts."

He rubbed a hand across his nape. "Then how to withdraw without shrieking cowardice?"

"Mitigation," Lady Gresham pronounced, as if it were a soothing draught. "I shall call upon Lady Partridge this very afternoon and ensure she understands you are still surveying your options."

Freddy felt relief uncurl, as tentative as sunrise. "You believe it will suffice? That she will not take it as a sign of favour?"

"It must suffice, and if I make it clear you have not singled out Letty in front of an audience, even she will understand your hand will not be forced." She tied a knot in her silk. "Your part is simpler: conduct yourself as a gentleman who is decidedly not on the brink of proposing. Call no more at Grosvenor Square. In the Park, divide your attentions between at least three young ladies—none of them Partridges. And, Frederick—"

He winced in anticipation. "Yes, Mama?"

"Never, ever allow yourself to be discovered alone. Antechambers, gardens, even the return corridor from supper should be construed as an invitation to ruin."

He spread his hands in submission. "I shall keep perpetual company or none at all."

"Very good." A final tug secured her thread. "We will invite a selection of close families to a house party at Gresham Park directly. I have been thinking, that with the Coronation so late, a break from Town would be quite welcome. If the Partridges receive no card; it will be understood that your interests have wandered elsewhere."

Freddy's shoulders eased. "And if my own interests settle during that house party?" He should tell his mother about Joy, but he was not yet ready to do so until he knew they were both free.

"Then, my love," Lady Gresham said, eyes softening, "I shall be delighted—provided no Partridge feathers remain to be ruffled in the process."

Released from this maternal tribunal with his spirits considerably lighter and a full repast weighing comfortably in his stomach, Freddy drove his curricle down Brook Street towards Hyde Park that afternoon. The horses were fresh and wanting to be given their heads. To distract himself from the memory of Letty's plaintive smile, he rehearsed a possible conversation with Miss Harriet Livingston—clever, musical, fond of dogs—who might profit from a turn along Rotten Row with him. Yet thoughts of Joy intruded unbidden, and each time he pictured her laughing, the prospect of other ladies paled.

He entered the Park by Grosvenor Gate just as the fashionable hour commenced. Riders filed along the tan stretch in twos and threes, the sun gilding plumes and brass harness alike. Near the Serpentine he reined in, intending to watch the flow and select a partner for a turn. Instead, his gaze at once alighted upon Colonel St. John's tall chestnut and the familiar black mare, Nightingale, dancing beside it. Joy rode light in the saddle, her face animated. St. John bent to say something; she laughed. A stab of jealousy, sharper than he expected, cut through Freddy's chest.

Anyone who cared to glance along Rotten Row that hour would

thus find Mr. Cunningham obeying his mother's edict with military precision, being occupied not with Miss Partridge but with several eligible misses.

"Miss Livingston, would you and your poodle care for a circuit about the Park?"

"Miss Mabel loves to ride!"

Miss Livingston laughed and settled her prized poodle between them. They rattled away at a decorous trot, Freddy saluting acquaintances with his whip. He took pains to linger near the fashionable hold-up by the rail, where Lady Pembury's landaulet hindered the traffic, ensuring ample opportunity for the onlookers to remark his passenger. Lady Pembury's lorgnette lingered pointedly; Mr. Beauchamp tipped his hat; even Lady Partridge, bowling along in a barouche with Letty and two younger daughters, was compelled to nod as Freddy guided the greys past. He noted Letty's faint pout, but pressed on, conversing with Miss Livingston about her latest litter until she was set down again by her brother's phaeton with thanks and a blush.

Without allowing the curricle's wheels to cool, Freddy rolled on to greet Miss Eliza Fairfax along the Serpentine where she walked with her aunt. Miss Fairfax—tall, witty, blessed with a contralto laugh—accepted the vacant seat with alacrity. Freddy repeated his circuit, this time quickening the pace as a knot of cavalry officers called to them from their cluster on the side. Miss Fairfax insisted on taking the ribbons for a furlong, so Freddy relinquished them and, for the benefit of every onlooker, praised her light hands and fearless eye. They returned flushed and laughing. Lady Partridge witnessed that exchange, too, for her barouche had not yet quitted Rotten Row.

Finally, Freddy acknowledged Miss Dinah Cavendish—a young lady famed more for fortune than conversation, though her dimples compensated. He assisted her up, arranged her shawl, and set off on a leisurely promenade so visible that his brother-in-law, Montford, cantering by on his dun, hooted a good-natured greeting. Miss Cavendish, delighted, waved to half a dozen friends. Freddy smiled, knowing the spectacle was accomplishing precisely what Lady

Gresham had prescribed: the *ton* now saw him as a gentleman distributing his attentions with amiable equity.

As he brought Miss Cavendish back to her chaperone near the gate, Freddy doffed his hat and felt, for the first time in weeks, a curious sense of ease. No one could accuse him of singling out Letty Partridge today. Hopefully the betting books at White's would, by supper, reflect new odds on whom Mr. Cunningham preferred—and perhaps leave poor Letty to more promising suitors.

He turned the greys towards the ring for one last circuit, intending only a solitary canter to restore his wits. The afternoon sun glinted on the Serpentine; carriages sparkled like the backs of beetles. Then, ahead, the distinctive chestnut of Colonel St. John again caught Freddy's eye, Nightingale's dark coat beside it. Joy's laugh drifted to him on the crisp air, as clear as a bell. Freddy tightened the reins and guided the curricle nearer—but not so near as to intrude—content, for the moment, to observe while his pulse settled into a rhythm quite unlike that calm he had boasted minutes before.

Montford's dun loomed at his elbow with a snort and a cloud of steam. "Cunningham!" Monty called, his grin broad. "You have become the veriest Don Juan—three fair companions in one afternoon!"

Freddy forced a chuckle, eyes still on Joy's graceful seat. "If diversity aids harmony, Monty, I shall compose symphonies till dusk."

"Varied melodies, indeed, though I collect Miss Partridge's mama is tuning her instrument for a different finale." Montford's gaze followed Freddy's. "Ah—but St. John conducts another performance."

Freddy's answering grin was tight. "Let us trust he keeps the tempo."

Suddenly an unseen blow snapped Joy's head back. Nightingale bucked upright, and Joy catapulted from the saddle.

Freddy's blood froze, and in an instant the day's calculated parade of partners was swept from his thoughts. He flung the ribbons to his tiger, vaulted down, and raced across to the only lady who mattered, all too conscious of how thin a veil his performance of indifference had truly been.

CHAPTER 17

*J*oy had spent the hours preceding her five o'clock engagement with Colonel St. John in a state of determined cheerfulness, outwardly calm yet inwardly reckoning every tick of the mantel clock. If she allowed herself the briefest pause, Freddy's wry grin from the Thornhill ball would rise before her mind's eye, followed quickly by the warm weight of his hand at her waist and the half-serious, half-desperate murmur. *Why not?* She had quelled that memory all morning, reminding herself that Freddy was, even now, engaged in disentangling himself from Letty Partridge's expectations. And reminding herself equally that, until such disentanglement was complete, she must do Colonel St. John the courtesy of treating his attentions in good faith. By no means would she accept him when she had hopes of Freddy. She was not certain if she could wed anyone when her heart belonged to another.

Of one thing she was quite sure: London's fever of gossip made no allowances for hesitation. Within a single day of Maeve's ball the news-sheets had blossomed with hints—some only a line, others whole paragraphs—that 'Colonel S——'s admiration of Miss J. W——d continues to be marked.' Joy, who had once calculated that plain spectacles would serve as armour, now discovered they offered no shelter at all against public conjecture. One half of her mind rehearsed the Colonel's merits—handsome, dutiful, a seat better than her own—while the other half kept slipping back to Freddy's crooked smile and the gleam in his eyes.

When the hour at last arrived, she met Colonel St. John at the entrance, vowing to bear herself with calmness. His bow was irreproachably gallant, and the chestnut he rode stood his equal in bearing. Nightingale, by contrast, seemed to catch her mistress's uncertainty and pranced sideways until the groom steadied her head.

"Miss Whitford," the Colonel said, bowing, "the Park will envy my happy advantage."

"Advantage is precarious where so many phaetons prowl," Joy returned, suppressing the urge to flee back into the house.

Joy gathered her skirts, accepted St. John's assistance, and settled into the saddle with a determined composure. He laughed, then mounted his chestnut with effortless grace.

Curzon Street, Park Lane, then Hyde Park Corner—each turning admitted new equipages: curricles rimmed in yellow, driven by modish whips, barouches lined with matrons and their nodding ostrich plumes, and mounted riders dressed in the peak of fashion.

"Behold," St. John said, guiding his steed to pace beside Joy's mare, "the Parliament of Vanity convened in open session."

"Then I trust you have prepared your speech," Joy replied. "This is a most particular and discerning crowd."

"My speech, Madam, is to prove I ride better than Lord Petersfield, and admire one lady to the exclusion of every other."

Joy felt her cheeks warm. Would she ever feel comfortable with such empty flattery? "You tempt the gallery to censure your partiality, sir."

"Let them," he murmured, yet the twinkle in his eye leavened the sentiment with humour rather than presumption. They drove on, conversing on the previous week's racing triumphs. Joy recounted Banquet's breath-stealing finish, while St. John recalled a time in

Portugal akin to a steeplechase, where a French battery provided both obstacle and incentive. His descriptions brimmed with dry wit.

"Nothing clarifies a horse's courage like a cannonball ploughing the turf three yards away. One need not even apply the spur."

Joy did not know whether to laugh or decry such morbid humour. They reached the Park's broadest sweep, where riders three abreast paraded for Society's inspection.

As Nightingale carried her at an easy canter beside Colonel St. John's disciplined chestnut, Joy's gaze strayed across the tan to a curricle painted dark green, its grey pair stepping smartly while Freddy, hat atilt, conversed first with Miss Livingston and then—barely a furlong farther on—assisted Miss Fairfax into the very seat the brunette had just vacated. A swift, unreasonable pang stirred beneath Joy's habit, only to be rebuked a moment later by sober recollection: Freddy's elaborate parade was no flirt's frolic but a calculated campaign to demonstrate impartial civility and thus free himself, gently, from Letty Partridge's expectancy. Resolutely, she schooled her features to pleasant interest as the Colonel recounted some Peninsula skirmish, yet the small tightening in her chest confessed that even strategic gallantry could kindle a spark of jealousy in a heart already leaning towards its oldest friend. Joy took pleasure in the rhythm of the greys' strides before they turned away towards the other side of the Park.

Then a curious incident occurred near Queen Caroline's Temple. They passed the same solitary gentleman loitering by the rail, wearing the shabby coat and hat brim pulled low. Joy might not otherwise have noted the connection but the Colonel's posture altered—and Joy knew it was no coincidence. Joy felt Nightingale catch the tension in the air. The mare's ears flicked, her stride shortened. She followed his gaze and caught the stranger's upward glance—an intent smirk—somehow familiar to St. John.

"An acquaintance?" Joy ventured, hoping to find a simple answer to the mystery.

"An importunate fellow," he answered too swiftly, too casually. "Pay him no heed."

But she could not dismiss the matter so lightly, for that stranger—shabby coat, narrow stance—resembled the very man who had lurked near the modiste's window a fortnight earlier, beside the rail at Ascot, and again in Berkeley Square. Her pulse quivered, the spectacles slipped faintly down her nose, and she forced a smile. The Colonel guided his chestnut past the loiterer, who lowered his head in apparent deference.

Then an object flew near them, and Nightingale took objection. "What was that?"

The Colonel's horse, used to war, steadied on. "I did not see what it was."

"Easy, girl!" she commanded, seat deep, hands firm. But something flew through the air again, and Nightingale, already afire with alarm, reared. Joy clung, balancing, aware only dimly of St. John wheeling beside her. Then another object flew straight at Joy and she was unable to dodge it whilst trying to manage Nightingale. It struck her in the head, her spectacles flew and her vision doubled. She felt the saddle slip, her right foot failed to clear the pommel, and daylight tumbled into a blur of mane and spinning sky. Her shoulder first, and then her head, bounced off the ground and sharp bursts of pain assaulted her. She fought to recover, but the world pitched and turned black.

"Miss Whitford! Joy!" St. John's voice, tight with alarm, penetrated the ringing in her ears. She felt hands steadying her shoulders, and smoothing hair back from her brow. The groom arrived, others with him, and a crowd formed, chattering.

"I am quite—quite well," she attempted, but the words slurred. She tried to focus: the Colonel's face hovered in a blur, yet only the left half seemed to be working, but the right dissolved into shifting greys.

"She struck her head," someone declared. "See, there is blood."

"It is nothing," Joy insisted—though even to her own hearing the claim rang thin. She attempted to sit up but the Park reeled, so she shut her eyes. A hush fell, punctuated by the intermingling of frightened conversation.

"We must fetch a surgeon," someone urged.

"No, carry her to a carriage," another counselled.

Joy opened her eyes again, but shapes glimmered like underwater shadows. Her right vision was absent, and while the left strove valiantly, faces still shifted like willows in the wind. Terror prickled cold along her spine. She felt St. John's arm supporting her, yet the comfort mingled with dread.

"Send for Lord Westwood," the Colonel ordered crisply.

Joy, half-dazed, saw Freddy's face—it drew her like a bell in fog. She wished fervently for him to be real, to laugh the fear away with some outrageous jest. The pain in her head throbbed, her vision wavered, and darkness fringed the edges of sight. She was lifted by what must be Freddy's arms, which she recognized by his familiar scent, and placed in a carriage.

She clung to consciousness as one clings to a slippery rein. In the swirl she caught St. John's whispered oath, an expression strained and desperate—not of gallantry but of a man cornered. Then everything dissolved into shadow again.

When awareness seeped back, Joy found herself reclining in a moving carriage. Faith's face hovered indistinctly above her, and somewhere opposite Freddy's anxious profile bent forward, blurred but blessedly familiar.

"Joy, dearest," Faith murmured, adjusting a folded cloak beneath her head, "lie still. We are nearly home."

Joy strained to see Freddy. Her left eye was blurred, but her right yielded nothing. Yet she sensed his presence, a strong tether against the fear flailing inside her.

"How—how is Nightingale?" she croaked.

"Unharmed," Freddy assured her, his voice husky. "A scratch to her hock, nothing worse."

The relief was dizzying. She tried to smile, but tears slipped out instead. Faith dabbed them away, murmuring soothing nonsense. Freddy's hand found hers, warm and sure, and she held fast, the way a drowning sailor might seize rope.

"Someone was lodging stones. There was the man," Joy whispered. Vague questions and remembrances crowded her mind, but pain smothered thought.

"Hush now. Do not trouble yourself," Faith soothed.

If St. John's attentions had once seemed flattering, they now felt weighted with enigmas. In her swimming vision she sought a steady shape, and found only the steadfast pressure of Freddy's fingers twined with hers—only familiar strength. She held to it, desperate, as the carriage rumbled towards Berkley Square. She surrendered again to darkness, convinced of only one certainty: she was now blind.

◈

Freddy paced anxiously in Westwood's drawing room while Dr. Harvey examined Joy in her chambers. The sisters were all present with Joy upstairs, while Freddy, Rotham, Carew, Montford, and Stuart waited in the drawing room. All the sisters had been sent for and had come as quickly as possible with their husbands.

When at last Dr. Harvey emerged with careful composure to pronounce that Miss Whitford had sustained no fracture of skull or limb, that a concussion must be allowed its course, and that, most troublesome to the patient, an abrupt disturbance of her vision had asserted itself. She was now resting quietly, and should do so for a least a week. He took his leave, promising to call again in the morning.

Joy's sisters soon followed.

"Joy is resting with cats strewn all about her," Lady Westwood said, dropping into a chair between Lady Rotham and Mrs. Stuart. "Grace is sitting with her for now."

Freddy, who had been pacing up and down by the window, turned. "How is the pain?"

"Eased, thank Heaven. She claims it is chiefly annoyance now—at being unseated before half of London Society."

Joy would say something like that.

Stuart, standing behind his wife, shook his head. "That is what puzzles me. Joy has as good a seat as anyone I know. Something had to have happened."

Freddy echoed the sentiment.

Before conjecture could ferment, the door opened and Westwood strode in and Colonel St. John followed close behind. Freddy felt his nerves tighten like a jockey's reins before the start.

"We have tramped the length of where they were riding and the woods thereabout," Westwood announced, "but found no spent shot, no wadding, no powder scorch on branch or rail. It appears no firearm was discharged."

"Joy said someone was lodging stones," Freddy said.

"Something did fly by us and agitate her mount," St. John concurred.

"A catapult? Perhaps young boys up to mischief?" Rotham questioned the unlikely behaviour with a deep frown.

No one said anything, since there would be little chance of tracking anyone launching stones. Someone was causing mischief, then. But was it related to the man tracking Joy?

Lady Westwood thanked St. John for his care. He bowed, murmuring hopes for Miss Whitford's speedy recovery, and excused himself upon business at Horse Guards. Freddy watched St. John depart yet thought again of the man Joy had mentioned.

The ladies went back upstairs to see how the patient went on.

When the door closed, Westwood exhaled. "St. John was genuinely distressed, say what you will."

"I do not doubt his distress," Freddy replied, unable to smother the edge in his tone. "I question its cause."

Westwood crossed to the window. "If he serves Joy's happiness, we cannot censure him for this misfortune."

"If we can rule him out as the cause of it," Rotham added. "Would that today's mishap is an awful coincidence, and that is all there is to be said about it."

"It seems something has occurred since Ascot for which someone is keen to have their pound of St. John's flesh. He is unlikely to confess it or he would have done so today. If it has reached the point where they are willing to harm Joy over the matter, then he bears watching and Joy protecting," Stuart said.

"They might not have been aiming for Joy, but she was nevertheless caught in the crossfire."

"If he is not in debt, then what could this be about?" Rotham asked.

"I expect a report from the Runners momentarily. They would not approach if St. John were here."

No sooner had Stuart uttered the prediction than the butler reappeared, as grave as a funeral, and announced Mr. Hamble of Bow Street. The Runner entered—a spare, sandy-haired, florid-complexioned man in plain coat and serviceable boots—carrying his hat respectfully beneath one arm and a folded sheet in the other.

"Beg pardon, my lords, gentlemen." He inclined his head before turning to Stuart. "We have followed the person you described—the tall fellow in the shabby greatcoat—from Hyde Park to the Rookery at St. Giles. I'm afraid we lost him in the maze of courts and alleyways, nigh half an hour ago."

Stuart motioned Hamble to continue. "Give particulars, please."

"Aye, sir." Hamble laid out his report: the suspect had loitered in the Park until the accident, then trudged east, hugging the mews on Oxford Street. Two men had followed. The quarry cut through a print shop—"Bold as brass, sir, straight through the rear door,"—and melted into Charing Cross. One Runner had circled, another had kept at heel. They had shadowed him as far as Dyott Street, where he slipped into the labyrinth behind the Rookery. "No constable dares venture far in there after dark without a troop," Hamble added dryly. "We posted men at the visible exits, but the cove must know bolt-holes the size of mouse-runs. 'E vanished."

Freddy clenched a fist.

"Did you see any badge of trade? Did they approach gaming dens or pawnshops?" Stuart asked.

"Not yet, sir. So far, we only tracked him to a nearby tavern called the Nag's Head—kept to a corner table, drank small ale, paid from a purse with ready coin." Hamble hesitated. "Beggin' your pardon, but when he settled the score he used a Portuguese coin. A ducat, I think."

"A soldier's pay from their time on the Peninsula?" Stuart's eyes narrowed. "Did he meet any companion?"

"No, sir—sat alone for twenty minutes, watching the door," Hamble answered. "I questioned the tapster. Man gave the name of Silva."

"Our bookmaker?" Carew queried of Freddy.

"Could be."

Hamble continued. "'Tis nay much to go on, but my men will continue to hunt."

Freddy paced to the window and stared at the flare of a lamplighter beyond the pane. "If Silva is pressing St. John for payment he cannot lay hands on, he must have hoped to speed matters by frightening Joy. That dowry would clear every note twice over."

Westwood drew a sharp breath. "You think he meant to injure her deliberately?"

"Not necessarily," Freddy answered, turning, "but a stone hurled to make the mare shy, a message to St. John was risk enough." His voice roughened. "Joy paid the price for another man's obligations."

Westwood drummed fingers on the mantel. "We must bring St. John face to face with this and demand explanation."

"Carefully," Stuart warned. "Rush a desperate debtor and he may flee—or strike first."

Hamble cleared his throat. "We can set four men at the Rookery lanes, but t'would be better to take him where streets are broader and the watch within whistle."

"Do what you must," Stuart ordered. "I fear we will not get answers without questioning him."

"Aye, sir." The Runner made a bow and left.

"Perhaps Silva serves as go-between for gentlemen too wary to approach the public hells. There may be someone else he does the dirty work for," Rotham prophesied.

Freddy's gaze drifted to the half-open door at the far end of the hall—the staircase lay beyond, up which Joy slept. A wave of fierce protectiveness surged within him. "Regardless of St. John's motives, Joy shall not see him again."

If anyone was surprised by Freddy's cold claim, no one mentioned it.

Carew offered a practical amendment. "We might persuade Maeve to insist that Joy accompany her to Thornhill Place—fresh air and a duke's security in the country—until this spectre is laid."

Westwood approved. "An admirable retreat—provided the journey is slow."

"My mother intends to hold a small gathering of close acquaintances at Gresham Park. I had intended to invite you all there. It might be more restful for Joy." Freddy did not mention he'd like very much for Joy to visit his home as his intended.

"Very likely. We will put the question to Joy when she feels more the thing," Westwood agreed, then clapped Freddy's shoulder. "Ashley and I will confront the Colonel after breakfast. If he means honourably, he will speak plainly with explanation. If not—" He let the threat hang. "—we shall know how to protect Joy."

Freddy inclined his head, his voice rough when he spoke. "Thank you, Dom."

Rotham and Montford gathered their wives and took their leave. Stuart lingered only long enough to scribble fresh instructions on thin paper before departing into the night, a shadow among shadows, every inch the army's old intelligence chief.

Freddy wanted to ask to see Joy if only to put his mind at ease. A week of rest, Hartley had said. Freddy vowed Joy would not know a moment's distress—whatever cost it laid upon his own conscience. Tomorrow, St. John would have to answer for his part in this. The debt, the danger, and the truth would be dragged into the daylight.

He reached the stairs as Grace descended.

"She sleeps," Grace whispered. "Faith and Patience keep vigil."

Freddy exhaled, relief sharp. "Thank you. I shall call in the morning."

Grace paused two steps above him, candlelight gilding her calm features. "She asked, before the laudanum took hold, whether you were still below. I told her you would remain until all was safe."

A lump rose in his throat, but he swallowed it.

She placed a knowing hand on his arm. "I will reassure her."

He nodded, knowing he should leave, though it was the last thing he wished to do. But as nothing was yet settled, he did not have the right. "Good night, then."

"Good night, Freddy."

CHAPTER 18

~

*J*oy's first clear memory after the tumble that had tilted her orderly world into murky half-shadow, was the scent of lavender and the faint purr of a feline kneading its paws upon her coverlet. She could not, at first, decide whether it was night or day. The room lay muffled in drab greys, its familiar contours melted, but someone—a sister—sat in a chair near the shuttered window, murmuring soft assurances that Dr. Harvey would come presently with laudanum and that no one, most particularly Joy, was to stir so much as a finger.

When next consciousness claimed her, the physician himself stood by the bed, spectacles glinting as he lifted the bandage at her brow. "A concussion, yes. Bruising of the optic nerve, temporary, I hope. The left eye retains parts of its faculty. The right—well, we must bid it rest until the swelling abates. No strong light, no reading, only rest."

"For how long?" she murmured, bristling at his brusque sentences.

"Miss Whitford, you must cultivate patience."

Joy could have sworn Patience snorted at that instruction. The curtains remained half-drawn thereafter and Joy submitted to her unaccustomed blindness with as much grace as could be summoned from aching limbs and a headache that pulsed like a drum.

Her sisters divided the first night's vigil. Grace brought barley water and bathed her neck with cool cloths. Faith read in a voice so gentle it lulled her to sleep. Hope silently re-plaited Joy's unruly curls, and Patience smuggled in an orange and laughed when Camilla swatted at the peel. Only Maeve could not sit long, but she darted in and promised country air at Thornhill Place once Joy might travel.

Yet it was Freddy who lifted her spirits most. He arrived in the morning with uncharacteristic punctuality, armed with Joy's favourite novels—including *The Mysteries of Udolpho*—Byron's poems, and a stack of daily papers. Lord Orville invariably abandoned the bedpost to sprawl across Freddy's lap as if claiming precedence.

"You must tell me the instant this tires you or vexes your head," he cautioned, opening *The Morning Chronicle.* Notably, he did not read to her what was said about her incident, though she knew it had been remarked upon.

"Your voice and presence soothe me far more than laudanum," Joy answered, settling deeper into her cushions. She dozed, lulled by the steady cadence of his voice, and woke to find him recounting plans for the small estate his father had bequeathed him—Heartsfield Grange, a comfortable greystone house in Kent which was bordered by orchards.

"It is no grand seat," he told her, "but the stables are sound, the south meadow ideal for a modest course, and the dovecote could be coaxed into a library if one bribed the birds elsewhere."

"A library in a dovecote?" Joy laughed softly at the absurdity. "You tempt me with visions of reading beneath fluttering wings."

"And racing Nightingale and Banbury along the hawthorn hedge," he added, the warmth in his tone painting scenes she could almost see.

But though he described orchards in blossom and a river ready for summer picnics, there were no more mentions of permanence. Each time the future hovered close, he redirected the conversation—asking whether her pillows were comfortable, whether the doctor had truly forbidden her from rising from the bed, whether Camilla's friskiness disturbed her head. Joy noticed the evasions and felt a tremor of impatience. When her sight cleared and her strength returned, the moment must come when neither of them could pretend the future was a neutral country waiting to be discovered. Joy dared not ask the one question that kept burning in her mind. Would he still want her if she was permanently blind? And then, she countered, could she thrust herself onto someone, knowing she was blind?

"Has anything more occurred with Miss Partridge?" she asked instead.

"Letty's happiness is no longer my affair," he added quietly, lowering the paper. "I have made clear that matter to her mama. All else seems trifling when—" His words fell away, but the meaning hovered, warming the air.

Joy, cheeks tingling, whispered, "I do not wish you to feel beholden to me, Freddy."

"I shall not be," he answered. "Nothing matters now but your recovery."

"What if I do not recover this time, Freddy?"

He leaned forward and took her hand. "You are perfect however you are, Joy."

She could not quite see him, only a pale shape at the bedside, yet she felt the conviction pulse between them like sunlight pressing the curtains. Her heart took courage.

On the fourth morning, when Dr. Harvey pronounced the swelling somewhat diminished, and allowed that Joy might be able to sit in a chair for a while, provided it caused her no dizziness or pain.

Faith then informed her that St. John had called and was below. "He has called and enquired after you every morning," Faith told her. "Do you wish to see him?"

Did she? Joy was not certain. But the unease she now felt must be for naught. If they had found anything against him, surely he would not be allowed into Westwood House.

"Perhaps it would ease his anxieties to see you are well," Faith suggested.

"A few minutes perhaps."

"I will be right over there and ensure the visit is short," Faith assured her, then helped her to sit up with pillows supporting her. She was now able to discern shapes and some colours with her left eye if she did not blink too rapidly.

St. John entered and advanced to the bed and bowed—Joy thought she detected stiffness in the gesture. Polite enquiries followed: her pain, her appetite, the doctor's predictions. She answered and thanked him for the violets he had sent, but she sensed that his thoughts darted elsewhere.

At length, he cleared his throat. "Miss Whitford, I have come—" He halted, his breathing shallow. Then, with evident effort: "I have come to renew my addresses, which must have been too faintly conveyed in our previous encounters. The accident has made me see that time is not to be taken for granted. Your fortitude, your good humour…these qualities command my esteem." He paused again, fingers tightening on his hat. "I wish to lay before you, therefore, the earnest hope that you will—when recovered—do me the honour of becoming my wife."

Joy's pulse leapt, yet not with the astonishment she had once imagined. Instead she felt a gentle sadness. The words, though honourable, lacked the living warmth she had grown to cherish in Freddy's presence. Moreover, courtesy demanded truth. She would not relinquish her freedom at the price of mere esteem.

"Colonel," she said softly, "your regard does me more honour than I can express but I cannot, in fairness, accept it."

St. John's shoulders sagged, whether with relief or disappointment, she could not tell. "I confess," he murmured, "I feared as much. Circumstances—" he broke off, straightened, then seemed to want to persist. "I spoke too soon. I beg you will forget this intrusion until you are stronger."

"There is no need for you to feel obligation for what happened, but my sentiment shall not change." Joy managed a small, earnest smile. "I do thank you for your offer."

He bowed again, still distracted, and withdrew without further protest. When the door closed, Joy pressed trembling fingertips to her eyelids—and felt as though she'd made a close escape.

He certainly had not displayed the ardour to be expected of a man making an offer of marriage, although to be fair, she could hardly see any nuances of expression.

Joy heard the house stir at his departure. Faith came closer, her tread betraying eagerness for news. "I could not hear all."

Joy relayed the essentials, and Faith's sigh expressed both relief and sisterly concern. "I feared he would press you," Faith said, smoothing the coverlet. "And that you might feel forced into agreement."

"Not in the least—but I do feel the need to get out of this bed."

Faith sighed heavily, but did not object when Joy's feet slipped over the side of the bed to stand up.

～

FREDDY MET ST. John on the landing outside Joy's chamber. The officer drew up short, offered a stiff bow, then descended without a word. Freddy watched the straight back disappear around the curve of the staircase and felt a tightness unknot inside his chest. At least St. John had not lingered to play the devoted suitor. One ordeal at a time was quite enough for Joy.

He tapped once on her door and slipped inside. The room lay mellow with filtered sunshine, the curtains half-drawn to spare her sore eyes. Dr. Harvey's bandage had been exchanged for a neat strip of linen at her temple, beneath which the right eye remained covered. Joy reclined against the chair while Faith sorted vials on the escritoire.

"Ah, good morning, Freddy. Dr. Harvey has permitted Joy to get out of bed and sit in a chair for brief periods. Do not let her talk you into more."

Joy's irritated smile followed her sister out. "You are late, Mr. Cunningham," she chided when the door clicked shut. "My daily novel arrives with you, and I have been quite starved for entertainment. Did something dire detain you?"

"No, nothing dire," Freddy said, perching on the chair beside her bed. "My mother demanded a full accounting. She had it on excellent authority that someone attempted to shoot you out of the saddle."

Joy made a face. "You reassured her that I am well?" She tapped her bandage. "Save for this refractory eye."

He sobered. "Harvey still hopes the sight may creep back once the swelling fades."

"So he says." Her left eye studied him. "What did Lady Gresham decide? I do not wish her to postpone her house party on my account."

"That was her first suggestion," Freddy admitted. "She asked whether we ought to delay the gathering at Gresham Park. I told her I would seek your preference." He hesitated. "The country air might do more good than darkened rooms in Town."

Joy's brows lifted. "I will not be the cause of overturning half a dozen invitations. Besides, Westwood speaks of Taywards in Surrey—close enough for others to visit."

"My mother proposed Heartsfield Grange as a compromise," Freddy said slowly. "It is in Kent—nearer than Derbyshire—and we could repair there in two short stages." He managed a crooked grin. "And you could advise me on the dovecote-to-library scheme."

Her lashes cast shadows on the bruised cheekbone.

"Unless you prefer pigeons to books."

"A difficult choice," she murmured, then grew thoughtful. "Kent would spare Westwood any objections. You are sure Lady Gresham would not object to an invalid among her guests?"

"Mother's precise words were: 'If Miss Whitford consents, I shall consider her presence a blessing.'"

Joy laughed—just a breathy catch of sound, but bright. "I would like to see Heartsfield above all things. Now to convince Dr. Harvey and Westwood."

He reached to cover her hand where it lay atop the coverlet. She did not draw away. "I will speak to Westwood this afternoon. If he agrees, we could travel down early next week—slow stages, plenty of cushions." He paused before lowering his voice. "Joy, you will not be pushed if your strength fails. One word, and the plan changes."

Her fingers curled around his in silent answer. For a moment neither spoke. The ticking bracket clock served as a heartbeat for them both.

Presently she said, softer still, "St. John was here five minutes ago. He asked for my hand."

Freddy schooled his features. "And how did you answer?"

"I declined his offer." She turned her head towards the muted window. "I still wish I knew if he even liked me or only my dowry."

Freddy's pulse drummed. "Must one be separate from the other?"

She smiled at that, releasing his hand.

"Shall I read *Evalina* or *Cecilia* today?"

"*Cecilia* I think," she decided, closing her good eye.

Freddy opened the book, his voice steady, his heart anything but. If fortune favoured him, Kent would offer more than orchards and fresh air.

Once Joy was resting, Patience relieved him, and Freddy slipped downstairs. Westwood saw him walk past and hailed him into his study.

Mr. Hamble, the Bow Street Runner had called.

Freddy had not hoped for much from Mr. Hamble after his last report, but he and two additional Bow Street men had ventured back into the fetid lanes of St. Giles. Already, four days had slipped past when the butler announced the Runner once more, and Westwood had sent for all of them to attend. Hamble, cap in hand, began without preface.

"We have the fellow, sir—name of Silva. Took him at the Cock and Bull in High Holborn, late last night."

Freddy motioned him to a chair. "Has he confessed to doings with St. John?"

"Aye. As soon as he realized he was trapped, his courage collapsed. His story's as queer as any Minerva Press plot." Hamble produced a crumpled paper. "Written deposition, witnessed by me and Sergeant Leigh."

Westwood scanned the first lines, brows lifting.

"He admits blackmail?"

"Aye. In so many words. He says Colonel Edward St. John owes him support for 'a wife and two children' in Portugal. Silva's sister, Maria, was landlady to British officers during the war. He claims St. John married her, and she bore a son and a daughter two years later. St. John has not been heard of in two years. The wife is dying, and St. John has not responded to pleas for help. Silva came to London to remind him of his duty—"

"—and found the Colonel dangling after a possible heiress," Westwood finished, his knuckles whitening on the paper.

Hamble nodded. "Silva began threatening St. John with exposure, and thought to milk him for enough to take care of his family. He says he hurled stones to alarm St. John's chestnut—meant only to force the Colonel's hand. Never aimed for her head, he says."

Westwood's jaw tightened. "Intent and outcome know little difference, Hamble."

"'Twas also my thinking, my lord. He seems shaken by the miss's injury—that part, I judge, was not contrived."

"Where is Silva now?"

"Clerkenwell. He will stand before the magistrate on Friday."

Freddy paced back and forth. "And the Colonel?"

"We 'ave kept watch on his lodgings. Word is he took leave from the Guards, and rides out for Portsmouth tomorrow—passage booked on a packet bound for Lisbon."

Stuart read the missive, then rapped the parchment on the desk. "Blackmail and a secret family—yet none of it meets open court unless we haul it there. What is our object?"

Westwood's face hardened. "Joy's future. If the fact that he was married becomes public, she is ruined. If they remain discreet and the Colonel departs, she is spared scandal."

"St. John must face us first," Freddy said. "And Joy must hear nothing of this. At least until her health is equal to it."

Carew frowned. "We summon him now. He has much to answer for."

Stuart reached for quill and ink. "I shall draft the letter."

Colonel St. John presented himself at Westwood House that same evening. Freddy stood by the mantel; Stuart beside the desk; Westwood, Rotham, and Carew formed a silent tribunal in chairs. The Colonel entered with outward composure yet an undeniable pallor.

"You asked for me urgently, gentlemen."

Westwood inclined his head and spoke first. "We have detained a man named Silva."

St. John's gloved hands tightened around his riding whip. "On what charge?"

"Assault," Stuart answered, holding out the deposition. "He has confessed to throwing the object that hit Miss Whitford—"

"Indeed!"

"—an act intended to warn you and secure funds for an unacknowledged family in Portugal. Your family."

The Colonel swallowed, colour draining from his face. "Silva talks for his liberty."

Freddy stepped forward. "Do you deny your flesh and blood?"

Silence boomed. At last St. John exhaled, his shoulders sagging. "I do not deny it. Maria—Miss Silva—was dear to me. I have sent what I could. My debts swallowed the rent of the estate. The inheritance I expected will never materialize thanks to poor investments." He met Westwood's eyes. "Your Miss Whitford stood to bring fortune enough to settle everything—my children, my estate. I am quite fond of her." His voice cracked.

"When you were already married. Were you waiting for your wife to die?" St. John opened his mouth to deny it, but Westwood stayed him with a hand. "You risked Joy's life to salvage yours."

"No!" St. John's denial rang with desperation. "I have never sanctioned violence, nor guessed she would come to harm. When I saw her fall I—" He faltered. "—I knew I must resolve the situation at once."

Westwood's lips thinned. "You still sought a betrothal only this morning."

"And are now set to remove to Portugal," Freddy scoffed.

Rotham folded his arms, granite-eyed. "Distance is precisely what you will keep. You will sail to Lisbon, and you will formalize a settlement upon Mrs. St. John, something signed before you leave, or you will never be able to show your face in England again."

"I shall leave England at first light. I wish Miss Whitford every happiness. Pray tell her—tell her I regret—"

Freddy's glare stilled him. "We shall tell her whatever spares her distress."

Stuart and Rotham oversaw St. John's writ of promise to care for his family, then St. John bowed, turned on his heel and was gone, his boots echoing down the marble corridor.

When the door's last echo died, Freddy's relief mingled with anger, pity with triumph.

Westwood clapped his shoulder. "Joy shall never learn the darker details."

Freddy nodded grimly. "Nor should Society. Let the rumours fade."

Carew, ever pragmatic, produced a brandy. "To Joy's speedy recovery—and to more honest suitors."

They drank to her health, but Freddy did not mention his intentions towards Joy. Even as the spirits warmed Freddy's throat, a new anxiety unfurled. He was now, unequivocally, free to declare himself. Would Joy accept?

CHAPTER 19

❦

*E*ach subsequent day brought minute progress: diminishing aches and bruises, more clarity of vision in her left eye. Dr. Harvey permitted a walk in the garden after one week—provided Joy wore a broad-brimmed straw hat and kept her gaze shaded. Freddy insisted on lending his arm, and while Lord Orville's grey was harder to follow than Camilla and Frederica's orange, Joy appreciated being able to watch them explore the garden. Every colour was brighter, every birdsong sweeter, as though convalescence had stripped away the commonplace veil.

The herbaceous border wafted thyme and sage, whilst lilacs drooped with their own weighty perfume. Lord Orville—now a lanky grey adolescent—sprang from behind a yew, pounced on his orange sister Camilla, and sent both of them tumbling through the foxgloves. Joy's laugh startled a goldfinch from the wisteria.

"So," she said, adjusting the tilt of her spectacles, "tell me when we quit Town for Kent. I have lost patience with waiting."

Freddy guided her around a sun-warmed stone urn. "We can leave as early as tomorrow, should you feel equal to the excursion."

"I feel equal to a dull carriage ride, certainly." Still, a flicker of disquiet crossed her mind. Heart-stirring rides, curricle races, the thunder of hooves—would those pleasures ever be known to her again? And would Freddy still wish to share them? She pushed the thought aside. "Who forms the party?"

"Westwood and Faith, naturally; Rotham and Hope; Stuart and Patience; and Montford and Vivienne."

"No Letty Partridge?" Joy's tone struck a teasing chord.

"No." Freddy stopped beside a double row of irises—deep purple against silver foliage. "Letty and her mother removed to Bath yesterday."

Joy could not prevent a small sigh of relief. "And Miss Finch?"

"I have no notion of her doings. You are spared tittering and taffeta for a fortnight at least." His hand tightened on her fingers. "My mother's invitations make no mention of unattached young ladies—at least, none foisted upon me. Heartsfield Grange scarcely holds more than fifteen beds. She claims the house is 'delightfully compact.' The guest list is trimmed to family."

Joy walked a few paces in silence, letting pebbles crunch underfoot. Butterflies flickered through shafts of light, landing on catmint blossoms. A small knot of dread coiled in her stomach.

"Freddy," she began, affecting a lightness she did not feel, "you are spending every daylight minute with me. When will you search out your bride?

His voice dropped to a soft scold. "We decided at Thornhill's ball—"

"We decided in a fit of pique," she interrupted. The brim cast patterns across his coat sleeve, and she traced them with her thumb and marvelled that she could see enough to do so. "You were irritated by Letty. You should not feel beholden to me now that matters have… altered."

His breath left him in a huff. "Altered? If you mean your vision, that is Harvey's battle, not mine. I dashed well do intend to keep my word."

"Words spoken when one believed the ground level may prove

burdensome once the ground tilts," she persisted. "You do not wish to be saddled with an invalid wife, Freddy. I will persuade Westwood to leave me in peace. You may return to London and court whomever you wish."

"Do not be foolish, Joy! Did we not decide we would rub along quite well together?" He halted so abruptly that Camilla mewled. Freddy scooped up the kitten with one arm and faced her squarely. "If I must repeat myself in Latin, I will, though I am no scholar. Vision or no vision, you are the only woman with whom I have ever wished to share hedgerow or hearth." He broke off, colour rising under his fair skin. "I have looked my fill, as you once advised. There is no other candidate. Do you take me for the sort of fellow who jilts because of inconvenience?"

His vehemence shook her more than she allowed to show. "People have done so for less."

He set Camilla gently atop a stone plinth, where the kitten commenced licking her paws. "Do not be insulting, Joy. It is the perfect solution for us both."

Joy's parasol drooped until its edge brushed grass. "Freddy, what if my sight does not return? Dr. Harvey gives no guarantee."

"Then we shall teach Camilla to find your misplaced gloves and Lord Orville to fetch your spectacles." He managed a crooked smile. "I will read your favourite stories to you—and argue over the endings as always. We will ride with a little more circumspection. The world need not be seen perfectly to be lived perfectly."

Her heart gave one great thump—that was rather poetic for Freddy. "You make it sound simple."

"It is simple." He offered his arm again.

She slipped her hand through the crook of his elbow, feeling the steady warmth beneath superfine cloth. "We must wait before telling anyone, Freddy. Wait at least until we know how much sight can be salvaged."

He inclined his head. "If that is your wish, I will grant it as long as I may."

"And you must continue looking," she added, attempting sternness. "For the sake of your mother's expectations."

"I have looked," he repeated, softer now, "and found an answer." Then, rallying, he adopted a teasing tone. "Unless you are pining for that blackguard, St. John?"

"Now who is daft?" She elbowed him lightly, then wobbled.

They reached the sundial, set in a small clearing ringed by peonies. Joy lifted her face, searching through shapes blurred beyond a few yards. "What is it you are not telling me?" she asked.

"There is news," he said, thumb making small soothing circles on the back of her hand, "of Colonel St. John."

Her muscles tightened, and he covered her fingers at once. "Nothing to distress you. He departs England at once, bound for duties abroad—he will not renew his addresses."

She exhaled, relief and something like sorrow mingling. "Is he well?"

"He has obligations." Freddy chose his words with care. "Obligations he must meet in Portugal."

Joy let that sink in. The small part of her that had felt flattered by the Colonel's attention, dulled.

The silence that followed was curiously gentle, as if the garden itself applauded a chapter ended. Somewhere behind the peonies a bird sang, and the scent of warm earth drifted upward. Joy drew a steadying breath, surprised that the relief outweighed the disappointment.

"We shall speak of him no more," she said at last, shaking off the lingering ache like dew from a rose leaf. "Tell me of Heartsfield, Freddy. Your letters always mention an orchard—what grows there besides apples?"

His face lit up, and he seemed pleased to change the subject. "There are plums and cherries as well, and a stubborn stream that refuses respectable boundaries and floods the kitchen garden whenever it rains heavily."

"I think I shall enjoy it very much." She imagined the place: low eaves and mossy tiles, a dovecote waiting to be emptied of feathers and filled with books. A pulse of excitement fluttered, eager for new places to investigate.

They moved on, following a path that looped beneath an arch of early flowering clematis. Freddy slowed her pace when the gravel thickened, guiding her foot past a jutting stone before she could stumble. The courtesy warmed her in spite of feeling incapable.

"There is one inconvenience you have not considered," she said, tilting her head. "You seek a wife that can ride to hounds."

"However I may ride with you shall suffice. We will forge a path forward that will make us both happy."

That declaration sent a pleasant thrill through her, though she answered only with a soft, "Your optimism almost convinces me."

They circled towards a half-shaded stone bench. Joy lowered herself gratefully. Even a short circuit of the walk left her dizzy. Freddy settled beside her, remarking that the brim of her bonnet cast shadows across her face.

How easy he made it all seem, Joy reflected. Even the worry lodged in her breast softened under the humour. Still, a question pressed itself upon her notice. "And after Kent?" she asked. "What will you do if—if I remain mostly or completely blind?"

Freddy's gaze was steady. "I shall marry you, if you will have me."

He forestalled interruption.

"Do not raise objections again, Joy. I have charted every possible difficulty and reached the same conclusion each time. Life with you is preferable to life without you. There is no argument strong enough to shake that."

As she looked down her vision blurred, not from injury but from emotion. A bright spot wavered in her left eye—sunlight refracted by unshed tears. She blinked them back, unwilling to lose even that little clarity.

Freddy stood and held out his hand. "Come. I have kept you out much longer than would please Dr. Harvey."

∽

FREDDY ARRIVED at Heartsfield Grange a few hours before the caravan of barouches and luggage carts. He had felt like a boy waiting for a new pony. He'd inspected every inch of the house, but would wait for Joy's arrival to inspect the grounds together, for he knew she would enjoy it. His mother had already sent an army of servants to prepare everything. The grass was shorn, the house was freshly aired and polished, and smelled of beeswax and fresh pies. He'd warned the household to remove any obvious obstacles that Joy might miss and stumble upon.

By the time the party rolled up the drive, he was fair to bursting with excitement. Who would have ever thought Freddy would be thankful at the prospect of becoming settled?

Lord and Lady Gresham arrived first, his father having left his beloved country seat to join them.

"Well, Frederick, your mother tells me you have found your match. I am quite pleased."

"Joy does not wish to announce anything yet." Seeing his father's concerned face, Freddy hastened to add, "owing to her recent injury, you understand."

"We may not even speak of it amongst family?"

"I will ask her."

"And how do you find your new home?" his mother asked, by way of intervention.

"It will do very well," he pronounced, which met with pleased smiles.

The carriages began to arrive one after the other.

From the first, Joy emerged on Westwood's arm, straw bonnet shadowing her fragile vision but cheeks flushed with the prospect of open country about her. Frederica jumped down from the coach, followed by Camilla and Lord Orville, the latter two quickly scampering off to explore.

"Welcome to Heartsfield Grange," Freddy said, executing a bow.

Vivienne clasped her hands and spun around. "It is just how I remembered it. Do you remember the swing over the river, Freddy?"

"It is still there, Viv," he assured her.

Within the hour they were shown to their chambers: Westwood and Faith in the east wing overlooking the river, Stuart and Patience over the library, Montford and Vivienne in her old chambers nearest the orchard, and Rotham and Hope with a view over the valley.

Joy, at Lady Gresham's insistence, occupied a south-facing chamber with French doors onto a balcony. Freddy lodged opposite, separated by a passage, 'for propriety's sake,' according to his mother, and "for strategy," according to Westwood, who winked.

When everyone came down for tea on the large terrace, there were steaming scones with fresh cream, honey, and fresh cherry preserves. Joy tilted her head to listen as guinea fowl chattered outside the open casement.

"Music," she said dreamily. "Though I grant their rhythm is irregular."

"Guinea fowl make no noise I would ever call music," Patience said. "They screech and cackle."

Stuart remarked, "Any bird capable of sounding the alarm at French trespassers deserves indulgence."

"Surely we need not worry over the French any longer?" Hope asked.

"We are safe, my dear," Rotham reassured her with a scathing look at Stuart.

Freddy, half-amused, half-entranced by Joy's quiet absorption, laid out the day's design. "I thought to walk about the orchard, if you feel up to mild exertion?"

"Any movement is welcome after sitting idle in the carriage for so long. I do not need to be coddled."

Freddy guided Joy down the path that led from the south lawn into the old orchard, every step accompanied by the faint hiss of meadow grass brushing their boots. Ahead, low boughs arched in profusion: pear and plum and apple, some already set with pale marbled fruit, others still sheathed only in leaves. The air, scented by a thousand petals fallen and crushed beneath last night's shower, was half-honey, half-cider—intoxicating in the lazy heat of late afternoon. Fat bees dawdled from blossom to blossom, their humming a contented buzz beneath the shriller tunes of chaffinches overhead.

Freddy guided her where the ground dipped. Where it rose again, the grass grew sparse and sun browned, exposing the roots like gnarled fingers clutching earth. To the west, glimpsed here and there through branches, the Medway flashed silvery blue as it uncurled towards the estuary. Freddy had ridden that crooked mile of water since he first sat astride a pony—yet, walking now with Joy on his arm, he felt as though he viewed the place through freshly scraped glass, every colour heightened because she named it beautiful.

He noted her cautious tread—still slightly unsteady from the lingering strain on her vision—and slowed when the path slanted unevenly, tilting his body between her and the rougher ground. He found himself wishing every orchard in Kent had a furrow long enough to keep her hand on his sleeve forever.

"I can walk on my own now, Freddy," Joy remarked, but her tone was laced with amusement.

"I rather like holding you near, Joy. Do you mind?"

She wrinkled her face—an adorable mannerism she had when she was thinking. "I do not. Rather, I would not have thought I would like it."

"It is rather a marked change, is it not? You and me."

"But it does make sense for both of us. That way we will always be together. You do not mind that I will not be an overly feminine sort of wife?"

"To spare me from feminine hysterics?" he mocked. "But in all seriousness, I did not think about it overmuch before, but when I was courting Letty, I always found her wanting and compared her to you."

"What a nice thing to say, Freddy!"

"Honestly, I hope being married will not change either our friendship or your hoydenish behaviour—at least in private."

Joy gurgled with laughter. "You will have to help me with that. You always encourage me when I always mean to behave."

"I suppose I do."

Joy tilted her head, half-smiling beneath her shady brim.

They reached the edge of the apple trees and stepped into an open glade. A roped swing, fashioned long ago for children now grown, hung from the stout limb of a sycamore beside the river's edge. Its wooden seat swayed lazily in the breeze like a pendulum waiting to be claimed.

They strolled on towards the river, the dialogue still echoing in cheerful counterpoint to the buzz of insects. When the swing came fully into view, Joy's step quickened, and she released his arm long enough to knot her skirt above sturdy kid boots.

"Do you think you would enjoy being a squire, Freddy?"

"I do, but I also enjoy Town. Would you mind if we went to enjoy some of the Season each year? Perhaps as Mrs. Cunningham you can cut a dash without censure."

"You mean I can be myself but it would be acceptable as long as I am married?"

"Something of that nature."

With an irrepressible grin she seized the swing's ropes. "Push me."

He planted his heels. "Are you certain you should be doing that?"

"Not at all, but what harm could there be in a gentle swinging?"

He would give her the moon if she asked—a measured push seemed harmless enough. Yet his caution proved laughable—Joy needed only the faintest impulse before she was pumping her legs with the vigour of an experienced circus belle, bonnet ribbons fluttering behind her like pennants.

"Was there ever anything better, Freddy?" she cried, soaring high. However, then—"But it also makes me very dizzy—oh!"

The "oh" lengthened to a squeal as momentum betrayed her. The seat tilted sideways, she lost her grip, tumbled, and with a spectacular splash vanished into the water's cool embrace.

Freddy's heart slammed once, hard, then instinct took command. Boots, coat, and dignity flew in three separate arcs as he hurled himself after her. The river, no deeper than his waist here, still closed over his head before he found the bottom. Sunlight fractured above; silt billowed. He reached, caught fabric—her skirt—and hauled upward.

They surfaced together, Joy sputtering, hair plastered to cheeks, spectacles dangling by one temple-piece. "Well," she managed as she wiped her hair from her eyes, "that was bracing."

"That took ten years off my life, Joy!"

"I am no simpering miss, Freddy. I must insist you do not coddle me!"

Freddy didn't think he could love her more in that exact dishevelled moment. He slipped an arm beneath her knees and waded towards the grassy bank, water sluicing from his waistcoat. She weighed little more than a bundle of drenched muslin.

Depositing her on the bank's turf, he eased the crooked spectacles from her nose, blotted them with his linen handkerchief, and set them back with ceremonial care. Her lashes were spiky, her cheeks glowed, and river weeds clung to her hat like absurd cockades.

"I am going to kiss you now, Joy."

He leaned forward, and their lips met. She tasted of river water and something fierce and new. The kiss possessed very little polish—their mouths met at an angle that bumped teeth and fumbled fingers at the same time—but passion answered in joyful disorder, steaming her spectacles until the world vanished behind fogged lenses.

When they parted she blinked, breathless.

"Well? Does that give you a disgust of me?"

"Oh, no, Freddy. Quite the opposite."

"Then I am going to kiss you again. And then we are going to go and announce our betrothal to the family."

"If you insist, Freddy."

A second kiss—surprisingly surer—followed, punctuated by the delighted yowls of Lord Orville as he pounced on their feet. Joy laughed into Freddy's mouth. He laughed back, and their mirth dissolved into the ripple of the water.

Ten minutes later, they trudged towards the house, dripping like newly landed fish, boots in hand, fingers locked. Freddy thought of Westwood's raised brow, and his mother's faintly scandalized gasp, but this proposal suited them to the ground. Joy squeezed his hand, as if divining each thought, and murmured, "Prepare yourself: Faith will prescribe warm baths, Hope will demand broth, and Patience will laugh."

"Let them fuss. Nothing will dull my happiness," he proclaimed.

"I never took you for a romantic, Freddy," she said, leaning her head on his shoulder.

"See, I did pay attention when I read you all those novels!"

CHAPTER 20

The morning at Heartsfield Grange was one of those that seemed to apologize for the very notion of melancholy. It was everything Joy loved about the country. Skylarks were threading through a canopy of trees and sky, south-westerly breezes floating across the orchard, and the river itself provided a sweet symphony in the distance to accompany the birds. Joy rose early and found the east windows shining in brightness she could almost catch with both eyes if she did not force the effort. A week of Kentish air had made all colours bolder, her aches and bruises fade, and though the right eye remained unreliable at best, the left had grown clever at compensating —much as a fond elder sibling might for its impish twin.

The rest of the party were already outside when Joy joined them on the terrace for breakfast. Faith loaded a plate with food for Joy and handed it to her. Freddy announced that today's principal entertainments included a fishing picnic on the lower meadow near the river.

That set a ripple of amusement round the table—save for Rotham, who, balancing his toddling son on one knee, was too occupied preventing the child's chubby fist from upsetting the marmalade. Hope, now several months increased, watched both father and son with indulgent resignation. "Men are born with an instinct for peril. They merely refine it as they age."

Joy could not disagree with the proclamation.

Patience, her cheeks aglow, murmured that she had news which might shake even Stuart's equanimity. Joy, prompted by that conspiratorial glimmer, leaned closer. "Another miniature cavalryman on the way?" she guessed.

"Or equestrienne," Patience confirmed.

Squeals of excitement greeted this pronouncement, and Joy reflected on what it would be like to be a mother. She adored Sylvester's lopsided grin and Benjamin's earnest toddle, yet she could not deny a flutter of doubt. What if blindness proved permanent? Would she memorize her children's faces by touch alone? Would they resent the mother who bumped into chairs and could not read to them? Then she recalled how Sylvester had once thrust a half-eaten apple into her hand, absolutely trusting she could mend its worm hole wound with a kiss. Sight or no sight, love was not measured in flawless vision. "I shall manage," she told herself firmly. And if I falter, Freddy will scold the furniture for tripping me." The thought made her smile and steadied her heart.

An hour later the cavalcade set out with Freddy and Joy in the lead, she astride placid Pandora, he on an older cob, Ganymede. This was her first time on a horse since the accident, and still required restraint—not to mention the fact Dr. Harvey's cautionary lecture about "jostling her head" still rang in her ear. Yet, seated on the mare's broad back, reins steady, she felt the old thrill of movement: the rhythmic sway, the subtle adjustment of weight, the creak of leather.

"For someone who protested at a plodding old horse," Freddy teased, "you manage Pandora with remarkable dignity."

"She is not plodding," Joy protested. "She is a dowager duchess who moves only when duly petitioned."

"I stand corrected, your Grace." He made a short bow from his waist to the horse.

Behind them, the rest followed at varied paces. Some rode and some were to take gigs and carriages. The orchards unfurled on either side of the path, their limbs not yet burdened with heavy fruit. Joy caught the smell of blossoms now beginning their slow alchemy into fruit, and marvelled again at how pleasure could still be had despite concession—slower pace, shaded eyes, Freddy's discreet watchfulness.

And so what did it matter if she could not do everything exactly as before? There was still so much she could do.

At a dip where the path met the river flat, Montford raised a pointing arm. "Salmon leap from the water!" he shouted in uncharacteristic verve. "Perhaps we shall catch our supper!"

"If you cannot catch one whilst they practically leap onto your hook, then you are not the angler you thought you were," Westwood taunted his old friend.

The picnic unfolded with cheerful chaos. Rugs spread, baskets unpacked, lemonade poured into thick tumblers that beaded with cold. Sylvester—Hope's sturdy two-year-old—escaped immediately, barefooted, to chase butterflies. Benjamin—Faith's one-year-old—toddled in wobbly pursuit, intercepted at intervals by Faith's quick hand. Freddy assembled three rods with line whilst Joy knelt on a rug, threading bait with fingers nimbler than her impaired vision would have suggested possible.

Westwood had already begun casting with the practised flick of a man who had grown up on angling, and promised a sovereign for the biggest fish.

"And if I bait, hook, and catch with one eye?" Joy asked with a challenge.

"Still a sovereign."

Freddy handed Joy the second rod and adjusted her grip. "Do not do anything foolish."

She blew him a mock-solemn kiss and turned her attention to the water. Sun spangles danced across the surface, willow leaves drifted like small ships. Once or twice she strained to see a shape flash beneath—a salmon testing the shallows. When the bite came, it yanked her arm nearly to the socket. She set her heels, angled the rod, and let the fish run. Freddy hovered, ready, but she needed only for the fish to tire a little to bring it to a glittering arc above the water. "Do not dare try to assist," she snapped.

Minutes later the fish lay in wet grass, still flexing powerful tails, and Westwood pressed a sovereign into Joy's palm as she gloated.

Westwood then landed the next—nothing to boast of but large enough to eat as well as make Sylvester cheer. Montford lost two flies to overzealous flicks and finally captured a salmon so small even Vivienne refused to praise his catch. Rotham hooked a submerged tree branch and spent ten minutes extracting his line with muttered curses. Stuart, leaning against a willow and observing Patience's glowing face, never noticed the gentle tug on his rod until the salmon shook free, leapt once in triumph, and vanished.

Joy's catch therefore remained the victor, and she brandished her sovereign like a medal pinned to a general. Westwood bowed, conceding defeat with good grace. "Joy, I should never have doubted you."

Lunch tasted better for the victory. The cook had packed cold roast fowl, pickled quails' eggs, fresh bread, and strawberries so sweet they needed no sugar. Conversation rippled like the river itself as they sipped on sweet elderflower wine.

The afternoon drifted towards lazy perfection: salmon safely packed for supper, children dozing in the shade, adults scattered in agreeable fellowship. Freddy guided Joy a little upstream where they walked hand in hand.

Here the current slowed, permitting reflections almost mirror clear. Joy sat upon a fallen tree, removed her spectacles to polish the lenses and studied him through the softened haze of near-sight.

"You look thoughtful, Mr. Cunningham," she said, as he guided Lord Orville away from the bank.

"I was just thinking…hoping that we will be friends as good as this when we are eighty."

"It seems a strange concern. Why would we not be? We were friends from the very first."

"I suppose so. It will take some getting used to, this notion of you as a wife."

"I think we are very lucky to have each other forever. That is what concerned me the most about having a Season. It meant I would lose you forever."

"Now you will have me forever."

She polished the spectacles, slid them on and blinked until the world steadied. "I have a worry, too."

"And what is that?"

"That I will trip when walking down the aisle at my own wedding. Would it not be appalling if you were forced to carry me?"

He laughed. "If necessary, I shall do so. We shall set our own style."

"No, no. I shall practise so I will not make a fool of myself," she promised, then added softly, "Freddy, are you absolutely content? You do not regret choosing convenience?"

He sat beside her on the trunk, their shoulders brushing. "Convenience?" He considered the word. "There is nothing resembling that word in what is between us. I belong to you, heart and soul."

"Oh, Freddy." She snuggled next to him and leaned her head on his shoulder. "Why did it take us so long to open our eyes to each other? I mean, I always thought that any lady would be lucky to have you, and then I wanted to claw Letty Partridge's eyes out when she would fawn all over you."

He chuckled. "I wanted to pop St. John's cork more than once just for making you laugh," he admitted.

"Was that love? I suppose it was," she said thoughtfully. "Thankfully, we are not now married to the wrong people."

"I shudder to think what almost was not. I will tell you one thing: I will never take for granted the gift you are to me. I love you, Joy Whitford."

She felt colour warm her cheeks. She turned slightly so that his face blurred into gentle shapes of light and shadow. "Then you ought to know," she murmured, "that I love you, too, Freddy."

His arm slid round her waist, her head nestled against his shoulder. "I do know. I think I have always known."

FREDDY HAD OFTEN HEARD CURATES declare that nothing on earth could fluster an English bridegroom once the banns were called, the licence signed, and the bride safely at hand. He now discovered that curates, like poets and prospective connexions, trafficked in half-truths. For although Joy was indeed 'safely at hand'—somewhere in the east wing with four sisters, two maids, and several felines—everything else about the blessed morning contrived to rattle his composure.

First, the weather: a July day that threatened to imitate April, scattering sun, drizzle, and mischievous gusts in hourly rotation. And—kittens. Six of them (and one dog, Patience's Xander) now toddled about, making war on wedding ribbons and lace. Cecilia and Mortimer remained with their new lady, but the remaining feline fraternity—Lord Orville, Camilla, Frederica, Theo, Evelina, and the house's current mouser, Mouser, had joined the fray.

Still, Freddy reminded himself as he paced the panelled passage outside the chapel, he had survived worse. London dowagers. Letty Partridge's mother. A few animals and capricious clouds could not sink him.

"Deep breaths, lad," came Westwood's rumble from the open vestry door. The Viscount, impeccably arrayed in navy superfine, leaned against the lintel as if he had personally invented matrimony. "She will not gallop away."

"I never doubted that," Freddy answered. "It is still an unnerving process."

Westwood gave his shoulder a squeeze. "I will see you soon with your bride on my arm."

"Not soon enough," Freddy muttered as his old friend walked away.

Next, his father and mother wanted to speak with him. His mother was dabbing at her eyes, and Freddy embraced her. It nearly made him cry to see his mother so.

"Well, son, I am sorry we had to force you and Joy, but the two of you needed a little push."

"What do you mean?" Freddy looked up at his father.

"It has been obvious to us from the start that the two of you were meant for each other. However, Joy was too young, and your friendship a bit...immature. You both needed to be brought to the bridle."

Lady Gresham whimpered at the rough phrase.

"However, when it was time for her come-out, we were afraid that neither of you would see what a treasure you had in each other."

"We almost did not." Freddy shook his head. "I thought it devilish odd that you'd come the heavy, but am nevertheless grateful."

His father wrapped him in a tight hug, and said no more.

Freddy let out a half-sigh, half-laugh and shook his head. He could not deny that he and Joy had been slow to see what had been right in front of them the whole time.

He stepped inside the tiny chapel: timber roof, white plaster walls, and windows of antique glass through which orchard-filtered light fell in shifting blues and greens. Two rows of polished oak benches flanked a centre aisle not five paces long. At the far end stood the rector, Reverend Clark, stout and placid, consulting his prayer book. Freddy took his position before the white-draped communion rails, Rotham at his left.

Guests arranged themselves with low rustles of conversation: Faith cradling sleepy Benjamin while Hope attempted to keep Sylvester occupied; Patience radiant beside Stuart on the right. Chairs were placed for the Dowagers Westwood and Aunts Flora and Rosemary.

Lord and Lady Gresham graced the other side of the chapel. Next came Thornhill, his gleaming duchess-to-be, Lady Maeve, Grace and Lord Carew.

The organ sighed to life, and Freddy's heartbeat matched the rising chord. The chapel door opened. The congregation gasped, then chuckled. Joy's laughter—soft, unmistakable—floated in as the cats preceded the bride.

Then Joy appeared on Westwood's arm. She wore a gown of soft ivory spotted with delicate silver embroidery, and a gauze veil pinned to a wreath of hawthorn. Her spectacles glinted in the light. She moved with quiet assurance, evidently seeing enough to step without pause, and the trust in her gaze—directed first at Westwood, then with her brightest smile at Freddy—nearly unmanned him. As it was, he had to wipe tears discreetly from his eyes.

The final pace brought her to his side. Joy's palm trembled once and then steadied, warm against his gloves. She inhaled deeply, but never stopped smiling. Freddy smiled back, finally feeling that all was just as it should be.

Reverend Clark began. "Dearly beloved…" Freddy scarcely heard, his heart drumming beneath his starched neckcloth. When the Reverend enquired who gave the bride, Westwood answered in a resonant baritone. When the vows came, Freddy found his voice surprisingly firm.

"I, Frederick George Marshall Cunningham, take thee, Joy Margaret Whitford, to be my wedded wife…"

Joy's replies came clear and unwavering. As she said, "With my body I thee worship," Lord Orville let out a plaintive protest, causing Rotham to cough behind a gloved fist. Reverend Clark soldiered on. The rings were exchanged, the blessing pronounced, the register signed. It was done.

As the bride and groom turned to face their friends, congratulations filled the chapel. Lady Gresham dabbed her eyes. Freddy bent and scooped Frederica, who had been sleeping at their feet, into his arms.

Joy reached over and scratched her behind the ears. "Do you know the day I first knew I loved you, Freddy?"

"When?"

"It was when you bought her for me."

"I should have known then how things would be. I never could say no to you."

Joy gurgled with laughter. "I think I am going to like being married, Freddy."

The words felt like sunrise in his heart. He tucked Frederica against his chest and offered Joy his arm and the new-made Cunninghams stepped down the aisle, preceded by their informal menagerie.

Lord Orville led the procession with the solemnity of a field marshal, tail erect, until Mouser discovered the long white ribbon trailing from Joy's bouquet and pounced. The sudden tug sent petals flying like an explosion and produced a collective laughter from the pews.

Before disaster could escalate, Xander sprang in to assist, seized the ribbon in his soft mouth, and attempted to trot alongside—so that bride, dog, and two cats advanced in a lurching, three-legged waltz perfectly timed to the music.

Joy only laughed harder, and Freddy melted into delighted chuckles. At the chapel door, Sylvester darted forward waving a nosegay, and Camilla sprang up, seized the posy and capered off, causing Sylvester to cry.

The Dowager's eyebrows ascended to the border of impropriety but before she could issue a rebuke, Evelina vaulted onto the pew and —decided to paw at the floral and fruit display atop Aunt Flora's bonnet.

Freddy bit the inside of his cheek. Joy's shoulders shook. Rotham and Carew's guffaws echoed off the plaster ceiling.

Outside, sunshine had conquered drizzle for the moment, gilding the gravel sweep where the wedding breakfast awaited. Two grooms held a brace of white doves meant for release from their repurposed dovecote; the birds, unnerved by kittens skirmishing round their boots, burst free prematurely and shot heavenward, brushing Freddy's hat and leaving a decidedly unceremonious token on Thornhill's immaculate sleeve.

"An omen of prosperity," Thornhill insisted gamely, flicking the mark with a lace kerchief while Lady Maeve tried—unsuccessfully— not to wheeze with mirth.

The newly wedded pair progressed towards the house, Joy pausing when she heard a frantic squawk. Camilla, bored with ribbons, had discovered the cook's pet bantam—who had somehow wandered over —and decided to herd it like a sheep. The flustered fowl zigzagged between ankles, which delighted the toddler boys.

Freddy dropped Frederica, intercepted the chicken a pace from catastrophe, tucked it under one arm, and breathed a sigh of relief.

"Cook would have my head if I let anything happen to her precious boy."

Joy was now doubled over with laughter. "I could not think of a more fitting scene for our wedding."

Freddy's answering grin promised pandemonium—and lifelong partnership in every antic yet to come.

EPILOGUE

Five years later...

Joy Cunningham woke to the unmistakable sound of a harried husband. That was how it felt when Freddy came pelting in half-dressed and announced, with exaggerated gravity, that "Your goat is eating the refreshment tent."

"My goat?" Joy retorted, dragging her spectacles from the bedside table. "Since when do I hold that title?"

"Since Sylvester christened her Lady Nibbleton and claimed she answers only to your voice."

That explained everything and nothing.

Somewhere down the passage, two shrill voices—a piping "Papa, goat!" and a toddling echo of "Go!"—announced that their own children were awake. Three-year-old Frederick George (Georgie to all) came charging in, nightshirt flapping, while chubby Amelia toddled behind pulling a wooden kitten on wheels. Freddy scooped both under one arm, accepted a gummy kiss from Amelia, and deputized Georgie temporary Goat Constable.

"They have escaped Nurse," Freddy remarked as though it was not a daily occurrence.

Joy laughed, kissed the tip of Freddy's chin—the closest available target—and quickly dressed in a day gown. Outside, early sun striped the lawn and cast Heartsfield Grange in gilt. Trestles, half-erected, and tablecloths lay in piles awaiting hands willing to assemble. Near the orchard gate, Lady Nibbleton was indeed sampling the tent skirt while a footman ineffectually waved his arms at her.

"Shoo, Madam," Joy commanded. The goat looked affronted but trotted off and transferred her attentions to an innocent hedgerow.

Quincy, their wedding pup from Lord Gresham, padded up, ears pricked.

"All livestock accounted for, save Lord Orville, who is presumably inspecting the neighbour's queen," Freddy announced. It was quite the task, keeping track of their menagerie.

Joy's left eye caught colours bright and sure; the right, a stubborn blur, filled in nothing but soft hues. *Even so*, she thought, *I see enough*. And today she meant not to miss a single absurdity.

By noon, sisters and families descended like a cheerful invasion. Faith arrived first, the ever-capable Westwood and Lydia at her side. Benjamin sprinted past, waving a wooden sword and enquiring whether goats could be pirates. Trailing them came Faith's youngest treasure—fourteen-month-old Edmund, gurgling approval at every goat bleat.

Hope's carriage followed, Rotham disembarking looking decidedly dishevelled, as Sylvester leapt out to join Benjamin in the quest as a pirate. Their twin girls, Beatrix and Briony, slept undisturbed through the commotion.

Patience and Colonel Stuart brought five-year-old Robert and four-year-old Rose, each clutching a tiny felt pennant bearing crudely drawn kittens. "Flags," Patience explained. "So they may cheer whichever creature actually stays on the course."

Grace's party made the grandest entry. Lord Carew helped her down, brandishing two familiar felines. Grace whispered to Joy, eyes twinkling. "I am afraid Theo and Evalina are too fat to race." Three more little Carews tumbled out after their parents: serious-eyed Augustine, now four, exuberant Charlotte, now three, and solemn

Nicholas—a one-year-old who clung to Grace's skirts with his thumb securely in his mouth.

Soon after, a ducal landau rolled up the drive, bearing a radiant Maeve, Thornhill proudly holding aloft a wicker basket. Inside lurked two more of Frederica's offspring, Mortimer and Cecilia, whom they had rescued whence Lady Marchmont passed on. They were groomed to celestial perfection and radiated disdain for the rustic venue. "Observe the opposition," Thornhill said, as though introducing prized bloodstock. A pair of rosy-cheeked Thornhill heirs were handed down next—James (aged two, brandishing a toy horse) and baby Eliza in Maeve's arms, wide-eyed at the scene around her.

Joy curtsied. "Welcome to Heartsfield."

A cry of "Aunt Joy!" burst out as soon as the last landau door clicked shut. Sylvester and Benjamin, wooden cutlasses aloft, charged across the gravel in full piratical array—scarves tied crooked, one eye circled with charcoal to suggest villainy. Joy braced herself for impact. They hugged her knees with such enthusiasm that Frederica, lying regally at her feet, had to whirl aside.

Behind the buccaneers came Robert and Rose at a more measured trot, their kitten pennants fluttering. Augustine followed, clasping what appeared to be a pocket stud book. Charlotte skipped in his wake, attempting twirls that ended in grassy somersaults, while Nicholas clung to Grace's hand and blinked owlishly at the commotion. Lydia made straight for Quincy, and he fell at her feet and rolled onto his back without shame. James, Thornhill's eldest, marched to pet Lady Nibbleton, who eyed the miniature person with wary interest. Eliza nestled on Maeve's hip, thumb in mouth, wide eyes reflecting everything with caution.

Joy spread her arms. "Goodness, I hoped all my favourite people would appear, and here they all are at once! Pirates, flag-bearers, breeders—what a company."

"Have you really a goat now, Aunt Joy?" Benjamin demanded, eyes sparkling.

"I have. Lady Nibbleton of the Tent Chewing Brigade. You may parley with her after luncheon, but mind your hat. She is indiscriminate when it comes to eating."

"And is it true," Augustine enquired gravely, "that Lord Orville once carried off an entire cheese?"

"An entire Stilton," Freddy supplied, arriving, "larger than your head, young sir."

"Oooh," whispered Charlotte, twirling again. "I want a cheese."

"There are smaller cheeses," Joy assured her, "in the food tent.

Joy stooped so they could all crowd around. "This year's fête," she announced, "boasts more delights than any May Day festival. You may test your arms at the Pie-Flinging Booth—Cook has baked special cream missiles—and at three o'clock there will be Blind Man's Bluff on the south lawn, overseen by Quincy, who refuses to wear the blindfold but promises to bark impartially."

Benjamin's hand shot up as if in school. "Will there be pudding?"

"After the sack races," Joy confirmed. "I have seen four kinds so far: lemon drizzle, ginger syllabub, gooseberry tart, and a chocolate sponge."

"Capital!" he answered.

"A boy after my own heart. And—" Joy spread her arms wider—"the jewel in Heartsfield's crown: the Cat Derby. Six famous racers, one velvet ramp, feather wands for reins, and a blue ribbon to the swiftest whiskers."

A collective intake of breath greeted this. Even Nicholas's thumb slipped from his mouth to express excitement.

Freddy adopted his most portentous baritone. "But derby racers must prove themselves worthy. There will be a Jockey's Inspection first. Clean boots, brave hearts, and no smuggling sardines under your bonnet, Master Sylvester."

"I would never!" cried Sylvester—though his grin strongly implied he might.

"Everyone present and accounted for," Freddy declared. "Pirates, accountants, and goat artillery, form ranks!"

Chaos obliged happily: pennants tangled with cutlasses, baby Edmund burst into delighted shrieks, and Rose attempted to fasten a

UNENDING JOY

ribbon to Mortimer's considerable middle with limited success. Westwood raised a hand like a drill sergeant and corralled the mass towards the orchard path, where tables waited under striped awnings. The children surged ahead, Lydia toddling after Quincy, Augustine already pretending to jot odds in his book.

Joy and her sisters lingered a moment, exchanging glances heavy with years of shared motherhood—and the faintest astonishment that they had somehow multiplied into such a carnival.

"Bless us all," Patience murmured, "but our nursery will soon outgrow the house."

Hope linked arms with her. "We always have Davenmere if needed."

"At least there will always be hands to wave feathers." Maeve adjusted Eliza's sun bonnet. "And small voices to cheer when the goats stage a coup."

Grace laughed. "We wanted adventure for our children. Joy has handed them a kingdom of misrule."

Joy felt warmth rise to her cheekbones—part pride, part that old shy disbelief that life could turn out so richly unexpected. She caught Freddy's gaze over a sea of bonnet ribbons and whisking tails. He lifted an eyebrow in silent invitation. *Ready?*

She nodded, her half-blurred vision swimming with colours: Lydia's saffron sash, the deep blue of Augustine's journal cover, the sleek black of Mortimer's coat, Charlotte's bright pink pinafore, and Freddy's steadfast figure in oat-straw tweed guiding them all forward.

"Come, sisters," she said, voice light and sure. "Before Lady Nibbleton relocates the pastry table, and before Lord Orville requisitions the cheese. The world may call this a mere country fête, but we know it for what it is: the finest fête ever assembled under one orchard's boughs."

When at last the time came for the actual derby, the children were sent to gather their assigned charges.

The Cat Derby of Heartsfield Grange had grown, over five summers, into a country legend: a velvet-lined ramp, twelve feet long, sloping from the start to a triumphal arch plaited with catnip and hawthorn blossoms. This year Frederica's original litter—six venerable kittens now grown in their dignified middle age—were each to be coaxed down the course by one of the cousins brandishing a feather wand. The notion delighted every adult present. It also reduced the stable-boys to helpless laughter, for middle-aged cats were scarcely given to obliging footraces. But the children took the assignment as solemn destiny. The competitors were:

Lord Orville—striped, long-bodied, and proud possessor of a half-missing ear from an early duel with a neighbouring tom. Jockey: Benjamin (Faith's eldest, six years old).
Cecilia—gleaming grey with a scandalous fondness for snacks. Jockey: Sylvester (Hope's eldest, now seven).
Camilla—silky tabby whose figure bore evidence of many cream dish triumphs. Jockey: Robert (Patience's first, five and three-fourths).
Theo—steady, mellow, black fellow. Jockey: Augustine (four and a half).
Evalina—orange tabby and white-pawed huntress, quick as thistledown, given to sudden philosophical naps. Jockey: Lydia (just barely five)
Mortimer—grey tabby whose girth suggested strategic pacing rather than sprint. Jockeys: Beatrix and Briony (just turned four).

The children gathered at the head of the ramp, feathers aloft. Freddy, acting course steward, tried to assume an expression of sober authority but betrayed himself with a twitch of laughter when Mortimer yawned hugely and flopped over the starting line as if to say, 'wake me when the cream arrives.' Quincy patrolled importantly; Lady Nibbleton lurked some yards away, chewing a stolen ribbon from the Dowager's bonnet.

Joy raised a handkerchief—today's official starting flag. "Ready—steady—GO!"

They were off—sort of...

Sylvester whooped, waggling a bright blue feather in front of Lord Orville, who sprang forward three aristocratic strides, ears flattened, then paused to glare back as if to question the futility of this exercise. Camilla advanced two dignified paces, decided the velvet was deliciously warm, and curled daintily upon it. Robert, scandalized, flapped his feather like a flag: "Charge, ma'am!" Camilla blinked regal indifference.

Cecilia surprised everyone by scampering half the distance in a fluid grey streak—Benjamin galloped beside her until a biscuit tumbled from his pocket. Cecilia reversed course to devour the prize.

Theo trotted methodically, Augustine pacing him at a distance. "Keep the inside lane, old chap." Evalina darted with airy elegance until Charlotte squealed encouragement. The cat, taking the squeal for rebuke, executed an elegant pirouette and sat down to groom her paws.

As for Mortimer—the twins' gentle coaxing induced exactly three waddling steps before he discovered a discarded sliver of pie at the side of the course. He settled upon it with the gravity of a Roman senator.

The crowd—sisters, husbands, villagers—roared approval of the chaos.

Joy's sides hurt from laughing. "We may finish by Michaelmas," she called to Freddy.

Halfway down, fortunes shifted. Lord Orville, offended by Camilla's public nap, delivered a gentlemanly cuff to her haunch, waking her in indignation. She shot forward, knocking Theo sideways. Augustine yelped. Theo decided the best avenue of retreat was directly over the steward's boots. Freddy hopped back to give way.

Evalina, startled by the commotion, opted for altitude. She bounded onto the arch itself, scattering catnip leaves upon the heads of the crowd. A sudden breeze sent catnip drifting across the course like green snow. Camilla inhaled bliss, rolled ecstatically, and collided with Cecilia, who was still pursuing biscuit crumbs. Both tumbled into a catnip-induced heap of wriggling purrs.

The children shrieked with delight. Lady Nibbleton, reading the excitement as invitation, trotted over, planted herself between Lord Orville and the finish arch, and began chewing catnip sprigs. Lord Orville halted in affront. Sylvester drew his wooden sword. "Yield the course, foul beast!"

The goat butted the air in answer.

Freddy, wiping tears, judged the moment ripe for decisive intervention. "Quincy!" he barked. The collie, awakened to duty, bounded forward, barking a summons to obey. Lady Nibbleton, being herded, gave one last tug at foliage and lumbered aside.

In the sudden clearing, Lord Orville saw destiny: tail lashing, he streaked for the arch. Camilla rolled after him in a sideways tumble. Theo plodded behind with Augustine, while Evalina executed a swan-like leap from arch to ramp and glided the final inch nose-first over the line mere whiskers ahead of Lord Orville.

The crowd erupted. Charlotte clapped so hard she fell backward into Grace's arms. Joy, wiping tears beneath her spectacles, declared, "Evalina by a whisker's breadth!" Reverend Hathaway, official judge, confirmed it—though confessed he'd lost sight of Mortimer entirely. A search party discovered him snoozing in the picnic basket, neatly curled around the pie's remainder.

Lydia proudly tied the winner's ribbon on Evalina's neck.

As dusk painted orchard leaves bronze, Joy slipped her hand into Freddy's. "Next year, we should add a dog sprint," she whispered.

Freddy laughed. "With Lady Nibbleton to officiate?"

"But of course." She left him to superintend the children's further entertainment.

Joy found a quiet bench beneath an old pear's shade. One by one, her sisters drifted to join her, husbands herding offspring at a discreet distance.

"Remember our first garden party in Town?" Patience asked. "We thought ourselves so grand...until Joy discussed fetlocks with half the bachelors present."

"And Faith sneezed on Lady Jersey's aigrette," Grace added, giggling.

Faith sniffed with mock outrage. "That feather was poorly anchored."

Hope leaned closer, voice low with contentment. "What matters, is all our roads wound back together."

"Yes." Joy traced the bench grain with a fingertip. "And I would not trade a step."

In the field beyond, children chased kites dangling on strings. Freddy organized teams, his laughter unmistakable. Joy's heart stitched the images together: family, laughter, resilient love glowing in her chest.

As the afternoon wore into evening, the cats curled on hay bales, and the laughter of children drifted skyward. The Whitford family's second generation had written its own way forward.

The meadow emptied slowly, as all good fêtes must: children yawning with exhaustion, and the villagers content with food and laughter. By eight o'clock the light had mellowed into dusk. Above the orchard, the sky shifted from amber to pink and purple, and shadows stretched long beside the collapsed Cat Chute.

Everyone gathered on benches or cushions, and lantern poles were already planted in the grass awaiting dusk. Night edged in, carrying rich scents of hay and woodsmoke.

"Come," Freddy said, his voice gentle amid the din. "There are lanterns to light."

Joy squeezed Freddy's hand. The whirl of colour and laughter shimmered, but through it she saw—truly saw—their entire world: friends, family, animals, imperfection, joy. Her right eye might fail, but her heart's vision felt startlingly clear—to love and be loved amid such uproar was the finest finish she could imagine.

Lanterns—thin paper globes painted by children during the afternoon—were lit, one by one: crimson, amber, palest green. Their glow set the orchard glimmering like hanging fruit on a fantastical tree.

They raised their lanterns. The children counted: three…two…one —release! The spheres bobbed skyward, trembling, then steadied, drifting over orchard silhouettes. A collective sigh rose with them.

Joy tipped her face to his, lantern light gilding his features. "I used to fear I should never see clearly again," she whispered.

"And now?"

"Now I know clarity belongs to more than eyes."

He pressed a kiss to her temple. "Mrs. Cunningham, you remain the finest vision in Kent."

She laughed—soft, unbelieving—and let the sound join lanterns, the summer breeze, children's shouts, and the cricket's song. The world blurred, sharpened and blurred again, but still shone: a constellation of small, perfect lights lifted by hands she loved.

And high above Heartsfield Grange, the lanterns sailed on, marking the sky with gentle fire, while below the orchards slept, guarded by goats, kittens, puppies, and the echo of unending joy.

AFTERWORD

Author's note: British spellings and grammar have been used in an effort to reflect what would have been done in the time period in which the novels are set. Yes, Jane Austen used -ize spellings, even though -ise is accepted now. While I realize all words may not be exact, I hope you can appreciate the differences and effort made to be historically accurate while attempting to retain readability for the modern audience.

Thank you for reading *Unending Joy.* I hope you enjoyed it. If you did, please help other readers find this book:

1. This ebook is lendable, so send it to a friend who you think might like it so she or he can discover me, too.

    2. Help other people find this book by writing a review.

    3. Sign up for my new releases at www.Elizabethjohnsauthor.com, so you can find out about the next book as soon as it's available.

    4. Come like my Facebook page www.facebook.com/Elizabethjohnsauthor or follow on Instagram @Ejohnsauthor or feel free to write me at elizabethjohnsauthor@gmail.com

ALSO BY ELIZABETH JOHNS

Surrender the Past

Seasons of Change

Seeking Redemption

Shadows of Doubt

Second Dance

Through the Fire

Melting the Ice

With the Wind

Out of the Darkness

After the Rain

Ray of Light

Moon and Stars

First Impressions

The Governess

On My Honour

Not Forgotten

An Officer Not a Gentleman

The Ones Left Behind

What Might Have Been

Leap of Faith

Finding Hope

The Gift of Patience

Only By Grace

ACKNOWLEDGMENTS

There are many, many people who have contributed to making my books possible.

My family, who deals with the idiosyncrasies of a writer's life that do not fit into a 9 to 5 work day.

Dad, who reads every single version before and after anyone else—that alone qualifies him for sainthood.

Anj, who takes my visions and interpret them, making them into works of art people open in the first place.

To those friends who care about my stories enough to help me shape them before everyone else sees them.

Scott and Heather who help me say what I mean to!

And to the readers who make all of this possible.

I am forever grateful to you all.

Printed in Dunstable, United Kingdom